Dedication

For my mum. You continue to inspire me every day of my life. I love you and I miss you. XXXX

Acknowledgements

To my publishers, Publishing Push – thank you for your fantastic support and utmost professionalism in taking me through the publishing process and having to deal with my endless questions.

Thank you to Tim Small from The Sealed Knot (www.thesealedknot.org.uk) for checking I had got everything right about them.

I would like to give special thanks to the following family members and friends who have stood by me through good times and very sad times and/or have supported me throughout the writing of this book:

Lynda Morrison, Adrienne Thomas, Chris Turner, William Kettle, Delia Burt, Sally Warrington, Geraldine Murphy, Steven Brown, Helen Powell, Niki Morrigan, Stephen Hall, Elaine Oxley (thank you for telling me about your incident with the cow pats), Joanne Holloway, Susan Wilson, Heidi Rossetter, June Bartlett, Janice Walsh, Gill Carpenter, Patricia Wilson, Jo Strickland (thank you for letting me use your seagull 'incident'), Zayren Veerapan, Uzma Chowdhary, Cathy Clack, Lyle Wray and Rex Beanland.

Contents

1

The Journey of Loneliness
and First Contact

My name is Beth. I am fifty-six years old and I have had enough now; more than enough. I have been rattling around by myself in this big empty place I call my home for over a year now, going from room to room, not knowing quite where to settle. The sound of silence around me is constantly overwhelming. It certainly doesn't feel like my home. It feels more like a show house. There should have been two of us here but there isn't; not since he went. I can still feel him near me though. I can feel his presence everywhere. I could almost reach out and touch him, stroke his hair and smell his aftershave. I speak to him every day. Some people might have found that odd but I don't. It helped me stay in contact with him. I had spent too long teetering on the edge of an abyss of despair. I had been stuck, unable to take a positive step forward. I often thought about what it would be like to just click my fingers and disappear. No one would have noticed I wasn't around anyway. I was no longer in the world I knew and now needed to adapt to a new and unfamiliar one. My life was black and white and I needed much more colour and light in it. I was constantly putting out fires, fires that flared up when my emotions erupted into flames. This is my story.

I live opposite a park. There are benches all around the edges. People would sit on them, make themselves comfortable and watch other people gathering on the grass to eat, play ball games or just chat. It was like an outdoor theatre. I always imagined those people on the benches clapping and shouting 'Bravo' when someone laid out an entire spread on the grass with cutlery and food and then, quick as lightning, removed the tablecloth, leaving every item still in place as neat as you like. There would be much bowing and repeat performances throughout the day and it was all for free.

The highlight of my life at the moment was the little things that other people might find ordinary and even routine. Other people wouldn't even mention the events I saw when asked how their day had been. One day, for example, I was taking a bulging bag of rubbish out. The air was crisp and cold with mist hovering quite still over the park. I saw a man sitting on a bench close by. He was bent forward, his head in his hands, slowly rocking backwards and forwards. It sounded like he was muttering into a phone but I couldn't be sure. From his body language, I thought he looked quite anxious. I thought about going over to check he was alright when he suddenly ran one hand quickly through his hair, got up, made a loud whooping noise and shouted, 'Yesss!! Oh yesss!! Whoopee!' and ran off across the park. On the way, he jumped in the air and clicked his heels together, something I have never been able to do. That was a while ago now. I never thought I would see him again and I often wondered what had happened to him and why he was so happy. I am glad I didn't make myself go over. That might have been too hard for me. Talking to people is now alien to me. When I saw a couple doing a little jig outside my house once, it made my week.

I used to have a stressful job in the city, one where you needed to wear a very, very thick iron overcoat, always tightly buttoned up to the neck, just to survive. Critical arrows were fired every day at anyone who fell below the high standards set by the managers. I was always being asked for financial reports, predictions on future financial and marketing outcomes, where to put money for the best gains and shouted at when things went belly up and money was lost. The pressure was immense and I didn't have the desire for it any longer. I knew I had to leave. I had reached an age where I could take early retirement so I did. I worked out how much I would need to live on each month and, surprisingly, it wasn't that much. Thankfully, I had paid off the mortgage following the sale of my previous property, so I signed on the dotted line and left. There was a little leaving party in the office with many kind words said about me, but all I wanted to do was get home and put my feet up. I now get a very nice monthly pension and I also received a big one-off lump sum payment. Everyone told me I could spend it on things I wanted to buy or things I wanted to do. Trouble was, I had nothing I wanted to do and nothing that I wanted or needed to buy.

The following Sunday morning, I got up early. I have always been an early riser and I did a wash just as the sun was coming up over the horizon. The street lamps were still glowing in the street. I put my wet clothes on a clothes horse to dry and then looked out at the park from a window on the stairs. I frequently did this. This was something I felt comfortable doing. It was 8.00 am and the park was empty apart from two figures, a man and his young child, throwing a ball to each other. Neither of them looked like they were talking to each other and neither of them looked like they were really enjoying themselves. One threw the ball, the other caught it and threw it back. Exercise didn't seem to be the main motivator as they didn't move very much at all, apart from using their arms. Without realising it, I found myself turning my head from side to side following the movement of the ball. It was like watching a fast-moving tennis match but with none of the excitement and with the feet of both players glued to the ground.

As I have said and will keep saying until things get better, I haven't been going through a good time at all. Actually, it has been crap and still is. I was spending a lot of time alone lounging on my sofa, binge-watching drama series after drama series on Netflix, Amazon, iPlayer; you name it, I watched it. All I did was gobble down the biggest bars of chocolate I could find and drink lots of wine. I had a large bowl of sweets on the coffee table too. The local off licence loved me. We were on first-name terms there. 'Hello, Beth. Your usual order?' I half-expected them to have my bags packed, sitting on the counter, ready for me to pick up every day. I was thinking of setting up a standing order with them through my bank.

I knew I had to do something. I imagined people would start whispering about me, pointing and saying 'That's where that really fat hermit woman with the nasty-looking hair lives. She never washes, you know. She's in that big house over there. Look at her horrible garden and horrible house. She has a very large wart right on the end of her nose you know, and people say she is really a witch. She only has one tooth, right in the middle of her mouth. I haven't seen her black cat yet though'. I imagined children would egg each other on to knock on my front door and run off screaming, particularly at Halloween.

I needed to start perking myself up. I needed to give it a go and try to start feeling happy again. It would have to be a little event first. Very small steps were needed. If someone was sitting on a bench, I would wander over and say hello or at least try to start a conversation. Just to see someone smile, to hear another person talk, another voice that wasn't my own or on the television would surely help me. I hadn't spoken to anyone in such a long time and was spending far too long talking to myself. It wasn't that I didn't want to talk, I just didn't know what to say. I hadn't hugged someone else in heaven only knows how long. I had spent last Christmas alone which was a very joyless occasion. I made myself a Christmas dinner and raised a glass to myself. When I watched the Queen's speech, I had stood up and saluted and sang the national anthem very loudly in my pyjamas.

The weather had been exceptionally cold for the last few weeks and it had been rare to see people out for walks, let alone spending time sitting on benches. Now that winter was finally waving goodbye to us all, more people have started to venture out. There is a nip in the air so a warm coat is still needed.

The next day, I sipped my coffee and looked at the park out of another window in my house. I stopped. There was someone there, sitting on the bench nearest to my house. It was a man wearing a bulky coat and a large woollen scarf which he had wrapped round and round his neck and the bottom of his

11

face. He had a deerstalker hat on, its flaps covering his ears. He was watching the man and his child throwing the ball back and forth. I could see his head moving. There was nothing much else for him to look at. I quickly finished my coffee, put my favourite big coat on, quietly closed my front door and walked over to the bench. This was a big event for me; why will become clear later. I had my doubts, though. Is this mad? Will it work?

The man was sitting at one end of the bench. The space at the other end seemed to have my name written on it. I sat down and exhaled rather too loudly. A bit too deliberately. *Oh no*, I thought, *he might think I am the local looney out by myself for the morning as an experiment to see if I can cope by myself*. Thankfully, it started off okay. He nodded at me and got out a handkerchief to wipe his nose.

'I'm glad the weather has cheered up a bit,' I said and looked at him with a smile.

'Yes,' he replied and said nothing more.

He folded up his handkerchief very neatly so that it formed an almost perfect square with no edges hanging out and put it back in his coat pocket. He got up slowly as if to leave. He steadied himself by holding onto the back of the bench. The knuckles on his hand turned white.

Finally, he looked at me and pointed at the father and his son, back here again, throwing the ball.

'There must be more to life than simply chucking a ball at each other,' he said and laughed.

I smiled. 'I agree. They don't seem to be getting much out of it. They were here the other day too, doing exactly the same thing. It seems very one dimensional and utterly, utterly boring.' And we were off. We were talking.

He straightened up, stretched a bit and then sat down again. 'Do you live nearby?' he asked.

I pointed over my shoulder. 'Yes, in that house over there. I haven't been there that long.'

'I thought I hadn't seen you walking around.'

'No, I haven't been out that much. I have a lot of sorting out to do like emptying boxes' I replied. I didn't want to go into the real reason why I had abandoned the outside world.

'I have been here a few times, always making myself comfortable on this bench. You might not have noticed me sitting here. I don't always wear this hat or scarf,' he said and smiled. It was a lovely smile. I looked at his hat and scarf. They covered up an awful lot of his face and all of his hair. It was difficult to see what he looked like so I doubt I would have recognised him. I was struggling to remember if I had seen him before but couldn't. He started to take off his layers. When he removed them, it was like someone removing a mask. He was an older gentleman with the most wonderful fluffy white hair. It looked like someone had attempted to backcomb it but had done a pretty bad job. If the sun had been shining, it would have glistened and shimmered. His face was a wonder to look at. He reminded me of a character from a fantasy novel about goblins and trolls. He had a hooked beak for a nose that looked like it had been made from Play-Doh. At the last moment, someone had decided to pull it slowly downwards a bit more so it was longer and thinner. I looked and thought you could possibly hang a very small coat off the end of it. His eyes were the most brilliant hypnotic blue. His eyebrows were large and curled up at each end as if he had wet his fingers and idly played with them for such a long time that they had dried and permanently stayed like that.

'My name is Elizabeth; well, Beth.' I got up a bit and put my hand out to shake his. He hesitated for a moment and then extended his hand and we shook. His hand felt so soft that I doubted he had ever done any manual labour in his life. I couldn't imagine him smashing boulders or working on a building site for a living. Maybe he just used really good hand cream though. I was often wrong.

'My name is Harry.' He looked straight at me with those pools of blue water.

I looked back at him. What do I do now? What should happen now? I had forgotten the etiquette about who does what first.

He sighed. 'I live in a care home for older people, very close by over there. I have done for the last five years, ever since my wife died and the powers that be didn't think I could cope by myself, even though I am very capable of looking after myself. Being there has helped me to look back on my life but it hasn't been great. There doesn't seem to be anything good on the horizon and the home really isn't my cup of tea. You know what? Looking back, I wish I had done more fun things. I wish I had taken my wife, Maisie, out more often and had a good time, laughed and joked more. We could have sat down together years later and talked about how happy we had been and still were.' He paused. 'Sorry; you don't want to hear this. I am warbling on too much.' He turned to me.

'No, please, if you want to talk, talk,' I said. I was enjoying listening to his voice and being in the company of another person.

I actually felt privileged that he had spoken to me.

'Being there has taught me one thing. You need to live your life. Grab it with two hands. I never did and I don't like to see anyone else just waste away like a wilting flower. I know you don't know me from Adam. I hope you don't feel offended by me rattling on. I apologise if I am taking up your time. It's been very nice to talk to you but I need to go now and continue sitting in God's Waiting Room.' He pointed at his care home on the other side of the park. He got up, waved goodbye and started to walk off. He had a nice bouncy step about him.

'Okay. See you again, hopefully,' I said and waved back as he went off.

He looked back and said, 'Yes, that would be very nice'.

I stroked my chin. What an odd conversation. I never imagined that someone I hadn't met before would suddenly start telling me how they felt and how I should live my life. I wondered if he was lonely and just wanted to open up to another person. I knew that feeling. He was the first person I had said more than ten words to in six months and now it was over. I felt very thoughtful. What an impact he had made. I thought about what he had said and it crossed my mind that I hadn't really done anything with my life either.

It felt like he had been sent to tell me to get off my backside, which seemed to be getting larger by the week, and do something - anything - that would bring joy back into my life. I had been far too sad. I got up and walked the short way home. Time to confront my emotions. Time for a good hard look at myself. I knew it would be a marathon, not a sprint.

2

David and My Next Encounter

I know why I looked out of the window a lot and why happiness and company have become strangers to me. I looked out my window because I hoped that maybe, just maybe, my partner, who was killed in an accident abroad a little over a year and a half ago, hadn't been, and would instead come running over the grass waving at me as I looked out a window, shouting at me, 'I'm here!! Look!! They made a mistake. A big mistake'. Mostly, I sat in front of the large window in my living room, on a large comfy lounge chair with a cushion at the back for my head. I had been sitting there as my main outlook on life for over a year. I had been unable to bury David or even go to where he had died as it was too dangerous for me to travel there. The army couldn't return his body intact and instead sent over a small box that was given to his parents. He had been killed helping the army in Afghanistan. I had never really been told how he died exactly, just that it was a terrible tragedy and what a great bloke he was. There had been no real inquest, just a letter of condolence from his boss and the commander-in-chief. I was unable to say goodbye properly and now, because there had been a rift with his parents, I had no idea where he

16

was buried. My world collapsed when David died. My walls had turned to rubble.

How could other people understand how I felt day in day out unless they too had lost someone so close, so precious that it almost felt like you breathed in unison when together? How could I explain that loss to anyone? My fingernails were turning into bloody stumps and I wasn't sleeping well as all I thought about was David. I felt like I was suffocating.

I didn't recognise myself now. I needed someone to throw me a strong rope ladder so I could climb up out of my pit of sadness and feel the fresh air on my face again and hold on tightly to someone else. What do you do when you have so much love still to give for the person you wanted to spend the rest of your life with and they are no longer here? That love needed to go somewhere, to someone, but I wasn't ready to do that yet.

David and I had been together for ten years. We met through a mutual friend in a pub near the River Thames. I was celebrating my forty-fourth birthday and David was celebrating getting a new job. We had raised a glass to both events and talked and drank throughout the night. The next day, we went to a restaurant and carried on talking and drinking. A month later, we were living together. Six months later, we had bought our first home together. We were never married. David said he didn't want to be restricted by the conventions of modern society with all its certificates and paperwork.

David was killed just after we moved into this house by the park, our second home. This was the place where we were meant to grow old together, watch old paint crack and peel off the walls and have heated debates about what colours to paint them while waving paint pots at each other. We would have planted bulbs and watched them come up year after year and nurtured the garden together, watching everything grow and bloom in riotous colours. If I had been given the choice, I would have had what was left of him cremated so he would always be near me in our house. I would have been able to talk to him in person every day and ask his opinion on things. I would have said good morning and good night to him and told him endlessly that I loved him. I had been unable to move on. I just couldn't. Everywhere I walked it was like stepping in treacle. Listening to Harry had said was like being shaken vigorously and poked in the eye.

After my first attempt at a decent chat with someone else hadn't gone all that well, I decided to hold a meeting. It would have to be with myself as there was no one else. I looked at myself in a full-length mirror, walked up and down and side to side and discussed my options with my reflected self. 'We' both nodded and agreed that I should try again. I needed to try again. If nothing else, I needed the company. My friends and family had all but given up on me and I didn't blame them. The phone never rang now. When it did, it was usually from someone trying to scam me out of money. I can't tell you what I shouted at the last person who tried that.

For it to work and to stop me desperately launching myself at the first person who passed by, it was decided following the meeting, that I would be the one to sit on a bench - any bench - first. I would relax and wait for someone to come to me.

I chose the following Saturday. I had looked at the weather forecast for the week ahead and Saturday was the best day and there would hopefully be more people out and about. It would be sunny with some cloud cover with a very small chance of rain. I took those odds.

I felt like it was my second and possibly last chance so I wanted to look my best. I wasn't too great at rejection. I got a nice trouser suit out and hung it up on the outside of my wardrobe along with an overcoat.

On the Saturday morning, I had a shower, drank a coffee, ate a slice of toast with marmite on it, got dressed and tentatively stepped outside. I took my sketchbook with me as I had just started to draw again and it would help distract me if things didn't work out. It was one pleasure I did enjoy these days. The sun was out. There was one small cloud in the sky trying as hard as possible to cover it but it was failing miserably. There was quite a strong breeze and I could hear birds singing loudly. *How lovely*, I thought. I walked around the park as I hadn't been on any real walks for a long time. I could also do with the exercise. There were a few people out, some moving slowly taking in the scenery, the usual few who had their heads bent down looking at their mobile phones with a finger sweeping up and down on their screens poised to text or call someone. They were going so fast that everyone else had to move out of their way. Then there was me.

I stopped suddenly on one of the paths. I looked at a particular bench. This was one that David and I used to sit on, eat sandwiches, talk and rock backwards and forwards while laughing together. The memory was both painful and joyful. The bench was dappled dark grey by the shadow of leaves on the tree above. They sang and rustled in the wind and danced and swayed gently, making the bench look like it was slowly being shaken. The movement blurred my vision of it. I walked on. I couldn't sit there. At the end of the path, running between two large squares of grass, there was another bench. I sat down at one end. I crossed my left leg over my right leg. I uncrossed it. I scratched my nose. I was nervous. There weren't too many people out, but to me, it felt like a large crowd was milling around me. I started to draw aspects of the park in my sketchbook. People walked by but no one sat down. I got out a bottle of fresh orange juice and drank some. I put it back in my bag. More people walked past. 'This isn't going to work,' I said under my breath. 'Go home and keep looking out that blasted window. Who would want to talk to me anyway?' I put my sketchbook down on the bench and put my pencil in my pocket.

I was twiddling my thumbs and thinking about leaving when someone did stop. A woman. She looked like she was in her late fifties. Her hair was all over the place as the wind had blown it out of its original combed neatness. She held a bag of shopping in each hand and was struggling slightly. She sat down at the end of the bench and gasped, 'Ooo, aahh'. I was hoping she would finish it off with a round of cha-cha-chas but she didn't. She put the bags on the ground with a bit of a clatter.

'God,' she said, 'why have I never bought myself a shopping trolley? I feel like I am carrying lead weights in these bags.' She looked over at me and smiled such a full-faced smile that her eyes disappeared. *Go for it*, I thought. *It's now or never*. I was beginning to appreciate smiles again.

I laughed at what she said. 'I got a trolley a couple of years ago as my back would kill me after lugging bags home. It also felt like I was losing height every time with the weight of the bags pushing me down.' She laughed back.

20

'Will we ever learn?' she said. She looked at me again and then down at my sketchbook. 'What are you drawing, if you don't mind me asking?'

'Different parts of the park and the people here. I used to draw a lot but haven't for a while so I thought it was about time I started again. Do you want to have a look?'

'Yes, please,' she said.

I handed her my sketchbook. She took her time to look at each drawing.

'These are good. I like them. You have talent. By the way, my name's Katherine. Kath.' She gave me a little wave.

'I'm Elizabeth. Beth.' I lifted my hand and waved back.

I know people say don't go on first appearances but Kath seemed like a really nice warm person, the sort of person I would very much like to get to know better.

'Do you live close by?' Kath asked.

'I do, yes, in that house over there.' I pointed.

'That looks like a nice house. I love that large bush at the front.'

'It's called a Burning Bush, I think. Can't think of its Latin name, though. It was there when we... I, moved in. Much smaller, of course. Are you nearby?'

'Yes. I moved into a maisonette on the other side of the park a few weeks back. I have access to a superb garden but I am going to have to get someone in to look at it. I haven't a clue what to do with it and it looks a total mess.'

There was a pause.

'This might be a bit forward, and please say no if you don't think it is a good idea, but I can have a look if you like. I used to help my family out with their landscape gardening business during the holidays and at weekends. I'm not an expert but I have lots of useful guides at home and know a bit about plants.'

'That is very kind of you. Very kind indeed. Thank you. How about tomorrow afternoon at 3 pm? We can have tea and cake. I will pay you for your time too.' I refused payment and said a nice cup of tea and a slice of cake would be fine. She gave me her address on a piece of paper and we swapped phone numbers just in case a problem arose and one of us had to cancel. I folded the paper up and put it in my pocket. 'See you tomorrow,' she added and she was gone with a slow flourish.

I remained sitting on the bench for a while and smiled to myself. That was easier than I had thought. For ages, I had struggled to bring myself out of my shell, a shell of reinforced concrete, in order to meet new people and open my mouth and just talk. Now, in the space of a week, I had spoken to two people. The first conversation had not been that great but what Harry had said was the kick up the backside I needed. The kick that had started to crack open my shell. I realised I had put too much unnecessary pressure on myself to get out and make contact with other people.

3

Tea, Gardening and More

The next day, I put on a pair of old jeans and an old top and put my wellington boots and gardening gloves in a bag. That was at 8 am. I wasn't going over to Kath's until 3.30 pm. I sat in my chair in front of the window and then pottered around until it was time to leave. I watered my houseplants, moved magazines from tables, moved magazines back to tables, tried again not to look out the window too much but did, hoovered the stairs again and then again, cleaned some kitchen surfaces, descaled the kettle and sorted out all my recycling. I did not want to let my house go to rack and ruin now. I didn't want to just give up and let the dust settle year after year. I needed to put personal items out and placed photos of family and friends and David and me around my living room. I put my favourite photo of David on the mantelpiece. He was looking full-faced into the camera with his hair flopping over his left eye, smiling. It looked and felt more homely. I wondered, *is this happening too quickly?* I knew I wouldn't change overnight. I couldn't sort out David's clothes. They were still in the wardrobe and chest of drawers.

When I looked out of the window, I could see Harry walking around the park. He was with someone else, another older man. They were deep in conversation. Arms were being flung up in the air and fingers were being pointed. They stopped a few times to look at each other, shaking their heads, but then, after a short while, they carried on walking. It crossed my mind to go and talk to him but thought it best not to interrupt. It looked like a serious discussion was taking place.

I had some lunch, did a bit more cleaning and then left my house at 3.25 pm. Kath's place was only a five-minute walk across the park. More people were out and I found myself tentatively smiling and saying 'Good afternoon' as I walked by.

I rang Kath's doorbell. It sounded like the Charge of the Light Brigade. It was very loud. I heard her inside running towards the door, thump, thump, a big thump and then silence. She opened it with her arms outstretched. 'Delighted to see you again, Beth.'

'Likewise,' I said.

'Come in, please.'

She ushered me through to a large hall reception area. I put the bag with the wellington boots and gardening gloves in it beside the front door. There were lots of big-leafed plants in pots scattered around, framed photos on the walls, a telephone on a table, a mirror on a wall and lots of shelves stuffed full of books. We went through to her living room. I stood by her French windows and looked at her garden. I could see why she needed help with it. The garden looked like a mini-Glastonbury had taken place on it over the last week. It was so muddy. I imagined there was a tent in a hidden corner of the garden desperately trying to remain upright but leaning over to one side rather forlornly.

'As you can see, it needs a lot of work. I really don't think I have been blessed with green fingers.' Kath was standing next to me. 'Tea, coffee, wine?'

'Well, it will give us something to do then and we will get it sorted,' I said. 'Sorry, yes, tea, please. Just milk. No sugar. Sweet enough, as they say.'

When Kath went to sort the tea and a slice of cake, I looked around the room. Like her hall area, it was full of furniture, plants and books. She had lots of books all over the place. There were several piles stacked high as she had run out of shelf space. There were two alcoves on either side of a very ornate fireplace. She had lots of ornaments on shelves. *I bet they are a bugger to dust,* I thought. Her sofa and armchairs had seen much better days and were covered in different coloured throws. When I did sit in an armchair, I sank straight into it and it felt very comfortable. She had several rugs all over the floor which covered her wooden floorboards. I could see papers and newspapers on most of the surfaces. There were photos of Kath with a man who looked about the same age as her on several shelves and on a side table. They looked very happy together. One of them seemed to show them on a cruise in Egypt.

Kath came in with a tray of cups, milk and a teapot. There were slices of a Victoria sponge cake on a plate. We drank, ate and talked. I only had one slice of cake as all my clothes were starting to feel tight. I could hardly cross my legs when I wore trousers.

'Is that your husband, Kath?'

Kath put down her cup and looked at the photo nearest to her on the table. She picked it up gently.

'This is my husband, Christopher. He passed away nearly two years ago.' Kath breathed in deeply and out slowly.

I leaned over and touched her arm. 'I am so sorry, Kath. I know exactly how you feel. I lost my partner just over a year ago.'

'Oh, Beth. We are in the same boat, aren't we?'

I was still finding it difficult to connect with people even on a very basic level, and, although Kath and I had only met each other twice, I felt a very close friendship was starting to take shape. Like pancakes and maple syrup. She seemed like someone I could have been best friends with at school or university. Someone I would have shared secrets with over wine and dinner and then lost touch with over the years. This felt like a wonderful reunion of sorts.

I told her about me and how I stood in front of the window every day, waiting, waiting for David to return; how I had lost the nerve and ability to see family and friends and how I had hardly been outside the house in the last year unless it was to go into the back garden or take the rubbish out. I ordered all my shopping and clothes online. Kath told me how she had finally got the strength to move to her maisonette. She had originally felt like she couldn't move somewhere else as she would be leaving all the memories of her life with Christopher behind and the guilt would overwhelm her. Then, after several bereavement counselling sessions and lots of talking with friends and family, she knew she could bring the memories with her. They would be in her head, in her own memories, her heart, their shared furniture, ornaments, Christopher's

26

clothes which she still had, photographs, letters and films of their holidays and day trips together. He would always be with her in spirit.

'Beth, have you tried any form of counselling at all? It helped me to deal with certain aspects of my marriage and my loss.'

'I did, Kath. I went for about two months but got bored with it. It isn't for everyone and I just felt I was burdening the other person with the same issues over and over again.'

'That is the point though, Beth, to be able to talk to someone else, to offload to a stranger.'

'I know but it just wasn't for me. I just wanted to hide away. I tried self-help books but ended up taking them all to a charity shop.'

'But now you are starting to resurface, by the looks of it.'

'Yes, I am and I like it.' I had been swimming underwater for a long time but was now putting my head above the waves.

After an hour or so, we finally remembered to go out and look at Kath's garden. The sky was starting to grow dark and slowly pull its curtains together. Kath got a couple of torches to light up our way. I put my wellington boots on. We had a quick look around and discussed options and plans. I left at 8 pm. I said I would look at plants and flowers and come up with some options for her. We could also go to a garden centre to have a look and get some advice. We arranged to meet again the following weekend. My life was starting to take a turn for the better and I felt good about that.

4

Making Plans

The following Saturday morning, I went round to Kath's. We had a quick cup of coffee and then went out to the garden. I could see more than last weekend, that's for sure, as the light was now much brighter. There were a few bushes around the edges that were quite skeletal and a sad-looking tree on one side which needed a good prune and spruce up. In the many beds scattered about, there were no flowers, no colour apart from grassy green and earthy brown from the lawn which had spread itself everywhere.

We walked around and both pointed at areas saying 'Um' and 'Yes, that's a good idea, yes that might work, oh, I like that' a lot. I wrote stuff down and after an hour of looking, poking and finding anything that might still be alive, we went inside and I went through my notes on what plants and flowers would be best for a south-facing garden. Kath led on drawing the plan of what her ideal garden would look like and I added bits here and there. It wasn't a huge garden so between us we would be able to get quite a lot done in the next few weeks. Kath said she had some friends who had offered to help as well but she would stick with me. Kath said we could use her car to drive to a garden centre and get everything we needed.

We had another cup of coffee and then decided to get on with some actual physical work in the garden. Kath had a shed at the end of her garden which contained an assortment of items including gardening gloves, wellington boots, spades, forks, trowels and even a wheelbarrow. It also contained a lot of spiders' webs and, no doubt, tenant spiders, so I stayed outside and Kath handed me all the equipment we thought we would need. Then, with the tools by our sides like soldiers with rifles on parade, we stood and surveyed the task ahead.

The beds needed tidying up so we started there first. We slowly lowered ourselves onto some knee pads, grunting and oohing, and began getting rid of weeds, ancient twigs and rogue grass that had sprouted away from the lawn. It was almost like the grass was trying to escape to pastures new as it had had enough of its current habitation.

We finished at lunchtime and decided to get some sandwiches from the local take-away and sit outside in the garden to survey what we had done and praise ourselves endlessly. It was looking a lot better already.

'Day one in Kath's house'. She said it in a strong Northern accent and giggled. She settled herself back in a garden chair and finished her sandwich.

I smiled and found myself giggling too. This was fun. I had missed doing things like this. Life can be tough or you can make life tough. Mine was a mixture of both.

'Do you work, Kath? I asked.

''Part-time, yes.' She didn't say anymore and I wasn't sure if I should ask again but did.

'What do you do?'

'I work in a place where we help people realise their dreams. We give vouchers out so people can go in a hot air balloon, drive a racing car, run with camels or brush alpacas. You know the sort of thing. I used to be a social worker but the stress was getting far too much for me so I changed direction completely. I won't stay in this job that long though. I have too many other things I want to do before I leave this planet.'

Kath looked at me. 'What do you want to do? What are your dreams, Beth?'

'Now, there's a question.' I thought for a while. 'I took early retirement from a job in the city. Like your previous social work job, it was getting too much for me. When David was here, we had lots of things we wanted to do, places we wanted to see but his work always took top billing and he was often away for months. We never really did too much, to be honest, even though we were together for just over a decade. We did have a wonderful three-week holiday once. We drove down the west coast of America from San Francisco to Los Angeles. Something I had always wanted to do. Fantastic views and we stopped off in some lovely towns. That was six years ago, though. My dreams? I can't think of any at the moment. Sorry.'

I stopped talking. I would tell her more about David, but not now. I realised that my life had been standing still for years, like waiting at a bus stop for a bus that was never going to arrive. I had spent too much time on one side of the road never crossing it to find out what was on the other side and beyond. 'Kath, I used to be someone. Now I am going to be one of those single people who doesn't get invited to dinner parties just in case I fancy one of the other women's husbands.'

'Don't be silly. You are someone now, Beth. We both are.'

Kath gave a little cough. 'Beth, can I suggest something? We haven't known each other that long but I feel like we could become really good friends. We get on well, I like to think. Beth, I have dreams. I know you have them too. You just need to dig them out. What if, and you can say no - I won't be offended - what if we did some dreams together? It would help cheer us both up. You never know, we might have some of the same ones. What do you think? Why don't we just go for it? Carpe diem and all that.'

I started to cry. I could feel my face change, losing its stiffness as if someone had grabbed hold of it like a piece of old paper and was scrunching it up to throw it in the bin, ready to be replaced with a softer, happier look.

'Oh, Kath. You don't know what it means to hear you say that. I need to get my life back in some order so yes, yes, yes!!' I got up and danced around a bit. Kath joined me and we ended up doing the conga out into the garden. The neighbours must have thought we were bonkers.

Later that day, we went to a local garden centre. Kath chose several bedding plants and we came back and planted them. The garden was starting to take shape.

Kath hosed it down and I put all the dead bits and pieces in a large bag.

'You could have a compost area, Kath. I could make one for you.'

'Thank you, Beth. I would really appreciate that.' She looked around.

This is going to look marvellous,' Kath said. She was standing with her hands on her hips surveying her kingdom.

'It is, Kath, it is.' I smiled. 'It certainly is.'

5

The Dinner Party

Over the next couple of weeks, Kath and I got to know each other better. We needed to, particularly if we were going to be spending time together fulfilling our dreams. We talked, we laughed, we cried together. We did more work in the garden. Kath invited me round for a dinner party she was giving for some of her friends the following week. I was very hesitant. I wasn't used to being around a lot of people. The last time was at David's memorial service and I really could have done without all the squeezing of my shoulders, the patting of my back and the awkward looks of sorrow with people biting their bottom lips and just staring at me. No one had really spoken to me at the memorial. It was all comfort very much from afar. David's parents ignored me. They partly blamed me for his death, saying I had encouraged him to go out to Afghanistan and help the army. I hadn't. It was his job. He had no choice.

'There are only going to be three other people apart from us, Beth. I wouldn't invite you if there was going to be loads. Like you, too many people all together is a big no-no for me, but like you, I need to get back into the swing of things and this is going to be the start.'

I decided to go to Kath's. *Bugger it*, I thought. This was the first invite out to a formal occasion I had received for ages and I could always leave early if I felt uncomfortable. I got out my smartest dress and polished my best shoes. I had a long shower and washed my hair with shampoo that David had liked to use. I often nuzzled into his hair after he had dried it to take in the aroma. I put on some make-up and perfume. I looked at myself in the mirror and suddenly felt very down.

'Who are you trying to kid? Eh?' I said. I had half a mind to take everything off and just go and sit in front of the telly as per usual, eat a Pot Noodle or two and watch yet more television. I would phone Kath and say I had suddenly come down with a cold. Something stopped me from doing this though. A photo of David clattered to the floor. It was the one on the mantelpiece and it had never moved before. The glass had fallen out so I put it back in. I looked at his smiling face, his stubble, his blonde hair and knew that he would not have wanted me to give up. 'Stop existing, Beth. Start living.' I could hear David talking to me. He liked having fun but it was all too rare for us to share any joy. I could remember us once running hand in hand towards the sea at Brighton beach, the pebbles beneath us shifting and moving. We had jumped in fully clothed. We had sat on the stony beach afterwards, shivering, covered up with beach towels. I could also hear Harry's words resonating in my ears too.

I thought I would go a bit early to Kath's just so I could talk to her as my internal mechanisms were rocking, causing my stomach to turn over and over. There was, however, already someone else there. She was about the same age as me, tall and slim with a mop of dark curly hair which fell down

33

around her shoulders. She had a hairband wrapped tightly around her head.

'Hello, my name is Bette. My mum named me after her favourite Hollywood actress, Bette Davis. Very nice to meet you.' Her smile and handshake were firm and warm.

'Hello, I'm Beth.'

Kath got us a drink each, a nice red wine and we all went into the living room and sat down.

'Kath said you live over the other side of the park and have become good friends recently.'

'Yes. We actually met in the park when we sat on the same bench.'

Bette leaned forward.

'She needs someone like you. Someone who has been through the same tragic event. Someone who knows what it feels like and how to recover. She told me about you. I hope you don't mind?'

'I don't know about how to recover. I'm still working my way through all that. The long and winding, very bumpy road and all that.' I laughed nervously. I was a bit annoyed that Kath had spoken about me to this woman but put it to one side. *Worse things happen at sea,* I thought, *and I am sure Kath did not mean any disrespect by it. I needed someone like Kath too, to be honest.*

Bette suddenly shouted at Kath who was in the kitchen. 'Kath, what was the surname of that Pearl woman whose husband ran off with the cleaner? She found a lovely man to settle down with after a couple of years.'

'Harbour,' Kath replied.

'No, it wasn't, silly,' Beth chortled. 'I can't remember it. Anyway, the point is, she is very happy now. I am too, as it happens. My latest boyfriend thinks I am heaven-sent and absolutely divine. You never know, Beth. It could happen to you given time.'

She was just about to carry on saying how wonderful she was when the doorbell rang and two more people came in, Tim and Harriet, a couple who, whenever they spoke, always said 'We'.

We did the usual round of introductions, drank more wine and then Kath called us all to sit down at her long oak dining table. She had not put name tags on the table, thank goodness, so we could all sit where we wanted. There were only five of us, which was enough for me and Kath, I imagined.

'So, Beth. We understand you live on the other side of the park.' Tim and Harriet leant forward, clutching at each other and spoke and smiled as one. I thought about possibly just standing up and telling them all about myself just to avoid yet more questions.

I felt like Bridget Jones at a dinner party with everyone looking at me. Kath wasn't. She was tucking into the starter.

'Yes, I moved in about a year ago. Still sorting a few boxes out.' Those few boxes contained most of David's things like his personal possessions and I was struggling to get them out, to let the light shine on them, to feel his touch on them again. They were all up in the loft.

'This is wonderful if I say so myself. Do eat up, everyone.' Kath winked at me. She knew what Tim and Harriet were like, wanting to know everything about everyone.

'Are you there by yourself, then?' Harriet asked. 'We have a lovely house in Hampstead. You and Kath should both come up sometime. We would love that.'

'At the moment I am. Kath, could I get some more wine from the kitchen?' The bottle in front of me was empty and I needed a drink. I didn't comment on their Hampstead abode.

Kath followed me in. 'I am sorry about Tim and Harriet. I forgot they can be nosey blighters. Just tell them as little as possible. Leave them guessing. They don't need to know all your personal details. They normally love to talk about themselves and how great they are.'

'Just like Bette, then. I know she is your friend but if Bette was made of chocolate, she would eat herself. She thinks she is that tasty.'

'I know. Ignore her too.'

We talked about climate change and who was to blame and the pros and cons of electric cars - 'Can I find a charger free when we need one? No' - what we were watching on the multitude of television channels available, which I was an expert at, and Kath's garden with people suggesting plants, flowers and different types of ponds.

Tim and Harriet told us all about their wonderful garden. 'We have a beautiful secluded place. We love being there. We spend time meditating, doing yoga and exercising.' We, we, we.

They carried on. 'Harriet and I know that we have had several changes over millions of years. It's a natural occurrence. It's just what happens. This is just another one of them. We certainly haven't caused it.'

They owned a petrol-guzzling Range Rover so their comments didn't surprise me.

We ate our main course and dessert and then all moved to the sofa and chairs. Kath could see I was starting to feel uncomfortable. I had stopped joining in the conversation and just kept nodding my head to make them think I was listening to them but I wasn't. I was thinking about Harry and how he had managed to cope and carry on after losing his wife.

I left at about midnight. My legs were loose from the wine I had drunk. The dinner party had been a bit of an ordeal but it proved that my shell had opened a bit more. Fresh air and warm light were starting to come into my dark world. I walked the longer way home around the edges of the park. I felt safe even though it was dark.

I got in and drank some more wine. I knew I was drinking too much. I didn't smoke or take drugs but needed something to help me. I would have to put a stop to it, though, or really cut down. I tucked into a bag of crisps I found in a fruit bowl that never had any fruit in it. Salt and vinegar, my favourite.

I went to bed and cuddled what would have been David's pillow. I had a large fluffy toy dog on the bed which I often grabbed hold of. I rarely, if ever, had dreams now. Before David's loss, they were almost like watching a programme on television, in colour and with lots of talking.

I slept fitfully. I kept waking up in a panic and throwing my hands down on the duvet.

'Just put all this trauma in a box and bury it. Hide it away,' I repeated over and over again.

I finally had enough of tossing and turning and got up at 6.30 am the following morning. I got my coffee, sat in my chair and stared out of the window.

6

A List Begins and Our First Trip

The next day, I decided to sort myself out. I needed to move forward and thought about writing a few ideas down, my bucket list of sorts; what things David and I had wanted to do together and what things I had wanted to do by myself.

I sat at my table, pen in hand and stared down at the empty page. After a few minutes, I still couldn't think of anything I would like to do. My mind had gone completely blank. It had shut the door to happiness and enjoyment and I didn't have the key. I needed David's input. I chewed the end of the pen as I thought about the types of things Kath and I would both like to do but I didn't know her that well. For all I knew, she might be an expert rock climber which I would baulk at doing. But then again, it would be better if it was something that neither of us had done before.

I know I certainly didn't want to do what everyone always seemed to do - all those long walks over mountain ranges in a foreign country or long coastal walks from one end of the country to the other. There really was no point in thinking about what David and I would have liked doing as we hadn't done a great deal of things together.

My list started as follows:

Skydiving	As if
Potholing	Never in a million years. Sticking pins in my eyes would be better
Basket weaving	No. no. no
Landscape painting	This could be an option
Life drawing	Do I really want strangers drawing my bits and bobs or me drawing someone else's bits and bobs?
Walking on a glacier	Knowing me, it would start crashing into the sea as I was standing on the edge

I gave up and had a coffee. I looked out of the window and saw Harry, who had spoken to a couple of weeks ago. I ducked behind the curtain in case he saw me.

I called Kath. 'Kath, hi. I was wondering if I could come over or if you can come to me to have a chat. I would love to start organising our dream trips together.'

Kath came over to me at 7.30 pm that evening. I opened a bottle of wine. Kath had had a very large lunch with a friend so said she didn't want anything to eat at mine. I still put out nibbles which Kath tucked into. I had eaten a crisp sandwich before she arrived.

'Ah, the stuff of dreams,' Kath said and laughed when I read her my list. 'Not my idea of a fab time, I must say. Life drawing though, sketching someone else might be okay.'

'I know. Not brilliant, is it? My list looks rubbish'.

'Can I make a suggestion? Let's look at unusual things to do here in the UK and what we would like to do abroad. We can decide if we both like any of them and go from there.'

We decided to use technology as neither of us could think of anything fun and exciting to do.

I got my laptop and typed in 'Fun things to do in the UK'. A ton of pages came up.

'Good to know that it's not all doom and gloom here, then,' Kath said. 'I jest.'

I clicked on one page and a maze came up; the longest one in England, apparently. We both looked at the photos of it. 'Jesus, it's nearly one and a half acres with nearly two miles of pathways. That is big.' I sat back on the sofa. 'We are going to have to take a rather large supply of food and water.'

'And a compass,' Kath piped up. 'It might help us get out quicker.'

'I have an adequate rucksack, small, but you can pack a lot in.'

We both squealed and leaned into each other's shoulders.

'Let's go for it. It's not the biggest event in the entire world but it is a good start to our new adventures. Let's start little and then look at going big.' She patted my hand and we drank more wine and ate more nibbles to celebrate.

We had organised to go to the maze in a couple of weeks' time. It was in the grounds of a stately home which also housed a safari park so we decided to visit those too. We agreed to go during the week on a day when Kath wasn't working as we thought there would be fewer people around.

Thursday. We set off early in Kath's car which was as old as the hills but got us there in one piece. My passenger door was a bit temperamental and Kath had to help wrench it open when we got there.

The first thing we both needed to do was find the ladies' toilets. It had been a long drive. Then we decided that before we did anything else, we would need something to eat and drink.

'For sustenance. We both need to keep our strength up.'

'Of course we do, Beth.'

We found the café and sat down outside. It was a nice day, not boiling hot, thank goodness, but warm enough.

'Now, I would have thought a place like this would have served up lark's wing sandwiches, peacock eggs and pheasant pâté,' Kath said.

We got tea and cake instead. We gobbled down the cake and drank the tea as if they were both going out of fashion. I could see us going into the maze, getting lost and being found five years later as skeletons, clinging to each other in the hollow of a large hedge.

'Have you got a map of the maze, Beth, by any chance?'

'I think the whole point of going in a maze is that you don't cheat and find your own way out unaided.'

'Yep, you are right. Come on then.'

We went into the maze and I immediately felt the utter silence all around me. I don't quite know how someone can feel silence other than not hearing a noise but I felt like my head had been wiped all over with a hot cloth and any sounds had floated upwards. It was how I had felt at home. We were the only ones in there.

'Now, how do you want to do this?' I asked Kath as I looked around. All I could see were curving pathways and very tall hedgerows. There were no arrows as you went in to say 'please take this path first'.

'Hum,' said Kath, who also looked around. 'Let's toss a coin. Heads we go this way, tails we go that way.'

It was heads.

We stood on the path and headed off. We walked for a few minutes, following each other as we wound around corners into constant dead-ends. We sat down on a bench we found in one dead-end and munched on some food. We pointed at hopeful pathways only to be repelled back again by a huge hedge wall. It was like playing chess but always being in checkmate.

'If you climbed on my shoulders, Beth, you might be able to see over the hedges and find the way out.'

'I don't think you could carry me, Kath. Do you remember seeing a map on a board just before we came in?'

'No,' said Kath. 'Anyhow, I wouldn't have the faintest idea how to get back to the beginning now even if there was a map.'

I thought I had seen a map but we were so sure we would get through it easily that we had ignored it.

We had gone into the maze at 11.30 am. It was now 1 pm. I needed the toilet again.

'I need a wee,' I said. 'I will wet myself soon.'

'Me too,' Kath replied as she started to squirm and cross her legs.

'Look, there's no one around. Let's go down one of the many dead-ends we discovered, tuck into a gap in a hedge and go there.'

'Be rude not to,' Kath said.

We scuttled off and were just taking our trousers down when a family suddenly appeared. We stood like statues and stared at them. The mother stared back at us; one of her children picked its nose, the other child swayed from side to side and the father looked away.

The mum put her hand across her son's eyes. 'Tarkas, Poppet, come on. Let's go.'

When they had gone, we quickly had a pee and pulled our trousers up.

'Who calls their kid Tarkas?' I asked.

'Might be short for Tarquin, I suppose. I like the name Poppet but that might be a nickname too.'

'Well, whatever, that wasn't embarrassing, was it?'

We laughed out loud. More people were starting to come into the maze so we made a promise not to pee in there again even if we were desperate. I had visions of the police waiting for us as we left. Then again, they might just give up as we had been in there so long and I couldn't see us getting out before 4 pm.

We walked and walked. We sang. I particularly liked us singing the Colonel Hathi Elephant March from The Jungle Book - my favourite - 'Up, two, three, four, keep it up, two, three, four.'

We completely lost track of where we were. Then it started to rain. There was no cover in the maze but at least we had hoods on our coats. The rain got heavier. I imagined the earth getting softer and softer and turning into a bog or quicksand with us sinking down until all anyone could see were our hoods. We ran round corners, down long paths, said 'Bugger' and 'Sod' a few times at more dead-ends, ran our hands along the hedges and then, suddenly, we saw the exit. We fell in a heap outside the maze and stayed there for a short while.

People had started to gather and look at us so we got up, wiped ourselves down and walked off very casually. We were covered in damp earth and had started to smell like wet dogs. We sat in the car with the heater on so we could dry out and then drove through the safari park. We really needed to wind the windows down as the smell was starting to make us gag but we couldn't in case a marauding animal stuck its head or claws in. We left the safari park in a bit of a hurry.

'I somehow don't think people will appreciate us going into the stately home looking like this and smelling like this. Another time?' Kath did look like she had been dragged through a hedge backwards, a very tall hedge with lots of twiggy bits sticking out.

7

Opening Up

I had a long hot soak in a bubble bath before going to bed that night. I slept really well. The next day, my legs ached like mad. The gardening and all that walking around the maze was the most exercise I had done in ages.

Kath and I agreed that it had been a very worthwhile exercise in all senses even though we had ended up extremely wet, covered in mud and smelt appallingly badly.

I decided that I needed to sort out several things in my house. For starters, I had the biggest pile of old bank statements to shred. I have since gone paperless. All my windows needed cleaning inside and out, my rugs needed a good clean and the doors and walls needed a wipe down. Over the next couple of days, my house began to look much better. Everything was spotless. I was very proud of myself and felt pretty content.

I hadn't been in contact with many friends for a while. I couldn't handle them wanting to know how I was when all I wanted to do was shout at them, 'How the hell do you think I am?'

Kath had been working Monday through to Wednesday making people happy and getting lots of thanks from them. We met on Thursday afternoon in a local coffee shop.

The windows had steamed up so we couldn't see outside. It did feel like a secret club. Whenever someone opened the door to come in, everyone stopped talking and looked up. I wanted to shout out, 'What's the password?' but refrained from doing so. We had coffee and a slice of cake each. We both agreed that we did like cake, any cake really.

'So, marks out of five for our first venture out together,' Kath said, biting into her cake which she declared was delicious.

'Do you mean apart from getting caught with our knickers down, getting lost and spending most of the day saying bugger, let's try this way, collapsing in a heap outside the maze and smelling like we had jumped in a pool full of stagnant water?'

We both laughed.

'Okay, so maybe a few things went wrong but it was alright, wasn't it? You did enjoy it, didn't you?'

'Of course I did, Kath. I loved it. Getting out and doing something new, something different was and is the best thing for me.'

People started to leave but Kath and I stayed on to enjoy another slice of cake each.

Kath cleared her throat. 'Beth, there's something I haven't told you about Christopher. I will just come out with it so please listen and then we can talk afterwards. Christopher and I were very happily married, or so I thought. We talked, we laughed and we smiled together. We loved films, going to the theatre, going on long walks, going to exhibitions, art galleries. We went on holidays together, both in this country and abroad.'

Kath paused for a moment. 'When Christopher died, we had the funeral. I knew everyone who attended, family, friends. As I gave my eulogy, I looked at all the people and saw a woman with a child. I didn't recognise them. I assumed it might have been one of Christopher's work colleagues. Afterwards, we had drinks and food in Christopher's favourite pub. This woman was there too, outside in the garden with her child. She smiled at me and I smiled back. I went to the bar and when I got my drink and went out to the garden, she came over to me with this child. She said she felt very awkward but needed to talk to me. We sat down in a corner and she told me that she was Christopher's wife too. Not an ex-wife, a current wife and that the child was his. Muggins here just sat there and took it all in. I didn't react. I didn't do anything. She said she didn't want to have to tell me at his funeral but she didn't know what else to do.'

Kath stopped and looked at me. I took that to mean I could now talk. 'Did you believe her? She wasn't the sort of nutter who looks in newspapers for the next available funeral and just turns up? Almost like a professional mourner? You do hear about people like that.'

'No, she was telling the truth. I checked her out later. She even gave me her name. Maggie Lofthouse. She kept saying she didn't want to cause any trouble. She wanted and needed to pay her respects quite rightly. She said they had been together for eight years. She didn't even know that he had died. She only found out when she saw his photo in a newspaper in the obituary section. It was then she realised he already had a wife. She had no idea about me. He had told her he had to go abroad for work on a regular basis and it was when he was with me on a small Greek island for a three-week holiday that he had had a heart attack in a small cove and died in a foreign land in a foreign hospital. I can't tell you how difficult it was to get him home. A dreadful storm had hit the island we were on. All power lines had gone down and no telephones were working. Forget about mobiles too. She, Maggie, said that she got worried when he hadn't contacted her after a couple of days. When she did phone his work, they had no record of him having to work abroad. Then she said she thought all sorts of things, that he had run off with another woman or that something dreadful had happened to him. She rang all the hospitals to see if he had been taken in following some sort of accident. Then she started checking the newspapers. She was actually okay. She didn't know about me and I didn't know about her so we didn't really have any reason to be angry with each other. We were both angry with Christopher, however, for his deceitfulness. Thinking back, there were lots of occasions when Christopher would go off 'for work' for two to three weeks. I always believed him. Why wouldn't I?'

'Sorry, Kath, and stop me if you think I am intruding. What about his will? Was there anything in it that made you suspicious?'

Kath shook her head. 'He left me the house and some money but there was, in fact, a trust fund for the child with a monthly provision for Maggie. Christopher had apparently put her down as a long-standing and loyal friend who he now wanted to help. I found out after talking to Maggie over tea and cake. It worked out that he had left roughly half of the money to each of us. There was nothing that made me question anything. I couldn't turn up for the reading of the will. I was too ill so I didn't meet Maggie there. All I wanted to do afterwards was hide under my duvet and sleep for a year. I just wanted to forget about everything; erase it all.'

I myself am an intensely private person. For Kath to tell me all this and trust me was huge for me. I felt she trusted me. I had never told anyone exactly how I was feeling and that was the problem but I felt with her I could start to let go and share. My only issue was maybe with her telling other people. She assured me that telling Bette about me was a one-off. Bette was asking questions about how we met and she wanted to shut her up.

People began to think I was alright when I wasn't and they didn't check. My actions were mostly to blame. I gave the impression I didn't need any help and that I was strong enough to cope by myself. I had cut people out of my life.

That night I had a dream about David. It was my first dream of him since he had died. We were dancing close to each other with my head on his shoulder. We were on a beach and our feet kept sinking into the smooth yellow softness of sand. Suddenly, I decided to run, run down the beach with my arms out and my head up facing the sun. It reminded me of our trip to the seaside. I turned around and David wasn't there. He had gone.

8

The Next Challenge at Sea

'How about husky trekking in Yorkshire?'

'Sorry? What?' I was digging a hole for a pond in Kath's garden.

'You heard me.'

'Kath, I think it's too late. I doubt there will be much snow in Yorkshire now, nor has there been for a while. I can't imagine they would use roller-skates instead to get us around.'

'Oh, yes. How about sailing in a boat and sleeping in a room on an old sea fort then?'

I put the spade down. I thought and thought. Yes, that sounded good. 'Okay. Where are you thinking of? I would rather it wasn't round the Cape of Good Hope or other stormy parts of the world.'

'How about the Kent coast then?'

'Well, that can have its moments,' I said and smiled as I remembered David and I went and stood at the end of a pier at Herne Bay once and got drenched by a large wave.

Kath looked everything up on her laptop. She was good like that. 'Right, if we want to spend a bit of money, there is a sea fort near the Isle of Wight in the Solent that has been turned into a luxury hotel. It looks lovely I must say. It's not Kent, though, but it means we could nip over to the Isle of Wight afterwards for a few days if you'd like.'

'Yes, let's treat ourselves and stay over,' I said. I hadn't done that in a long time.

As it was not the height of the holiday season, we were able to book a double room for a weekend on the sea fort in two weeks' time and then rooms in a lovely hotel in Ryde on the Isle of Wight. I hadn't told Kath yet that I suffered badly from seasickness. I hoped that if I took some tablets beforehand, I wouldn't have to stand leaning over the side of a boat on our way to the sea fort with my head in a bag, waving any help away with a flailing hand while continually making retching noises. I didn't want to mention it to Kath.

The following weekend, I went over to Kath's and she was exercising. She was flat out over a large gym ball, arms and legs stretched out, balancing precariously. I knew that with just a small nudge......

'What are you doing?' I asked.

'We are going away and I want to look good. I'm not doing this crap for fun, you know. What if the sun comes out and I want to put a bikini on? Two Ton Tessie or a beached whale is not what I want to look like.'

'It's not going to make any difference if you only started exercising this week, you know.'

'I know, but it will make me think I have made a bit of an effort.'

Kath rolled slowly off the ball and onto the floor. I helped her get back to her feet. She let out a few 'Ooohs' and 'Aaahhs' plus one loud defiant 'Bollocks' and then 'Please excuse my French' and finally managed to stand up.

I packed my bag a few days before we were due to go to the sea fort. I then repacked it every day. 'You don't need to take the kitchen sink,' I said to myself as I took out a large radio CD player.

Kath and I met on the side of the road outside her flat and got into a pre-booked taxi with our cases. We sat next to each other, my seat belt eventually clicking into place following a few minutes of shouting, 'I can't find where to put it.'

'Said the virgin to the sailor,' Kath chortled. We both roared with laughter. That's what I liked about Kath. Her humour.

We got the train from Victoria Station to Portsmouth Harbour. It started to rain when we were halfway there. A short while later, it started to get very windy. My toes started to curl. All I could think of was how rough the sea might be. I looked in my bag for my tablets, popped one out of the packet and subtly put it in my mouth and drank water. The tablet stuck in my throat so I coughed and drank some more water.

'You okay, Beth?'

'Bright and breezy, Kath. Bright and breezy. Couldn't be better.' This was the complete opposite of how I was actually feeling.

We got off the train and walked the short distance to the harbour. The last time I had been here was with my mum to see the Mary Rose. It was shocking weather then and it was shocking weather now. It felt like invisible hands were flapping about and pushing Kath and me from side to side and backwards and forwards

'Well, this is utter cobblers,' Kath said loudly. The sound of her voice was quickly being blown away down the pathway and I was too slow to chase her words and catch them.

We got in a small boat which was going to take us to the sea fort. There were six of us. The captain had been umming and aaahing about going. He kept waggling his hand from side to side whenever another passenger asked him when we would be leaving.

After several minutes, the captain tossed a coin in the air and decided we could go. He got on the loudspeaker system. 'Just to let you know we will be leaving imminently. The sea is going to be somewhat choppy so please sit down in the galleried area. I wouldn't want any of you falling over the side.' I think he might have been trying to joke but it fell flat on the deck around him like the calm, still sea it should have been.

I should have told Kath about 'my condition'. How could I have put it? 'Oh, Kath, I forgot to mention that I can be violently sick, well not can be, am, whenever I set foot on a boat. Hope you don't mind as I can make loud almost dinosaur-like noises to accompany any sickness.'

We set off and I immediately felt like someone had stuffed me in a large bin, fastened the lid down and was violently shaking me up and down. I felt dreadful. I clutched a plastic bag in my coat pocket. I lurched forwards to get out to the side of the boat and threw my head over the side. That was that. I won't go into the gory details but the noise alone would have woken the dead. I am surprised no one videoed it on their phone and then stuck it on YouTube. 'Oh, you're the woman I saw on YouTube. That was really funny to watch.' 'Yes, funny to actually be doing it too,' would have been my response.

The captain snuck past me as I was in my last throws. He stood watching me for about five seconds and then quickly galloped off.

'He was very light on his loafers, wasn't he? Couldn't get away quick enough.' Kath had come out to see how I was. 'You would have thought he would at least have asked you how you were. Talking of which, how are you?'

'How do you think I am?' I said in between gulping down water from my bottle.

'Well, we are nearly there if that helps.' Kath pointed out to sea.

We were approaching the sea fort. I had never seen anything like it. It looked like a large round drum made of concrete and was incredibly thick. There were windows near the top of the drum spaced out to cover all views of the sea. The captain's voice came over the airwaves with a very brief description; 'This sea fort was built for use during the Second World War. I am not sure how much action it actually saw but it was heavily fortified just in case the enemy got close.'

'Once we settle into our room, I would like to have a good nose around. We could skulk.' Kath was interested in almost anything. If a garden gate creaked, she would want to know why it creaked, when it creaked most, if the noise was the same on all garden gates and what preventative measures there were to stop it creaking in the future. One thing she wasn't interested in was the mating habits of scorpions.

The small boat finally docked and we climbed up the steps to the top of the sea fort. I turned this way and that. I felt like a spinning top. If you looked one way, you could see the Isle of Wight, our next port of call, and the opposite way was

Portsmouth. The sea also played a big part. I looked at it, my enemy. You know when someone gets a long thin piece of coloured paper and runs a pair of scissors down it to make it curl? That's what some of the waves looked like.

Someone took our cases to our room. This sea fort certainly didn't disappoint. The room we had was lovely; two single beds with a window in the middle of them. There was a lovely wardrobe, chest of drawers and a little table between the beds. Plenty of space to put clothes in. There were only six of us staying and I got the feeling that the other people thought that Kath and I were a couple. It was the looks we were getting of 'Oh, I'm fine with you being a couple'. The person who brought our cases to our room even asked if we wanted the beds put together. Kath hooted with laughter at that suggestion and then said with a downturned mouth, 'No, we've only come away together as we had originally booked it as a romantic weekend ages ago. Now, sadly, we are no longer together so this is like our farewell holiday before we go our separate ways. I need a partner like I need a sixth toe.' She snuffled into a tissue. 'Kath! Please ignore her,' I said to the staff member who nodded and left.

We unpacked our cases and laid on our beds staring at the ceiling. 'This is nice,' I said. 'This is wonderful,' Kath said. At least the room wasn't moving from side to side.

It was nearly 1 pm so we changed into our lunch outfits and went to the restaurant. We had brought clothes to change into for both lunch and dinner. We weren't sure how posh this luxury hotel would be. As it was, we could have turned up in ripped jeans and t-shirts.

55

We had a browned butter honey garlic salmon fillet each with crème fraîche, new potatoes and broccoli. I wondered if they had caught the salmon fresh today off the side but couldn't imagine salmon swimming in the Channel. For afters, I had a chocolate fudge cake with fresh cream piled on it and Kath had a vanilla cheesecake with sliced strawberries on top.

We went back to our room to lie down again. I felt ready to pop. Before we knew it, we had both fallen asleep.

Four hours later.

I was awoken by Kath squealing loudly, 'Jesus, Mary and Joseph. Look at the time? Beth. Beeetttthhhh!!!!' She was shaking me. 'We've missed the trip out to sea!!!'

'Oh no, we haven't. Have you looked outside yet?'

Kath went to the window and said, 'Dear, dear me'. The sea wasn't looking at all happy. The waves were flying over the deck of the sea fort. We hadn't heard the storm as firstly, we were asleep, and secondly, the windows were double-glazed. I was so thankful that we hadn't gone out on a boat again. I doubt I would have survived it.

This was our first day in the sea fort. We were due to leave on Sunday and the storm lasted our entire stay. It only stopped an hour before we were due to depart. Kath was very disappointed as she hadn't had the chance to put on her all-in-one swimming costume. She had decided that a bikini was a bit much. We did get to see the gun towers and went to a talk on why sea forts were erected in the first place. All we did was eat, sleep, look at the sea, watch telly and go on walks around the sea fort.

'When we get to the Isle of Wight, we are going on several bike rides and long walks to get rid of the extra tyre developing around both of our bellies. When was the last time you rode a bicycle, Kath?'

'1886 when Raleigh started making them. To be honest, I can't remember, Beth. Ten years ago, maybe?'

Even though it seemed like we were on a British version of Alcatraz, we did have a lovely time on the sea fort. Lots to see and lots to eat. Now to the Isle of Wight.

9

The Isle of Wight and How Not to Bowl or Cycle

We had to go back to Portsmouth to get a ferry to Ryde. The sea had calmed down enough for me not to keep feeling sick again. I noticed that there was a couple who had been at the sea fort with us. They were waiting for the ferry to go to Ryde too. They hadn't been particularly friendly and had kept themselves to themselves most of the time. They were in their thirties and looked completely and utterly bored and miserable in each other's company.

When the ferry arrived and we boarded, they got on and immediately went off in different directions. She went to the front of the ferry and he went to the side and looked down at the water, gripping the railing. I had a horrible feeling he might decide to jump in and nudged Kath.

'What?' she said.

''Do you think we should go and stand near that man? He looks like he might take a leap over the side.'

'Whatever makes you think that, Beth?'

'He doesn't look very happy at all,' I replied.

Suddenly, the ferry horn let out a loud blast and off we went. I looked at the man and he was walking to the front of the ship.

'Right, Beth, to take your mind off any thoughts of sickness, let's go through the sayings about the places on the Isle of Wight. I'll start with.... Ryde where you walk.'

I couldn't think of one and had to think for a bit. 'Ah yes. Cowes you can't milk'.

'Needles you can't thread.'

'Freshwater you can't drink. Is that right? I can't think of any more, Kath.'

After about forty-five minutes of calm sailing, we reached the harbour at Ryde. The harbour was lovely with a huge array of boats in it, all bobbing up and down in excitement at our arrival. I could hear the bells from the boats. They sounded like a herd of cattle with cowbells on making their way down to greet us.

We had booked rooms in a hotel that looked like a castle. It wasn't far from the harbour so we decided to walk. It was a nice sunny day with a slight breeze coming off the sea. We needed to stretch our legs as we had spent the last few days either on a round concrete block or a ferry.

We had booked two single rooms, both of which faced the harbour. We unpacked our bags, put on some good walking boots and met back downstairs in the main reception area. We got a map from a constantly smiling woman on the desk. We looked at it, pointed at it and scratched our heads.

'You know what? Maybe we should have planned what to do before we came here,' I said.

'And where's the joy in that?' Kath replied. 'Spontaneity, that's what we need.'

After an eternity of chin-scratching and pondering, we decided that as it was close to lunchtime, we would walk back down to the harbour and find a nice restaurant. We found one with seating outside. We sat down, looked at the menu, and, as we were near the sea, both ordered fish.

'I wonder if it was caught locally,' I said.

'Not sure cod swim round here but then again, I'm not great on knowing where fish live in the sea, or rather seas, as there are many.' Kath took a large swig of her wine. 'That's better.'

The bells on the boats now sounded like people at their first bell-ringing lesson - no real tune and all over the place. It was, however, surprisingly relaxing. I looked up at the sky, a clear blue sky with no clouds. I could see two birds flitting about looking like two enemy planes fighting each other.

'Madam,' the waiter said as he laid down my plate of food.

'Madam. Well, I haven't been called that in a long time,' I said to the waiter and smiled.

We chatted, laughed, spent time in silence looking at our surroundings and then both closed our eyes and sighed in contentment. Suddenly, our peace was shattered by a group of people arriving who sat near us. There were four of them. They all looked like they were in their late fifties or early sixties.

Kath smiled at them and they all smiled back.

'What are we going to do then?' One of the group was looking anxious.

'That really wasn't on for him to pull out so close to the competition. We were sure to win with him bowling.'

I could see Kath's ears pricking up.

'Well, we can't cancel now. It's tomorrow. If we only knew someone who was good at tenpin bowling…'

'Excuse me.' Kath had suddenly vanished and was standing at their table.

Oh no, I thought. *Oh no*. 'Kath, what are you doing? Come back.'

'Forgive me, but I overheard your conversation and understand you are short of a player. I used to play regularly with my bowling team and we won lots of trophies.'

What Kath had failed to share with them was that yes, she did bowl but was always the last person asked. Very similar to when children picked their teammates from a line-up. Most, if not all of her balls, ended up in the gutter. They had indeed won trophies but they were all token ones for simply taking part in a competition, or, more often than not, for coming last.

Kath sat down and discussed the finer details with her new teammates. She came back and beamed at me.

'Tomorrow evening, my dear, I will be part of the Ryde It Home bowling team who will be in competition with other teams from the island, including their arch-rivals, Cowes Who Will Milk You.'

'Kath, you can't bowl. You told me you were terrible.'

'I know, I know, but they don't know that and it's only a little island competition. Nothing global.'

One of the team came to the hotel later and gave Kath a pair of smart blue tracksuit bottoms and a yellow top with Ryde It Home on the back of it. They were all to meet at the local bowling alley in Ryde the following evening at 6 pm. The bowling alley was huge, with lane after lane of people hurling balls down to the other end. All I could hear was a loud rumbling noise and then the clattering sound of pins falling. Kath and I went over to the team who were all warming up at one of the lanes. Arms and shoulders were being stretched and a couple of them were even leaning over and touching their toes.

'Hi, Kath,' said the captain, Leo. He introduced the others to Kath and me. 'This is Harold, Edna and Judith.' Everyone said hello and shook hands.

'Right, Kath. Join us in a warm-up before the battle commences,' Leo said as he stretched his head from side to side. 'Let loose the bowling dogs of war. Shakespeare of sorts.'

Kath did some token stretches and then picked up a bowling ball. She held it in her hand and stroked it gently like it was a big fat round watermelon. She stood at the top of a vacant bowling alley and threw it down. Luckily, no one else was watching as it went straight into the gutter.

Kath looked at me and grinned. 'I haven't played for a while. Just need a bit of practice.'

'Are you sure about this, Kath? Look how many teams there are and the press are over there.'

Kath looked over. There were at least ten other teams, a local TV news team and journalists with photographers from all over the island.

'Oh, God. I thought this was just going to be a bit of a knockabout; a bit of fun.' Kath's mouth was drooping and she fell onto a seat.

Someone somewhere was making an announcement. 'Welcome, everyone, to the annual Isle of Wight bowling competition. It is so good to see so many teams here.'

'No, it isn't,' Kath said under her breath.

'It is great to see Ryde It Home back again to defend their title. Just a reminder that we are streaming this live tonight.'

At that point, Kath tried to sneak out of the building. I grabbed her. 'Kath, you never know. It might all come back to you.'

'What, the horror of being the crappiest bowling player ever with the whole island and beyond watching? Why did I say I could play?'

'Well, just put your best smile on and pretend you have an injury or something after your first bowl.'

'Brilliant, Beth. Brilliant.' She patted my shoulder.

Ryde It Home were up against the Freshwater Light Brigade first. Kath asked if she could start first. She stood at the end of the bowling lane. 'And first up for Ryde It Home is Kath!' People clapped and cheered and I whooped loudly.

Kath picked up a ball, looked at it and then put it down again. She wanted to look like she was a complete professional and be seen judging the pace and weight of the ball, she told me later.

She decided on a rather fetching pink ball. She held it, walked forward, bent her knee and literally threw the ball in the air. It landed with a thud and whizzed off down the gutter again. There was a deafening silence in the building. It even felt like the cleaners had stopped wiping floors and tables and were staring at her, all open-mouthed.

What Kath did next was superb. She bent forward and held her back with one hand and her knee with her other hand. Someone walked towards her but she gestured them away. She looked like she was crying. I helped her sit down slowly and with great care.

'I am so sorry,' she said to the team. 'My back went just as I was about to unleash hell down the lane.'

There were cries of 'That is a shame' and 'I do hope you recover soon.'

Kath leaned on me as I led her out of the building. Once outside, she let go and straightened up. 'Thank goodness for that,' she said. 'Right, let's go to a pub.'

'We might be seen by someone,' I said.

'You're right. Okay, there is a bar in the hotel. Let's go there instead. If we see anyone tomorrow, I can say it was a spasm and righted itself overnight.'

We had a few glasses of wine and ended up roaring with laughter. 'I may well end up on the front of the local rag and God forbid that streaming service,' Kath hollered.

She was on the streaming service. We checked later. Kath had about 1,000 likes so far.

The next day, we decided to hire a couple of bicycles and go on a tour around part of the island. Neither of us had cycled in years but both reasoned it couldn't be that difficult.

We went to a nearby cycle shop. The assistant there gave us the option of getting electric bikes but we both chose not to. Wanted the exercise, we said. He gave us some maps of bike trails around the Isle of Wight and pointed out some good routes. We looked at some including a ride to a mill which did look interesting.

The most difficult part to work out was whether to go clockwise or anti-clockwise. A coin toss decided that. Anti-clockwise. We thought Cowes looked like a good target to aim for so we both tentatively got on our bikes. After some initial wobbling and planting our feet on the ground a lot, we set off. It was only about six miles to Cowes. We had prepared food for the journey. The weather was beautiful. It was warm enough to avoid having to wear great big coats but not so hot that we would have ended up sweating as if we had spent all day in a sauna.

We cycled as close to the sea as we could without the risk of having to call the coastguard out if one of us fell over the side. We stopped at one point to take a breather and looked at the water. There were a number of small boats dotted about, some with swollen sails and some with motors heading in straight lines to Portsmouth.

As we turned inwards, we saw the woman who had walked off from her partner on the ferry and had also been on the sea fort with us. She was standing on a small hill with her arms stretched out. We cycled over. She immediately waved at us to stop. 'No, no!' she shouted. 'Move. You are ruining the photo.'

'Photo? What photo?' I asked.

'My husband is taking photos of me to show what the compartmentalisation of loneliness and despair look like.'

'The comp what?' Kath said, shaking her head.

'We are doing a project on separation and how it makes people act and feel; those who are the victims and those who instigated it'

I nearly told her that Kath and I were experts on separation but decided against it just in case we got roped into helping out with the 'project'. We turned around and saw her husband coming towards us, camera in hand with a scowl on his face.

'Well, we really need to get going. Lovely to see you both again,' Kath said and we got on our bikes and quickly rode out of Dodge City.

'They must have been practising on the sea fort and the ferry. You know, walking off and leaving each other all the time,' I said. I got no reply. I couldn't see Kath.

All I heard was 'Weeeeeeeeeeeeeeeeeeee! Oooooooooooooooh nooooooooooo!!!'

I looked around for her. She had managed to cycle very fast down a steep path heading towards a small wooded area. She was bouncing around all over the place with her legs straight out in front of her.

'Kath! Kath! Are you okay?' I yelled at the top of my voice.

'I am fine, thanks,' she shouted back. 'I felt like a pea on a drum just then. Goodness me,' she said rubbing her bum. 'Come down. Slowly, that is. This wood is wonderful.'

I made my way down very carefully pushing my bike by my side. It was a lovely wood. All you could hear was birdsong, the rustle of leaves in the wind and waves rhythmically crashing against a cliff below. There were bunches of daffodils everywhere. We sat down, ate a sandwich and had a drink of fresh orange juice. We both lay on our backs and looked up at the clear blue sky.

'David would have loved this,' I said.

'Christopher would have too.'

We closed our eyes and fell asleep for an hour. When we woke up, the first thing Kath said was 'I need a wee'.

'So do I,' I replied.

I got up and walked around several tree trunks, feeling their rough wood. I bent down and smelt flowers scattered on the forest floor. This was paradise. I didn't want to leave it but we had to.

We got back on our bikes and continued our cycle ride to Cowes. We went at a leisurely pace, stopping every now and then to point at things of interest or to look at the sea and to catch our breath. We didn't go to the mill.

'They have yacht racing here, you know,' said Kath as Cowes came into view. 'International, no less.'

It looked like a lovely place.

'I had a look at things to do here last night. As you have mentioned yachts, do you want to go to the Maritime Museum? Or there is the Classic Boat Museum or Cowes Castle which is, and I quote, a Device Fort originally built by Henry VIII in 1539 to protect England against the threat of invasion from France.' I had the tourist book in my hand.

'Are you wearing a t-shirt with I Love the Isle of Wight on it?' Kath asked and smiled. 'Okay, can I make a suggestion? It's nearly lunchtime. Let's get something to eat and then go to a museum or something. I think I might faint if I don't eat something else soon.'

We found a seafood restaurant at the harbour and enjoyed a superb fish lunch with lots of wine to help it go down. We pondered over which dessert to have. We spent some time reasoning that we had done a lot of exercise cycling and therefore deserved a large dessert each. We had chocolate fudge cake with 2 scoops of ice cream and a Banoffee cheesecake, this time with lots of whipped cream. We divided them up equally and sat eating them really slowly and saying 'Scrumptious' after every mouthful.

After lunch, we cycled up to the Classic Boat Museum. We walked around and looked at lots of classic yachts, lifeboats and motorboats. We read about the history of maritime activity and spent time saying 'Well I never knew that. Every day's a school day'. After a couple of hours, we left and cycled back to our hotel.

For the next couple of days, we spent time on the local beach, went into shops and bought touristy things like a test tube of all the different coloured sands on the island. We indulged in lots of restaurant meals and wine and decided that we loved watching the local news programmes. We cycled some more and walked a lot.

'When was the last time our London News mentioned that a tractor had overturned on a major road?' Kath said.

We got the ferry back to Portsmouth and then the train to London.

'We can tick that adventure off now, Kath.'

'We can, Beth. We can.'

We stared out of the window, both wishing we could have spent longer on the Isle of Wight.

10

A Rest for the Good It Gives

Kath and I met up a few days later. Kath had things to do at work and I wanted the time to relax and straighten my place up a bit more. I had left it in a bit of a mess before our journey. There were clothes on my bedroom floor and bed where I had chucked things I wasn't going to take. My plants were drooping somewhat so I gave them some tender loving care.

Kath and I met and went to a local pub that had an outside area and got a couple of gin and tonics.

'Mother's Ruin,' Kath said after taking her first mouthful.

'Sorry?'

'Mother's Ruin, Beth. In days gone by, women became addicted to it, much more than men. They started to mistreat their children and turned to prostitution to pay for more drink. I read that somewhere. Hence the term Mother's Ruin.'

'I thought it was because women wanted to get rid of unwanted pregnancies. They drank gin until it forced a miscarriage or supposedly did.'

'I suppose it was that as well, but I would need to confirm that by asking Mr Goggle.'

'Google.'

'Goggle.'

'Oh, Mr Beeswax Goggle.'

Kath and I enjoyed this humorous sparring. We both knew there was no malice involved and it always ended with the pair of us either giggling or smiling.

As we sat talking, we realised that neither of us had written down a list of things to do together, a joint bucket list.

'Well, we could start now and backdate it to include the maze, sea fort and Isle of Wight.' I suggested.

'Sounds like a plan,' Kath said. We were eating a plateful of chips each with lots of mayonnaise and ketchup. We each had a side salad as the healthy option. 'May I suggest that our next venture isn't overseas and doesn't involve a lot of exercise?'

'Yes, I like the sound of that. I could do with a rest, actually. All that cycling has certainly built up my stamina and my thigh muscles but goodness, I do feel like I have just cycled in a mini version of the Tour de France with lots of walking included,' I said.

'I have to catch up at work too. I need to make a few more dreams become reality.'

We decided that we would have a break from any excursions. We would take the time to write a few things down on our own bucket lists and see where we both thought of the same thing.

I spent some time linking up again with a few family and friends. After David, I had lost myself and had drifted away on a lonely boat to a deserted island. It felt good to hug people I hadn't felt able to in a long while. I apologised a lot and tried to explain why I had done what I had done. It all came out in a bit of a muddle but people understood. Some said they hadn't been in touch as they thought I needed space and time from everyone and everything. They apologised as they realised they hadn't made the effort to even send one supportive text to me. Relationships all round were starting to get back to normal.

I found myself going to places that I couldn't go to after losing David as they reminded me too much of him. My first nervous outing on my own was to St Paul's Cathedral. Neither of us followed any religion but it was the nature and grandeur of the building we had both loved. The height of it, the strength of it, the size of it. On our first visit there, we had gone up to the Whispering Gallery, stood on either side of it and said very softly to the wall how much we loved each other.

I entered St Paul's feeling very overwhelmed. I thought I might collapse, such were my emotions. I had a gap next to me where David should have been. My stomach felt empty. I found myself turning to look for him. I wanted to talk to him. My eyes started to water. I steadied myself, took a deep breath and sat down for a while. I wanted to hear every noise so closed my eyes. I went up to the Whispering Gallery and placed my ear against the wall. I wanted to hear the words 'I love you'. I wanted to look up and see him opposite me smiling, blowing a kiss at me and then running over to hug me. Again, this was a small step for me but it felt excruciatingly difficult. I felt like I was trying to climb a twenty-foot wall with no support and equipment. But I did it. I left St Paul's lighter. The large heavy stone slabs were starting to lift from my shoulders. I was starting to fly a bit. A flutter at first but I knew it would get better.

I sat and drank a coffee in a small place nearby. I treated myself to a chocolate éclair. I walked home. It took over an hour but I wanted to be one of the crowd. I wanted to be there with everyone else. I didn't want to be that person who did nothing and just stayed indoors.

A few days later, I met up with Kath again. She came to my place. We drank tea and ate lots of custard cream biscuits.

'These are my absolute favourite biscuits,' I said as I crammed another one into my mouth.

'Me too. Love them. Right. I have my list,' Kath said. She went through it and talked about canoeing down the River Thames, visiting a lighthouse and going to life drawing classes.

'Sorry, life drawing classes? What, as a drawer or the person being drawn?'

'Oh, don't be silly, Beth. A drawer. Look, you were sketching the first time I saw you so how about it?'

I hadn't even started writing a bucket list so I just nodded and said yes why not. It was something I had thought about when I was thinking about what to do.

'I shall look into it then,' Kath said. 'The person modelling had better be a man and have a very good-looking face. It will distract me from other parts of his body.'

We finished the tea and biscuits and started on a bottle of wine. Kath left in the early hours of the following morning. We had ordered a Chinese takeaway and were watching episode after episode of a police drama series we both loved without realising what time it was.

Kath contacted me the next day. 'I have found somewhere close by that does life drawing classes. I have booked us in for next Wednesday evening. Is that okay with you? You can have it on me as a treat.'

'Fine,' I said. 'Looking forward to it and thank you.'

11

I Can't Draw That,
Not after What's Happened

We arrived at our life drawing class early. Kath wanted to get the low-down on everyone and everything as she put it. She wanted to know if we would be drawing a man or a woman. She asked a few people who arrived a bit later but no one was quite sure as it was the first session of a new class. I smiled at a few people and talked to others about never having drawn a nude person before and what was expected.

The tutor greeted us and took us to the large art room. There were several easels set up with paper attached and lots of pencils and charcoal. We sat next to each other and giggled. Kath was fiddling with her bag when the model arrived; a man in his fifties. He climbed on to a raised platform, took his robe off and stood there naked. He then laid back on a sofa and placed one arm across his chest.

'Okay, ladies and gentlemen, please start whenever you are ready,' the tutor said. 'I will be coming round to each of you during the session so please let me know what help you would like, if any.'

Kath put her bag down on the floor, looked up and suddenly gave out a small yelp. She looked quite pale like she had seen a ghost.

'Kath, Kath,' I whispered. 'What's the matter?'

'I, I, I know him. It's Christopher's brother Mark,' she replied. 'I can't draw him. Not like that. I've never seen him in his birthday suit before.'

'Just pretend it's someone else. Don't look at his face.'

'And where exactly do you expect me to look then?'

'Well, just anywhere else. His chest or something.'

'Okay, I will give it a go but he can't see me.' She shuffled behind her easel which made it hard for her to see him. She had to peer round her easel or try and stand on tiptoes to look over it.

The tutor suddenly appeared beside her. 'Is everything okay?' she said. Her hands were clasped together.

'Oooh,' Kath said a bit too loudly as she jumped in the air and dropped her pencil. 'Sorry,' she said much more quietly. 'No, everything is fine. Just trying to look at the, er, person from a different angle really.'

The teacher nodded and then went through a few things with Kath about her perspective and what types of pencils or charcoal she could use to emphasize certain points.

After she went, Kath turned to me and said, 'I really don't want to emphasize certain points on his body, I must say. Goodness no.'

I chuckled to myself. This could only happen to Kath. Of all the places to be and of all the life drawing models in the country it had to be someone she knew.

The class continued for another hour. I had managed to complete most of my sketch. The tutor said we could leave our drawings rolled up in a cupboard in the room for next week or we could take them home and finish them there. We both chose to take ours home. I wasn't sure we would be coming back next week, particularly as Mark would be the model again. Kath told me she certainly didn't want to come back.

I looked at Kath's drawing. She had only managed to draw the top half of the model and the rest was a blur. She had vaguely drawn his bottom half but had left all the more delicate bits blank.

We packed up and noticed that the model had gone.

'That was Christopher's brother then?' I asked Kath.

'Yes,' she replied.

I sensed there was more to this. Why was Kath so angry and upset? I couldn't tell which emotion was affecting her most.

We left and had a chat with a couple of people outside the room.

Suddenly, we both heard, 'Kath, Kath!!'

I looked up and saw a man further down the corridor waving in our direction. Kath ignored him and carried on talking. It was the life model Mark.

'Kath!' He repeated himself and was almost shouting now. He came over and stood next to Kath.

At last, Kath stopped talking and looked at him. If Kath played cards, she would have been told she had a good poker face. I had no idea how she was feeling.

'Kath, it's so good to see you. Fancy you being here. How are you?' He looked at me and then said 'Hello, I'm Mark.' I smiled and told him who I was.

'How do you expect me to be, Mark? Happy? Over the moon to see you?'

I had never seen Kath like this. She had always been very laid back and had dealt with any problems with a smile on her face and a 'Keep calm and get on with it' attitude. Now she looked like she was about to explode. I hoped she wouldn't hit him.

Mark didn't know what to say and moved away. Kath and I left the building and quickly walked up the road. 'I need a drink,' Kath said and we headed towards a pub.

We sat in the pub garden, each holding a large glass of wine.

'I am sorry about that, Beth. I really wanted to enjoy that experience but seeing Mark there ruined it for me.' Kath stopped and took another gulp of her drink.

'Do you want to talk about it, Kath?'

'Yes, I think I do.'

It was warm and there was still some light in the sky. We decided to finish our drink and then walk back to Kath's and sit in her garden.

We got more drinks from Kath's kitchen and settled down on the garden seats. I wrapped a blanket over my legs. I could see this was going to be a long night.

Kath started. 'Right, here goes. I had been married to Christopher for a couple of years. Mark had been away working in the Far East for a few years on some building project, so, I hadn't yet met him. Christopher was very excited as Mark was finally going to be coming home. Christopher said he could stay with us as he had been through a divorce before heading overseas and his wife had got their house. I agreed. It would be nice to finally meet Christopher's older brother.

Mark arrived home six weeks later. Christopher was overjoyed and they spent many a night drinking, reminiscing and laughing at shared memories. Mark seemed really nice, very attentive to Christopher and always willing to help out.

Then it started. I gave him a glass of wine once and he held onto my fingers a bit too long as he took it and looked too intently at me. I just had an inkling something wasn't right and I started to feel uncomfortable. Mark would help out, like washing up in the kitchen, but he would always make sure he had to put something in a cupboard or on a shelf where I happened to be standing so he could lean in close to me. I was in the garden once when it was dark, collecting plates and glasses, and he came up behind me and grabbed my waist. I jumped and he laughed. I told him there and then to stop. He just looked at me and walked off.'

'Did you say anything to Christopher?' I asked.

'No. Mark was his hero. It would have destroyed him. In the end, though, it did and I am convinced that whatever Mark told him is the reason why he went off and had a child with the other woman. We never had any children ourselves. I had come home one night from seeing some friends and Christopher was sitting downstairs. It was very late so I asked him why he was still up. He said he was waiting for me. We needed to talk. I had no idea what he was about to say. He told me that Mark had left that day as he had found a flat. He said Mark had told him he needed to go as I wouldn't leave him alone. Apparently, whenever Christopher was out or in another room, I would practically throw myself at him.'

'But you didn't, did you?'

'Of course not, Beth. What do you take me for? I was in love with Christopher. It caused a huge rift between Christopher and me and we never got back to how we were at the beginning of our relationship. There was always the odd distance between us. I never forgave Mark. Even at the funeral, I couldn't bear to look at him. I was also deeply, deeply hurt that Christopher could even imagine that I would do something like that.'

'I am so sorry, Kath. That sounds horrible. Why do you think Mark did that?'

'Jealousy? Spite? They are the only things I could think of. Mark had gone through a nasty divorce, lost his home and when he came to stay with us, we were a happily married couple, devoted to each other, laughing together, liking the same things. I couldn't think of anything else.' Kath got up and poured another glass of wine for herself and one for me.

'I didn't want to say it but that college was fairly close to where we both live. You don't think he has moved into the area, do you?' I asked.

'Don't worry. I will check with a friend of mine who works on the electoral register. She wouldn't be able to tell me where he does live but she could say yes or no.' Kath did a sneaky check the next day and thankfully, Mark didn't live close by.

I sat and thought. Just when you think life is starting to do you a good favour, something like this happens and slaps you in the face. Kath was trying to act tough but I could see it was affecting her. I saw her wiping her eyes when she went into the kitchen.

'To make up for this disaster, how about we look at doing something thrill-seeking, something that will make us scream our heads off in delight?' Kath was eating an apple.

'It wasn't your fault so don't worry, Kath. I like the sound of a thrill.' We sat in front of Kath's laptop and put 'Thrill-seeking adventures in the UK' into the search engine.

Up came loads of pages with things to do. I read some of them out.

'Hang gliding, hydro speeding, camping off a cliff face, abseiling, rock climbing, kite buggy riding on a sandy beach, skydiving indoor and outdoor, Zip wire rides. Shall I go on?'

Kath sat for a moment staring at the opposite wall. Then she turned to me. 'The thought of camping off a cliff face fills me with absolute horror. I have no desire to climb up a very large rock either. Skydiving - do I want my face scrunched up with the distinct possibility it could stay like that? Hang gliding or a zip wire ride sound okay. I have no idea what hydro speeding is but it sounds more scary than fun.'

'What are you like on rollercoasters?' I asked. 'I have an absolute fear of them but what the hell.' *Be brave*, I thought.

'Never been on one so have no idea,' Kath replied. 'If it isn't too high it might be fun.'

'Do you want to give it a try?'

'Yes, Beth. Feel the fear and do it anyway.'

'That is very philosophical. Let's do it then.'

I told Kath that I was going to stay with David's parents the following week. We had been in touch and wounds had healed. I would be heading down to Sussex on the train. I was born in Sussex and had been itching to go back.

12

My Journey Downwards

David's father John met me at Brighton station. They lived in a square near the seafront. I remembered visiting it shortly after David and I started seeing each other. His parents were away and we stayed for a long weekend. We had gone on the pier and screamed ourselves silly on the ghost train ride. We had eaten fish and chips with lots of vinegar and had sat hand in hand on a bench looking out at the sea.

David and I had gone back after his parents returned from their holiday. We had travelled down by car to see various towns and villages near Brighton and David had bought me a gold necklace in an antique shop in Brighton.

I was more than apprehensive about going back to stay as there would be lots of memories of David there. His mother, Sybil, had struggled to move anything from David's room and I had images of walking in as if David had just popped out to get some milk and would be back shortly.

'It is lovely to see you, Beth. It really is.' John gave me a hug, one I had missed so much. David looked like his father which I found to be a comfort. We decided to walk rather than get a taxi. My suitcase was on wheels and wasn't heavy. There were lots of people out and about. It wasn't quite the tourist season but I could hear accents that weren't local and children getting excited about all the things they could do on their weekend excursion.

Sybil had been looking out the window and when she saw me, she rushed to open the door. Her arms were beckoning me forwards to have another hug. We held each other for what seemed like ages. There was no awkwardness, no uncomfortable silence.

We went in and coffee was served with a selection of biscuits on a plate. We sat in the living room and talked about how we all were, how time had passed but the pain was still there, what we were doing now and what we were going to be doing in the future. I didn't feel it was quite right to tell them about all my activities with Kath. It might have sounded like I was just going out and about without a care in the world for David.

That evening we went to a vegetarian restaurant. David's mum and dad were both vegetarian like me. The food was delicious. We walked back along the seafront and stopped to look at the horizon. It had reached that stage where you couldn't tell where the sea ended and the sky began. It was only when I saw a light from a ship that I worked it out.

When we got back, Sybil asked if I would like a night-time drink, a hot chocolate or something. I couldn't remember the last time I had had a hot chocolate so said yes. John and Sybil both went into the kitchen and I could hear them talking. The way they were emphasising words made it sound quite urgent. I got up and moved closer to the door.

John sounded like he was instructing Sybil. 'You HAVE to tell her. Take her for a walk tomorrow. I will come up with an excuse not to go.'

'Okay, John. I really don't know how she is going to take it.'

I went back to the sofa and sat down quickly, pretending to look at a magazine.

'Here you are, Beth. I forgot to ask if you wanted sugar. There is some in the bowl on the table if you do.' Sybil said.

We sat and drank, making small talk. I really wanted to say that I had heard them talking in the kitchen but didn't want it to sound confrontational. Luckily, Sybil began.

'Is there anything in particular you wanted to do tomorrow?'

I was very tempted to say yes, I had planned to visit friends, but really wanted to know what Sybil had to tell me. 'No, I hadn't planned anything.'

'Would you like to go for a walk? There are lots of new shops and places to eat. We could walk on the beach too. John, will you be joining us?' Sybil took another sip of her hot chocolate.

I knew the answer to that.

'No, unfortunately, I won't be able to. Meeting up with a couple of old golfing mates for lunch. Right, I'm off up to bed. Beth, if I don't see you in the morning, have a good walk. Night, night, one and all.'

Sybil and I sat up for a while longer until I suddenly felt terribly tired. My bedroom was opposite David's old room. I wanted to say to Sybil, 'Look, I can stay in David's room. He won't mind at all.'

I slept fitfully. I tossed and turned, got up, looked out the window, went back to bed and then went downstairs to get a glass of water. As I went through the living room, I jumped. I could see the outline of a figure in a chair.

'Oh, Beth. I am sorry. I didn't mean to frighten you.' It was Sybil. She couldn't sleep either. I made a decaffeinated tea for us and got the biscuits out.

Now was the time to talk. 'Sybil, I didn't mean to but I heard you and John talking in the kitchen earlier. John was telling you to say something to me on our walk. Why don't we chat now so we can both get some sleep and have a nice relaxing walk tomorrow?'

Sybil looked relieved. 'Yes, let's. I am not sure where to begin. You have noticed we have a lot of photos around the house of David when he was young.'

I had noticed.

'The thing is, Beth, they aren't all of David.'

'Sorry, I don't quite understand. What are you saying? Are you saying he has a twin?' I was dreading what she would say. I couldn't bear the thought of there being someone else who looked just like David. There was a horrible silence.

'No,' Sybil finally said. 'The photos are of David's son.'

I didn't know what to say. David and I had been trying to have children with no success and David had never mentioned that he already had a child.

'Whose, who, goodness, dear me, who is the mother?' My words came tumbling out.

'His first wife. Oh, dear Beth, no, David never cheated on you if that's what you are thinking. The photos are of his child when he was much younger. He looks so much like David.'

'David never said anything,' I said. I was finding it difficult to think straight. David had never wanted to get married to me and I couldn't understand why when he had been married before. Maybe it had put him off.

Sybil went into the kitchen and I followed her.

'I know,' Sybil said. She started to wash up, clanking the plates loudly as she put them on the draining board. She stopped and put her hands down on the work surface. 'David didn't want to upset you. He said you had been trying for a baby and he thought that if he then mentioned he already had a child it would complicate things more and upset you. When he divorced his first wife, she moved back to New York to be with her family and he started to lose touch with his son. The only time he ever spoke to him was when David called, but by then, his first wife had re-married and his son had started to call his ex-wife's new husband daddy. He was desperate to be part of his son's life but it never came to anything. He felt really pushed out.' Sybil looked relieved after she told me this. It was almost like she expected me to shout and throw things about but I was very calm.

I simply didn't know how to act though. I had too much grief for David to deal with still and couldn't even think about having to deal with another type of feeling or emotion. Part of me was glad that David was living on in another person. He was still around.

'Beth, Carole, his first wife, is going to be here tomorrow. She will be staying in a hotel in Brighton with John Junior, her and David's son. It is all very sudden and we didn't know until she phoned me yesterday. I couldn't put her off. We both really want to see our grandson. They are going to come over tomorrow evening for dinner and I would very much like it if you could stay on for a bit longer to meet them both.'

I couldn't cope. I staggered a bit and clung onto the back of a chair. What the hell? This was like a really horrible version of This is Your Life, with all the people you never wanted to meet again being there to wish you a happy day and share memories with you; ones that you really didn't want to remember.

'I, er, need to get back to London tomorrow evening as I need to prepare for something.' Could I be any vaguer? 'In fact, I think I am tired enough now to go back to bed. Sybil, before I go up, I need to know where David is. I would very much like to see him, pay my respects.'

Sybil looked at me and pointed at a casket on the mantelpiece above the fire. There was a long pause. 'He is here with us.'

I slowly moved towards the fireplace and gently touched the casket. My hands were shaking. I picked it up and held on to it for ages. *You are back*, I thought. I looked at Sybil and started to cry. She came and hugged me and we both wept.

'I am so sorry I didn't tell you, Beth,' she said. 'Things were too difficult but it was wrong of us not to say anything.'

I forgave her. I thought I might have erupted with rage but doing that didn't feel right; not now. David would not have wanted me to behave like that. He always wanted me to get on with his parents. After we chatted some more and shared memories about David, I said goodnight and ran silently up the stairs, two at a time, and fell on the bed. I slept badly and woke up feeling dreadful the next morning. I freshened myself up with a lukewarm shower and put on comfortable clothes and walking shoes. This time away was meant to have been a wonderful reconciliation but now I was starting to feel myself head downwards again. I was worried we would bump into Carole and John Junior on our walk.

'Come on. Pucker up.' I slapped my knees and went downstairs for breakfast.

Sybil and I had a long and interesting walk. We went down onto the beach. Brighton has a shingle pebble beach and it isn't the most comfortable thing to sit on. We got a couple of deckchairs. The sun was out so I bought two ice creams and we sat down and talked.

'I am sorry about telling you all that last night, Beth. I know it must have come as a bit of a shock to you. Carole didn't know about David and I had no contact details for her. It was only through a computer whizz friend of John's that we tracked her down. It was difficult as she had got married again and changed her name. When I told her about David, she said she would come over. John Junior is a teenager now and she felt he needed to know his grandparents here in England.'

'Please don't worry. Yes, I was confused and surprised but David did have a life before me, even if he didn't tell me everything about it. I just don't think I could cope with seeing them tonight. I hope you understand. I don't have to go home today but I think I will now, later this evening. Forgive me for my lie but I couldn't think of anything else to say.' I was glad Sybil and I were relaxed enough in each other's company to be able to talk like this.

'Please. There is nothing to forgive,' Sybil said.

We walked further down the beach until there were fewer people around and then doubled back and went into the Lanes.

We wandered around lots of shops and bought lots of things. I had got a large bag that I could wear on my back and ended up filling it with new clothes and shoes. I also got boxes of chocolate truffles for Kath, Sybil and John. We had lunch sitting outside a pub and drank some locally brewed beer.

We decided to go to the Royal Pavilion. I remember my mum telling me she had worked there when she was a student. I wanted to walk where she had walked and look at things she had looked at. The Pavilion was like an exotic palace with turrets shaped like peaked meringues. The further we walked through it the more splendid each room became.

Carole and John Junior were due at 6 pm so I packed my bag and bade farewell to John and Sybil at 5 pm. I had decided not to go to the station straight away. I parked myself in a local coffee shop that had a good view of their house and waited for them to arrive. At 6 pm I saw a woman and boy walk down the street and then walk up the stairs and knock on the door. I could see them clearly. I got my mobile phone out, zoomed in and took some photos.

I walked back to the station, got my train and looked at the photos. It was like seeing David again. His son was the image of him. Would I have wanted to meet him? Would I have regretted not meeting him? I still don't know.

13

Up and Down and Round and About

I met up with Kath a few days later. I told her what had happened and showed her the photos of Carole and John Junior. She was very supportive and understood why I didn't want to meet up with David's son. It would have been too hard for me.

The days were starting to get longer and we spent time sitting in Kath's garden. The hedges, flowers and trees were looking lovely. Everything looked taller, healthier and more colourful.

I hadn't let what happened in Brighton get to me. I wouldn't. David was there and he was closer to me than he had been in a long while.

Kath and I had decided to go to a very large amusement park in order to fulfil our dreams of feeling extremely queasy on a rollercoaster. We knew it would be full of children if we went at a weekend so decided to go during the week and definitely not during the school holidays. We might look out of place with no children or grandchildren in tow but we could get away with it.

The train journey up was a bit fraught. A couple were arguing a few seats away from us. One would get up, make a rude passing remark and stomp off. A few minutes later they would come back. The couple would make up with a kiss and a cuddle and then a few minutes later the row would start all over again. We couldn't work out what the issue was.

'Please don't get off at our stop,' Kath whispered, crossing her fingers. 'Please don't get off at our stop.'

They didn't, thank goodness. We got a special bus to the amusement park and queued up outside. Kath had downloaded tickets so we went through a fast entry turnstile. The first thing we did was find the toilets. Then we went and sat outside a coffee shop and ate cream buns and drank a coffee each.

The first ride we went on was a very slow one indeed. We found a large lake with huge plastic swans going round it in figures of eight. We queued up and eventually got in one and laid out. We rested our heads on the back of the swan seat which had a soft covering. It was incredibly relaxing. We could stay on the ride for up to half an hour. It was a sunny day, nice and warm so we settled down and looked up at the sky.

An hour and a half later.

'Hello? Can you hear me? Are you alright?' Someone was knocking on the side of our swan.

We had fallen asleep and were both curled up as if we were in bed. I looked up and saw several park staff looking down at us from two boats either side of us.

'Another glass of wine wouldn't go amiss but don't tell anyone,' Kath mumbled. She was still half asleep.

'Kath, Kath, wake up!' I prodded her. She woke up a bit startled and looked at me. Her eyes followed where mine had settled. There was a rather large man all in green standing in one of the boats with his arms folded. He didn't look at all happy.

'We have been calling out to you, even used a loud-hailer at one point, a very loud-hailer,' he said. 'Your boat was out and was the last one being recalled when it got stuck on an underwater cable. We couldn't get out to you as we had to wait for two boats ahead of you to be brought in. None of the swans will work while you are stuck here and now, we have a queue building up.'

We looked over and saw a huge line of people all standing on the side of the lake. Most of them had their hands on their hips and they were glaring at us. Several children were crying.

'We need to get you out of this swan so we can move it. Come on. Give me your hand.'

We got up, wobbled about a bit and got in one of the boats with help from the man in green. They even had a diver there who was sorting out the underwater cables.

'I don't believe this,' I said very quietly to Kath. 'How utterly embarrassing.'

'Yes, but one to tell the grandchildren about!' Kath sniggered. She looked at me and could see I wasn't amused. 'Well, yes. Sorry, Beth, you have a good point there. It is embarrassing. I hope they don't chuck us out. They could ban us for life.'

'Why us? Look what happened when we went into that maze? Remember?'

'Yes. Ha!' Kath forgot that I was not best pleased at the present time. 'Where's my scarf?' She stopped saying anything else after that.

I turned to the man in green. 'We are so sorry. Please accept our apologies.'

He didn't smile. He just stared at us.

We got a good talking-to by the amusement park manager. I felt like we were back at school being told off by the headmistress. We both had our heads down. When she had finished reading us the riot act and we had apologised profusely, we were allowed to continue with our day in the park. I did think though that we were due an apology of our own as it wasn't our fault that the swan had got caught on a cable. That was until the man in green with the unhappy face came up to us with Kath's scarf in his hand. It had been cut to shreds.

'Our diver found this wrapped round the line from your swan leading down to the cable which all the rides run off and normally makes everything run really smoothly for the enjoyment of everyone. As you probably realise by now, that didn't happen. I am sorry your scarf is not in the same condition it was when you entered the park. Our swan ride isn't either, funnily enough.' He handed over the scarf still wet, turned around and walked off like a triumphant sheriff in a cowboy film. His legs were bandy enough to sit on a horse very comfortably. He had got his men, or rather, women.

'I think we should get some lunch,' Kath said and ushered us in the direction of a pizza place.

'I bet they have all their surveillance cameras on us.' I looked up at one nearest to us. It looked like it had its head tilted towards us, following us as we moved. 'I bet we will be on YouTube again or similar now.'

'We could go viral then,' Kath said.

At that point, we both spluttered with laughter. 'Never a dull moment doing things with you, Kath,' I said.

'Likewise,' Kath said.

We ate a large pizza each with cheese in the outside crust with a side accompaniment of coleslaw and onion rings. We felt stuffed afterwards.

'I hate to say this but do you think we should go on that rollercoaster ride now?' I rubbed my stomach.

'I think if we walk around a lot, we can work all this off and then go on it.' Kath seemed to have worked it all out.

'I have just looked up details about that rollercoaster in this leaflet. Apparently, you go round with a G force which is out of this world and you are literally thrown upside down and roundabout all over the place. If you close your eyes and then open them again, you have no idea where the ground is or where the sky is. The final insult is that at several points, you go round and round in a circle one way and then go round and round in a circle the other way. Really fast. Really, really fast. It sounds horrific. I think I would rather have my toenails pulled out very slowly and then rubbed with lemon juice. My toes where my toenails would have been, that is.' I folded up the pamphlet and laid it back on the table.

Kath had a mouthful of pizza in her mouth while I had been talking. She ate it quickly once I had stopped talking. 'Okay. No rollercoaster ride then. I don't think I could cope with being that high up. I would have my eyes closed the entire time. We should have planned this better and had lunch afterwards and not before.'

We sat and chatted over coffee. The amusement park was close to a large river. I looked up and could see a number of seagulls hovering right above us.

'Look at them, Kath. It must be wonderful to fly like a bird. They can see so much.'

As Kath looked up, I saw something large and white whizz past beside her and splatter on the ground.

'That was lucky. It missed you,' I said.

'No, it didn't,' Kath replied. 'I felt it hit my head.' She touched the back of her hair and then showed me the muck.

'Well, that was a very good aim then.'

I got up and looked at her head. It was covered with seagull poo. I couldn't stop laughing. I got a napkin and wiped it.

'You might need to rinse your head in a sink, Kath. I have got as much as I can off but there are still a few bits left.'

'Sod it. I can't be bothered. Let's get going.'

As we walked around the park, we decided not to go on any rides that would have the potential to make us throw up. We thought about going back on a swan ride but realised we would have to heavily disguise ourselves to even be allowed to queue up. They probably had our photos up too at the kiosk with a message telling the staff not to allow us on the swan ride UNDER ANY CIRCUMSTANCES WHATSOEVER. We found a log ride instead. I love log rides, always have. When I was little, I went on one with my mum and we went back on it loads of times and got thoroughly soaked.

We stood in the line for it, slyly looking around to see if any staff from the swan ride disaster had been transferred to other duties in the park to help calm their nerves.

As we went to get into our log, someone handed Kath waterproof plastic macs to put on.

'I don't think we will need these,' Kath said and handed them back. Luckily, the person put them behind us in our log and crossed his fingers. I thanked him. We had an entire log all to ourselves.

'Kath, I really think we should put these on.' I put mine on and handed the other one to Kath who shooed it away with her hand. 'It's only a bit of water, Beth. Nothing to write home about.'

The log ride was peaceful at first. We just went around a couple of times like we were on a little river. There were animals on each side of the banks waving at us; squirrels, badgers, rabbits with happy smiling faces. I waved back but made sure no one in the other logs could see me. Then we started to go up a hill. We were on a cable which worried me as all I could think about was what had happened with the swan. We were going higher and higher. Kath closed her eyes. I could see parts of the park we hadn't gone to yet. People were starting to look like ants. I grabbed hold of the rail in front of me and then sat sideways. We reached the top and went through a little tunnel in a make-believe mountain with more animals waving and smiling. Some even talked and squeaked. It was at this point that I realised what was just about to happen.

'Kath, I really think you should put your mac on. Please.'

'I honestly don't think...arrghhhhhhhhhhhhh!!!!!' Kath had opened her eyes.

She suddenly saw what was in front of her. The exit to the mountain tunnel was coming up fast and there didn't seem to be a waterway ahead. All of a sudden, it became a sheer drop down. As quick as you like, we were over the edge screaming our heads off. I felt like I was flying but at a hefty speed facing downwards with the ground coming up towards me very quickly. I clung on for dear life and closed my eyes. Kath was beside herself with panic. Suddenly, we hit the water with an enormous bang. Huge amounts of water came pouring over us. I had my waterproof mac on which protected me from getting completely wet but Kath...? My goodness. I looked across at her and found it so difficult not to burst out laughing. She was drenched to her core. She could hardly breathe. Water was coming out of her mouth and ears. Her hair was flat against her face and neck. She looked like she had grown a moustache she had so much hair clinging to her upper lip.

'At least it has got rid of the rest of the seagull poo,' I said.

'I...I...I need to get out of this. I need, ooooh, this is horrible, I need to get out of this log. NOW! I need to get....out.' Kath shook herself like a dog coming out of the sea. We sat in the log for another few minutes while it meandered its way down to ground level. The log was half full of water so both of us had sodden shoes. I thought I might develop trench foot.

When we stopped and were able to get out, our shoes hit the deck and made such loud noises it sounded like we had both eaten food that had made us fart ourselves silly.

We kept apologising; 'Sorry, not me. It's my shoes.' 'Oops. Oh dear, my shoes do seem to be talking to each other.' 'And there's another noise. Well, I never.'

The queue of people just stood and looked at us. No one said anything apart from a child who said far too loudly, 'Why are those women making farty noises, Daddy?' The child's father didn't respond.

We walked to the nearest toilets and Kath kept turning her head around under a dryer. Kath's hair looked like it had had a terrible fright and was standing up on end in sheer terror.

'Have you got a hairbrush on you, Beth?'

I rummaged through my bag and found a comb. 'I'm not sure this will help but here you go.'

I stood back. Kath tried to put the comb through her hair.

'Jesus Christ!!!' she yelled. 'Mother of all that is evil and unworldly!!! That is a killer!!!' She threw the comb back at me.

After Kath had spent an hour under the dryers, we reappeared. I half expected to see bookmakers outside handing out money to people who had successfully bet that Kath would take longer than a month of Sundays to get dry again.

It was now 4.30 pm so we decided that it was time to go home. It would take at least two hours to get back to London. Kath did smell like a dog who needed a proper bath but I didn't say anything. I just breathed through my mouth all the way home.

'I am never, never, ever, ever, ever, going on a log ride ever again. Never, ever.' Kath sat staring out of the window.

'That's a shame as I have entered us both in the Log Ride World Championships next week. All expenses paid trip to the south coast.'

Kath stared at me. We didn't say another word to each other until we arrived at our London station.

We got a cab and when we got out, we hugged each other.

'Can we have a bit of a break from doing any more excursions, please?' Kath said.

'Of course,' I replied. 'I can always help you with your garden instead.'

14

Harry

I was hoovering the stairs the following day and I looked out of the window. I saw Harry sitting on the bench outside. I finished up and wandered out to see him.

'Hello, Harry; how are you?'

'Hello to you. Lovely to see you again. I am fine, thank you for asking. How are you, Beth?'

'I'm good, thanks. Do you mind if I join you?'

'Please do.' Harry beckoned me with his hand to sit down. We sat and looked at our surroundings. There were more people out walking. It was a warm, sunny day. We watched the spectacle of people walking, talking, running, throwing Frisbees at each other, setting up a cricket match, putting suntan lotion on and laying on the grass, putting out a picnic or sitting on benches reading a book.

'This is what life is all about,' Harry said. 'Look at all those people enjoying themselves.' Harry pointed at several groups.

'The sun does that. The minute it comes out, people flock to absorb its rays.'

You could hear animated conversations full of laughter and see people with arms around each other, slapping friends on the back and drinking bottles of beer. People were trying to light barbeques but without much success, as local wardens were going around telling them not to. All that uncooked food was going to waste.

I wanted to know more about Harry. I almost felt sorry for him as I remember he had told me he was made to move into the care home after his wife had died. I wondered if he had made any friends at the home.

'Harry, would you like to come over to my house and have a cup of tea and a slice of cake? It doesn't have to be today if you are busy. I would like to get to know you better and I hope we can become friends.'

Harry turned and looked at me. He gently took hold of my hand. 'I would very much like to take up your kind offer, Beth'. He smiled. 'How about 2 pm tomorrow? I have the toe person coming in to saw my nails off this afternoon.'

I told him the number of my house and pointed to the Burning Bush as a reference as it was the only one on that side of the road.

I went to the local Waitrose the following morning to get a Victoria sponge cake, a Lemon Drizzle cake and some delicious chocolate bites. Before Harry arrived, I set out my finest tea set. It was another nice day so I prepared everything out in the garden.

Harry rang the doorbell at 2 pm precisely. He looked very dapper. He had a very smart suit on and looked like he had got his hair cut. He was holding a small bunch of flowers.

'You shouldn't have, Harry, but thank you.' I took the flowers and put them in a vase. 'They are lovely.' I smelt the scent. Freesias. 'My favourite.'

Harry wanted a tour. He pointed out books he had read, paintings he admired and took a keen interest in the history of my house.

We sat in the garden and Harry spouted some Latin names for various flowers and plants. He was very knowledgeable about a lot of things and I was keen to find out more about him. He seemed like a good egg.

'Harry, where were you born?' I asked.

'Sussex,' he replied. 'Lewes, to be precise. Delivered at home by my mother and aunt.'

'I was born in Brighton,' I said, 'but my home town is Lewes too. My family are from Lewes and some of them still live there. What a coincidence.'

Harry continued, 'My family moved up to Croydon when I was about sixteen years old. We lived in Gloucester Road where there was a pub called the Drum and Monkey but we always called it The Shit and Shovel.' Harry laughed out loud. 'My family went in there for a pint, a chat and a singalong while the piano player worked her fingers across the keys. Lovely times. The piano player's name was Beth too. Elizabeth. She was a wonderful woman. I knew her husband, Henry Ketson. We were best friends until he was killed in the Second World War. I was in the army too. Got a few wounds here and there but nothing too serious. I spent quite a bit of time in an army hospital and by the time I was ready for duty again, the war was coming to an end. I celebrated along with everyone else when it was all over but there was this huge space next to me where Henry should have been. We both loved football and used to go and watch Arsenal play. We would drop stink bombs on the ground so everyone would move away from us. Then, we always had a clear view watching the game. Those were the days. Always been an Arsenal supporter. We would take our rattles with us and make a hell of a noise with them.'

I sat in silence. Harry had known my grandfather. I was named after Elizabeth, my grandmother. This couldn't be right. I felt like I was being set up and a camera crew would suddenly appear with a presenter, grinning from ear to ear, yelling, 'Well, you thought you were just having a nice friendly chat with this man when in fact you have been chosen to appear on our show 'Well, That's A Coincidence, Or Is It?'

Harry continued with his story.

'After the war, I went to work in the family business. We were making new heating systems. We had some really good ideas but my father was made a derisory offer and sold everything to a company. They went on to make a fortune and we were left with nothing. My father liked to drink too much and it messed his brain up with his understanding of what was a good deal and what was a bad deal.'

Some of my family had moved up to Croydon from Lewes and they too lived in the same street as Harry and his family and went to the same pub. I remember them giggling telling me they used to call it that name too. My grandmother, Elizabeth, played the piano in pubs in Lewes before moving up to south London.

'After all that, I met my future wife, Maisie, in a dance hall and we got married. We had two children. My son moved to Canada years ago and I have a daughter but neither of them want anything to do with me. I joined the police force and retired fifteen years ago. I did a bit of gardening for neighbours, painted walls, cleared out rubbish and then looked after Maisie until she passed away. I was going through a very bad time, couldn't cope with not having Maisie with me, and lost a lot of weight. Neighbours and friends got worried and those in the know thought it would be a good idea for me to move to the care home here. I think I told you that once before. I wanted to come up to North London to be near close friends.' There was a pause. 'I often think my marriage to Maisie was based on lies though. When she passed over. I had so many different emotions and sadness. I was also angry at myself. I have had to learn to deal with how I feel in a different way now.' I didn't ask him what he meant. He would tell me when the time was right.

Listening to Harry made me feel incredibly sad. His life seemed to have stopped and started so often it reminded me of a rickety old car. I wanted to find something that would make some good memories for him again.

'Harry, would you mind? I want to show you some photo albums. I never told you my family surname. It's Ketson.' I had to be certain.

Harry looked at me without saying a word.

I came back carrying as many photo albums as I could. I put them on the table and sat next to Harry.

I balanced the first one on my left knee and Harry's right knee. 'Please, Harry, look as long as you like. Do you recognise anyone in these photos? These are my family.'

The first group of black and white photos were of large family outings with everyone lying on grassy areas smiling. More photos were of family and friends. Harry looked carefully at them and then suddenly he took the album and pointed at a photo of four young men holding pints up to the camera, laughing.

'I, I...' Harry couldn't get the words out.

'What is it, Harry? Do you know someone?'

'That's me,' he said very quietly. He pointed at the young man at the end who was a bit shorter than everyone else.

I looked closely and could see it was Harry when he was younger. You couldn't see his blue eyes in the black and white photo but he had the same nose and chin.

'Oh, my goodness, Harry. You are standing next to my granddad. You knew him!' I spluttered. I was starting to feel tearful. I had never known my grandfather as he had died before I was born. There was sadly no one left alive who knew him now, except Harry.

Harry started to cry and got his trusty handkerchief from his trouser pocket to wipe the tears away. I couldn't hold back and we both sat on the sofa weeping.

'This is almost like it was meant to happen,' I said. 'People are not going to believe this.'

I wanted to know all about my granddad. He died before I was born so I only had other people's memories to rely on. My mum didn't have many memories either as she was two when he was killed.

'Harry, what was my granddad like? I know you have told me some things, but was he a decent man?'

'Goodness me, yes. He was the most decent man I ever knew. He was wonderful and had such a great sense of humour. That's why some things were and still are so difficult for me to deal with as he isn't here anymore. I can't explain things to him.'

Harry was silent and then looked at me. 'There is something I would like to share with you, Beth, but not now. I'm not quite ready to just yet. It might help explain why my children haven't seen me in a while.'

'Okay, Harry. There's no rush.'

'But there is, Beth, there is.'

15

In an Art Gallery and Up, Up and Away

I thought about what Harry had said over the next few days. I knew he would tell me what his secret was in time and I didn't want to pressure him.

Kath and I decided that in order to avoid the possibility of any more accidents happening on our trips, we would have a relaxing day at an art gallery. We thought about going to a local one but instead travelled into central London. We got a bus and as we were been driven along, I told Kath about my afternoon with Harry. I told her the whole story, how we had first met on a bench and how important our friendship had now become because of our newfound link.

'That feels like it was written in the stars, Beth. That is amazing. I have never heard anything like that before. You should tell the national newspapers.'

We got off not far from where we needed to be and walked down through Leicester Square. There were a few performers there, one small group singing, a woman walking around on stilts, a young man swinging himself round in what looked like a large hula hoop and someone pretending to be a statue. Two young Japanese girls walked past him and he threw his arms out towards them. They both cried out and rushed off. We arrived at the National Gallery and went in. We were both interested in art and we both liked to stand in front of paintings looking at the finer details that other people may have missed or try and find where the artist had deliberately hidden clues.

We walked around in awe, standing still or sitting in front of the most exquisite paintings, some small, some large and some very large. It felt like we were in a cathedral. There was hardly any noise except the sound of people's shoes squeaking on the floor as they walked around. Everyone was there in revered silence or whispering out of respect for the paintings.

We treated ourselves to lunch in the restaurant at the top of the building and looked out at Trafalgar Square. Cars and buses were so close to each other it reminded me of a long and winding snake, stopping every now and again at traffic lights before moving on again. People were milling about in the square, dipping their hands in the fountains. Photographs were being taken of people standing still next to the lions, pointing up at a lion's jaw with pretend fright etched on their faces. There were no longer loads of pigeons there now which I found a shame. I remember when I was little and my mum took me there and bought some bird food. I had pigeons all over me.

A tourist bus went past and I watched as everyone on board simultaneously turned their heads upwards to look at Nelson on top of his column.

'Do you fancy walking down to look at the Thames?' I asked Kath.

'Yes, why not? It's not far.'

We finished lunch with the obligatory dessert each and made our way to the river. It was much windier walking along the embankment. We both kept dabbing our eyes with tissues.

'Not sure this was such a good idea. I can't stop my eyes from weeping,' I said.

'Tell you what, why don't we walk down a bit, cross over to the other side and go to Borough Market? It's a bit of a plod but worth it. We can look at The Shard, too.' Kath started walking in that direction so I followed her.

If we lost track of where to go, we only had to look up at The Shard to get our bearings. We walked on a bridge over the river and craned our necks to look up at the huge glass building next to London Bridge railway station. For some reason, it reminded me of a very long ice cream squirted from a machine that someone had then smoothed down on all sides to a point at one end. I have no idea why I thought that. Maybe subconsciously I wanted an ice cream.

We stopped off at Southwark Cathedral and sat in the grounds for a rest and then went to Borough Market and ended up buying far more food and treats than we had planned to. The cheese stalls were wonderful and we spent time tasting samples and then chose our favourites. We bought biscuits, cakes, jams, fruit and vegetables, homemade takeaway meals and lots of fudge. We had so much that Kath bought a large bag to help carry some of the increasing amounts of food and treats we were buying.

We sat on a long wooden bench to have a rest and looked around at how busy the market was. Stallholders were shouting and handing over food items in paper bags one at a time to a queue of patiently waiting people. We ate a couple of biscuits I had bought and drank a takeaway coffee each. I then ate some fudge.

'This is delicious. Have some, Kath.'

'Oh my. That is wonderful.'

After eating all the fudge, we went back and got some more.

'This has been a good day,' Kath sighed and took the last bite of a biscuit.

'It has. You are right and nothing has gone wrong yet.'

We both smiled. We sat for over an hour taking in everything like sponges until we were saturated. I wanted to wring myself out to absorb more but we both decided it was time to go and look at other things. We stood underneath The Shard and looked up at it with some difficulty. Both our necks ached like mad. We couldn't decide whether to go up it or not.

'Right. Paper, rock, scissors,' Kath said.

'Why?' I asked.

'Whoever wins two out of three attempts can make the decision. Do we go up or do we stay down?'

I won, my paper covering Kath's rock and my scissors cutting Kath's paper. It would be my decision.

'I know it is up to me, Kath, but I really don't want to make the choice and then it turns out to be a bad one.'

'Okay, let's go for heads or tails then.' Kath got out a coin. 'Heads we go up, tails we don't.'

Kath tossed the coin in the air and I was praying for tails.

Kath caught the coin, put it on the back of her hand and uncovered it. 'Heads it is then.'

'Great,' I said trying to sound enthusiastic. 'Whoopee do. Can't wait. Really, I can't.'

We got the lift up and I kept my eyes closed the entire way. When the lift stopped, I opened my eyes and thought we had been catapulted up to the edge of space. I was normally okay with heights but it was far too high for me. I was struggling. I felt like the glass around us would crack. I looked around for Kath but couldn't see her. Then I did. She was lying in a crumpled heap near the lift door. A couple of people were standing over her looking concerned. I walked towards them and told them I was a friend of hers and she would be alright once we got back down. A fear of heights had caused her to collapse.

'Beth, I am sorry. I can't do this. Can we go? I get dizzy standing on a thick carpet.'

'Music to my ears, Kath. Come on, let's go.'

Once in the lift and heading down, Kath said, 'I am sure the view was spectacular up there, the dreamy spires of London and all that. Listen to me; that's Oxford. I'm all of a dither. Even so, I think I would rather look at photos of it on the internet.' Kath sounded relieved when we were on the ground again.

'Let's get a drink,' I suggested.

We went down to The George pub, a former coaching inn, which was near Borough Market. It was off the main road set in a courtyard. You really noticed how much quieter it was there. It was full of oak beams, squeaky floorboards and lots of nooks and crannies. I loved it. We sat outside with a bottle of wine.

'What a wonderful place.' Kath looked around and made contented sounds. 'Look how old it is. It says on that board over there that Charles Dickens drank here. I can see why.'

We went up the staircase to the galleried area. Every other step up and down made a creaking noise like the wood was about to split. I wanted to lean over the balcony and shout out something Shakespearean but decided I would need a few more drinks to have the courage to do that to the crowd below. We finished our drinks, exited right and got a bus home.

16

Camping Out

Kath seemed to have developed an obsession with camping. She had started to watch programmes about people living in the wilds of Scotland or on desert islands and had even watched Carry on Camping while drinking wine and cackling with laughter.

'Kath, is everything okay?' I asked the next time I saw her. She was practising cooking on a very small outdoor barbeque set.

'Oh yes, Beth. Don't worry; I haven't gone mad. I found my dad's diaries recently in a chest and when he was young, he went camping all over the country. He wrote so eloquently about it and it just got me interested in wondering what it would be like to sleep under the stars, so to speak.'

'Where are you thinking of going then?'

'Where are WE thinking of going, Beth,' she stressed. 'I would like you to be part of this adventure too.'

I had never been camping before. I had always stayed in hotels or rented apartments. I had the money now to go first-class anywhere I wanted. Camping would certainly be something I could tick off on my non-existent list of things I never imagined I would end up doing. I wasn't entirely happy with the thought of having to get up in the middle of the night if I wanted a pee though.

'Do you know anything about camping, Kath, like how to put up a tent?'

'Diddly squat, Beth, but that's part of the fun, isn't it, learning how to do new things? You know the call of the wild, the thrill of the chase.'

'Not sure I want to be chased thank you. We do need to have a think about our destination. There are lots of options. We could go and camp up anywhere in the countryside where we would be allowed to, stay on a campsite or camp out in one of our gardens for a test run.' I preferred the last option.

Kath picked up a notepad and wrote Preparing for Camping on the first page. 'We need to go to one of those camping shops to get a tent and whatever else we need.' In her notebook, she wrote a list of things to take when camping, such as a tent and pegs.

The next day we went up the main high street and found an outdoor clothing and equipment shop. We got a sales assistant to talk us through all the tents, which ones were waterproof and, most importantly, which ones were the easiest to put up.

'Have you any experience camping?' the sales assistant asked.

'None whatsoever,' I replied and smiled broadly.

The sales assistant raised his eyebrows. 'Right then. I would recommend this type of tent. It is very easy to erect and won't let any rain in. Are you thinking of two single tents or a two-roomed one?'

Kath looked at me. 'What do you think, Beth?'

'Well, we could get a two-roomed one as it would save time having to put another one up, wouldn't it?'

'Okay then. Can we have a double one and everything that goes with it to make it as comfortable and secure to sleep in as possible? Beth, we need to look at suitable clothing and boots now.'

We came home in a taxi as we had far too many bags to cope with. We had bought a rucksack so rolled up the sleeping bags and attached them to it. The tent was in a large bag. We went back to Kath's and dropped everything in her hall.

'I need a drink,' Kath said. She came back with two glasses of fresh orange juice. I was half expecting a large glass of wine but was thankful for the soft drink. We sat down and drank them with much relish.

'That was nice,' I said. I got up and brought all the bags into Kath's living room. We decided that we would put the tent up first. 'This won't take long at all,' Kath said. 'It looks easy enough.'

Kath and I took the tent out into the garden and while Kath looked at the instruction booklet, I laid out all the pegs and poles on the lawn in order of size and colour coding.

'Lay the outer part of the tent out on the ground and zip up the doors.'

I did as instructed.

'Next, put the red colour-coded poles through the sleeves on the flysheet and then bend them so they form the shape of a tent.'

I did that too.

'It looks like a very large melon with a flat bottom,' Kath said. 'Next, peg out the tent using the pegs and whatever guy lines are.'

After a bit of a struggle, I found the guy lines and all of the pegs and got a mallet and banged them into the ground.

'Make sure they are all even and tight enough so the tent doesn't flap like crazy in the wind or we will end up on the other side of the garden in the morning.'

'Is that what it actually says, Kath?'

'No, don't be daft.'

Kath continued with all the other instructions, and, after forty-five minutes, we stood back.

'That looks perfect. Easy peasy, lemon squeezy,' I said. I was particularly pleased with it as I had done all of it. Kath had managed to wangle her way out of helping by just reading the instructions to me.

'I am very impressed,' Kath said as she walked around the tent and ran her hand across the top of it. 'It says in the instruction book that we should practice a few times before setting off on an adventure. How about we both sleep in it tonight in my garden to make sure we feel alright sleeping outdoors and also to make sure it doesn't collapse?'

'I feel like I am having a sleepover with my best friend. Okay. Let me go home as I have a few things I need to do. I can grab some pyjamas, clothes for tomorrow, a book and a lamp and I will see you at about 5.30 pm.'

I came back to find Kath sorting out board games. She had Monopoly in one hand and Risk in another and a chessboard on the floor.

'Kath, I once played Risk with my mum and it went on for five days. I still can't remember who won. I didn't think we were going to be in the tent for that long.'

'Cards then. I have a pack somewhere.' Kath rummaged through several drawers. 'Aha!' she said when she finally found them. 'I also have burger buns and veggie burgers in my freezer and there is some salad too. We can have all that for dinner.'

'Great. I will cook them, Kath, and then we can go into the tent and pretend we are enjoying a wonderful meal in a field full of wildflowers. We may need to close our eyes to get the full pretence flowing though and wear earplugs so we don't hear any traffic. Should I cook all the food outside, Kath? Then we really will be experiencing outdoor living.'

'No, not this time. We can cross that bridge when we are in the actual countryside.'

We did go the whole hog with clothing though and took our pyjamas into the tent to get changed into them. I brushed my teeth outside but drew the line at digging a hole in Kath's garden to use as a toilet.

We settled into our sleeping bags and I put a radio drama on for background noise. It was odd sleeping outdoors in someone else's garden. I felt like I was six years old again in a tent, squealing with delight, turning my torch on and off. As I lay down, I felt I could hear every noise in and out of the tent. There was a scrabbling sound outside. I could hear an animal snuffling and it was very close. It was sniffing near my side of the tent.

'Kath,' I whispered. Kath seemed to have fallen asleep. 'Kath!' I said loudly.

116

'Oh er, what is it?' Kath woke up and I could hear her get out of her sleeping bag. She unzipped the tent door to my side and sat on the end of my sleeping bag.

'What's the matter, Beth?'

'Can't you hear that noise outside? It's really close.'

We both listened.

'Oh, that? Don't worry, it's probably Barney,' Kath said.

'Barney? Who on earth is Barney?' I asked.

'The local fox. I always put food out for him and he is probably wondering what this thing we call a tent is doing here. I just hope he doesn't bite into it.' She went back to her side leaving me to cup my ear against the side of the tent.

We couldn't sleep so we sat up again, whispering when we spoke.

'Why are we whispering?' I asked.

Kath shrugged her shoulders. 'You don't want Barney to hear what we are saying, do you?'

We stayed up and talked until the early hours and then went to bed.

'Arrghh! What the hell?????' Kath was screaming.

I rushed in. She had a tissue and was thrusting it into her left ear.

'There's something crawling about in my ear!' she yelled.

I went back and got my tweezers. I always carry them with me as you never know when you might need them, like now.

'Let me have a look.' I put my torch on and carefully put the end of the tweezers in her ear and pulled. A large earwig came wriggling out.

'Euwwwwwwww!' Kath said and shook her shoulders. 'As much as I love nature, having an earwig crawling towards my brain is not my idea of fun.'

'It is quite appropriate, though. An EARwig in your ear.'

Two hours later, we were in trouble. Neither of us had checked the weather forecast properly. It was a brief look with both of us saying 'It will be fine' while waving our hands in the air.

I was dreaming about being covered with a wet marshmallow and suddenly woke to find the tent over my face. It was very wet. I quickly pushed it off. I felt like a bucket of water had been thrown over me.

'Jesus. Kath!!' I yelled at the top of my voice. I heard a muffled noise and then the sound of someone realising they were covered with water.

'Hashtag what in the name of all that is good is going on??!! Beetthhhh!!!!'

'The tent has fallen down and now I can hear the sound of thunder and lightning. It sounds really close.' As I finished, the tent lit up as the first strike of lightning came down nearby.

'Jesus Christ Almighty!!!' Kath shouted. 'We need to get out of here and back in my flat.' She raced towards the living room doors and flung them open. She came back after putting a mac on and helped me get everything out of the tent.

'At least lightning doesn't strike in the same place twice!' I shouted.

Neither of us had shoes on so running backwards and forwards in bare feet did not make for a jolly experience. We left the tent where it was. We slumped in chairs completely exhausted. We sat in silence drinking coffee and munching on biscuits.

The next morning, we woke up in the chairs we had sat in the night before. We went out and looked at the tent. Three tent pegs had been dislodged and the flysheet covering the top of the tent was nowhere to be seen.

'I blame that fox, Barney,' I said.

'You did hammer them in properly, didn't you?' Kath said.

'Of course I did,' I replied. 'I checked it out too before we went inside. Gave everything a good tug to make sure it was all secure.'

'Well, it is a hard lesson to learn for both of us then. In future, check, check, check.' Kath went into the kitchen to make another gallon of coffee.

We sat and talked. We both agreed that maybe camping was not the best option for us. We were total novices and I had visions of us being rescued by a helicopter somewhere with a lot of fuss being made and with us looking dishevelled on the local news. 'Well, we never expected this to happen but at least we didn't have to be airlifted from the edge of a cliff just before it collapsed,' I would have said to camera.

'At least we have done a bit of camping, albeit in my back garden.' Kath ticked it off her list with a small tick.

'We need to have a think about what to do now instead of camping,' I said. 'Maybe we could think about glamping instead.'

'Not today, though. I think we should just relax. Maybe watch a film or four on the telly.'

We looked at the TV guide. There was one film about a group of people with kayaks going along the coast and finding a cave. When they enter the cave, it is enormous and they get totally lost.

'Beth have you ever been in a kayak before?'

I looked at Kath with a blank expression on my face and then looked away.

'I take that as a no, then.'

'And I don't intend to go in one either.'

'Did you sleep at all in the tent, Kath?'

'Yes, slept like a log until the avalanche of water descended. Actually, I feel like I have slept *on* a log.'

17

Giddy Up and Moving In

We both came to the conclusion that kayaking wasn't for us. Kath had never been kayaking before and after the tent escapade, she didn't want to do something that involved getting wet again. I had no desire to sit in something that could quite easily capsize. Not a good look when you did finally turn up the right way, eyes bulging.

We both loved horses so I said I would look into us having a horse-riding lesson. Kath had been on a horse a couple of times before but only to sit on. She was full of enthusiasm for another go and a proper trot around a field. I had ridden a donkey once in a nativity play when I played Mary. I was about seven years old at the time and found it a most uncomfortable experience. Couldn't walk properly for at least a week afterwards. I had sat on a very large horse a few times as well when I was about five years old. Horse riding wasn't really on our 'bucket list' as we had both been on a horse before but thought it would provide us with some calm and relaxation after some of our recent exploits.

There was an Equestrian Centre in a very, very large forested park to the north of where we lived. If we decided horse riding wasn't for us, we could try the nearby golf course instead.

I booked a lesson for us on the following Saturday and we drove up in Kath's car. We had ticked all the boxes to say we weren't experienced riders. We both decided to wear loose-fitting tracksuit bottoms rather than material-splitting tight trousers.

Kath parked the car and we walked the short distance to the horse-riding centre. I could hear the sound of horses whinnying. It was a very happy sound.

We went to the office to confirm we were there and then waited for our teacher. Kath and I stood close to a horse as it waited for its rider. We were fairly close to its backside which was a huge mistake. Suddenly, there was a dreadfully loud sound like a lot of people blowing through rolled-up paper.

'Beth how could you?' Kath said and giggled.

'It wasn't me, thank you very much.' I burst into a fit of giggles too and then laughed out loud. This was followed by a short burst of crying. 'I needed that,' I said.

The smell was unbelievable - like very overcooked Brussels sprouts. If someone had lit a match, we would have all gone up in flames.

'Goodness me. That is some smell. What on earth has that horse been eating?' I said and waved my hands in front of my face.

A woman suddenly appeared. 'Apologies for Winston. He has a habit of doing that in front of visitors. If I didn't know him better, I would say he gets a kick out of it. Forgive the pun. So how are we today? My name is Barbara and I will be showing you both the ropes.' Barbara smiled at us as if we were six years old and she kept bending forwards to put her hands over her knees.

Kath whispered, 'I think I might have just entered my second childhood. Or perhaps Barbara thinks I am much younger than I look.'

Barbara took us to a roofed paddock area, the floor of which was covered with sand. Two horses were waiting for us. They looked bored. They were both chewing on something and looked like they were talking to each other.

'I bet that horse on the left is saying to that horse on the right, blimey, not more beginners.' I snorted as I said it.

'Right then. Do you think you would be able to get up on the horse yourself or would you like a step ladder?' Barbara was patting one of the horses down. 'This is Goliath and that is Hercules.'

'I do hope they are not as feisty as those two characters,' Kath said to Barbara who laughed out loud.

'No. They are a couple of cuties. They are very used to having people on their backs who are not experienced riders.'

We both tried to get up on the horses by ourselves but only managed to lift our feet off the ground by about a foot. After a few minutes, it looked fruitless.

'Could we use the step ladder, please?' I asked.

We finally got up on the horses. I had Goliath and Kath was sitting on Hercules. They looked pretty big. I wasn't sure how many hands tall they were, but when I was on Goliath, he seemed to be the height of a two-storey house. I felt like I could see the centre of London from my lofty position. Barbara told us about the structure of our horses, what was where and what to avoid. Its backside was what I considered the most important thing not to stand close to in the future. She told us about balancing correctly on a horse. How not to fall off, basically.

Barbara got someone else from the centre to help lead me around while she took Kath and Hercules. I found it very uncomfortable again and it reminded me of my last time on that donkey. I felt like I was doing the splits. I could hear Kath making noises.

We went round the sanded area several times with the horses walking slowly. I wasn't yet prepared for even a gentle trot. We stopped and started several times.

'Shall we try going just a little bit faster?' Barbara asked, and, without waiting for an answer, we found ourselves trotting. I kept bouncing up and down opposite to the movement of Goliath as I couldn't quite get used to the rhythm. I felt like I was being smacked in places I really didn't want to be smacked in. Kath was bobbing up and down too and suddenly shouted out 'STOP!!'

We both came to a halt. 'I am struggling to bob up and down in time to the horse bobbing up and down,' she said.

The horses stopped. Maybe they were used to people suddenly yelling and knew what to do. Barbara went back to basics.

'Right, I want you both to sit comfortably (*that will be difficult* I thought) and then almost stand up in your saddle and then down and then up and then down and then up and then down.'

God, how many times did she say up and down? I lost count. All I wanted to do was shout out 'Up, down, up, down, turn it all around. You do the Hokey Cokey and you turn around. That's what it's all about.'

After an hour, we both felt less stressed and were allowed out of the paddock area. Barbara and her helper got on a horse each and led us out into the park. It was like being in the countryside. You wouldn't believe we were so close to the heart of the city. All you could hear were birds singing, leaves rustling in the gentle breeze and the sound of the horses' hooves thumping on the grass. We had paid for the whole day and luckily the sun was out. It wasn't too hot and it wasn't too cold. Just right like the three bears and their porridge.

I thought that nothing could go wrong. Everything was perfect. We chatted, we laughed, we asked questions and Barbara went through an awful lot about horse care, using the reins correctly, how to stop and start and how not to freak the horses out. This last bit would come in handy.

Suddenly, a large dog appeared from nowhere followed by its owner who was shouting at the top of his voice, 'Quincy, QUINCY! Come back here NOW!!!'

The dog ignored him and bounded towards us. Barbara and her helper held on to our reins as our horses started to rear up. 'Come, come, Goliath and Hercules, you have been trained for this sort of situation.'

I think she was trying to reassure us as the horses certainly wouldn't have understood what she was saying.

I could see Kath was getting nervous. She started to squeal and then clung onto her horse's neck. Hercules was moving and Barbara was struggling to hold onto him. He trotted off quickly. I was dreading what would happen if he suddenly galloped but he didn't. Goliath turned this way and that. I held on for dear life and closed my eyes but he suddenly stopped and just looked down at the dog. It really looked like he was saying 'Go. Go now or else'. The dog moved away and its owner managed to put his lead on and apologised.

'I am so sorry. He got out of his lead.'

Barbara was furious. I could hear her yelling, 'Take your dog away this minute'. I could see she was moving further away on her horse. So was Kath.

I looked up at the sky in relief for a few moments and then turned to see where Kath was but she was nowhere near me. I looked around frantically. My horse wasn't bothered in the slightest and kept munching on the grass.

'Excuse me,' I said to my helper who didn't seem to have a name. 'Where are they?'

She looked around and said, 'I have no idea but don't worry, Barbara will look after your friend'.

We waited for a few minutes. The helper had a mobile and rang Barbara. 'Is everything okay, Barbara? Where are you? Shall I take Beth and Goliath back to the paddock? Okay then. See you later. Barbara and Kath have just gone for a little trot. They will meet us later,' she said to me.

How much later I wondered. I couldn't hear what Barbara had been saying but we went back to the paddock to wait for them. My helper took the long route back so at least I was getting my money's worth. When we got back, we waited and waited. I tucked into one of the sandwiches we had saved for lunch. Then Barbara and Kath appeared both smiling and looking very relaxed. I, on the other hand, felt like an overcooked microwave meal, very hot and turning crispy.

'Where have you been? I was getting so worried,' I said.

'We have had a wonderful time. Hercules settled down and Barbara took us for a lovely stroll through a wooded area and then over a few fields. We even saw a few golfers teeing off.'

I was so glad nothing dreadful had happened knowing what Kath's track record was like.

We stayed a bit longer and helped brush the horses down. We decided we would go back sometime in the future.

The next day, neither of us could move properly. My legs felt like two people had grabbed each of my feet and then pulled them out to each side as far as they would go. If and when we went back, I decided I would need to warm up and stretch my legs and nether regions out beforehand.

Kath asked me to come over. It took me twice as long to walk to her flat. I kept wincing. On the way, I met Harry.

'Hello there,' he said and waved at me. 'What has happened to you? You look like you have done three rounds with Muhammad Ali.'

'You know we went horse riding yesterday? Well, we forgot about the after-effects,' I managed to say.

'Well, at least you are out and about now. Come, sit with me for a bit.'

Harry and I sat and talked. We had met up a few times since our last chat. He was such a lovely man. He talked more about my grandfather and told me a few more funny tales about what they used to get up to. He was the last person who knew the older members of my family, who had all now sadly passed on.

'I am not sure if you saw it in the local paper but my care home is closing down. There aren't as many residents now as there used to be and the company want to move us all to another home which is miles away. I have no family left now but I love this area and don't want to go. All my friends, like you, are here.'

I didn't know what to say. I didn't want Harry to go either. I told him that his new place might be even better than his current one, but I knew it didn't matter what I said. He wanted to stay here.

'Come over for lunch tomorrow, Harry. We can talk some more. 1 pm okay?'

'That would be lovely. See you then, Beth.'

We said goodbye and I carried on with my slow walk to Kath's. As I walked, I had an idea that was beginning to sprout in my head. The first stem had shown itself, and, as I walked, I thought more and more about it.

I got to Kath's and she looked just as dreadful as me. We both walked around like we were treading on eggshells. Kath got some food together and we sat out in her garden.

'Kath, I want your advice on something.'

Kath looked intrigued.

'I saw Harry again before I came to yours. His home is closing down and he doesn't want to move to the new place as it is too far away from the people and the area he knows. I have my house which is far too big for me and have this thought that he could live with me. What do you think?'

'Well, it would be an admirable thing to do, Beth. Is he okay? I mean is he fit and healthy? Nothing wrong with his mind? Would you need to look after him?'

'No, he is perfectly okay. He has all his faculties about him and can do everything himself. He can manage stairs too. I just don't like the idea of him vegetating somewhere.'

'Well, find out what you need to do, talk to Harry and the home and go for it.'

That was exactly what I wanted to hear.

The next day, Harry came over with a small bunch of flowers and some chocolates. I had cooked a quiche and made some salad. As it was a warm day, we went out into the garden. Harry didn't have his hat and scarf on and had made a special effort to comb his hair so it sat neatly on his head.

We made small talk and then I made my move.

'Harry, I've been thinking. You said you were going to have to move away and didn't want to. Why don't you come and live here? I have plenty of room and would love you to stay. What do you think? I can talk to the manager of the home and see if I need to talk to social services too.'

Harry looked up and started to cry.

'Oh, Harry, I'm sorry; I didn't mean to upset you. I will understand if you don't think it is a good idea.'

'Beth, I think it is a wonderful idea. None of the staff in the home have had any time for me since my wife passed away. I have often felt so very alone. I have friends there and I talk to them but you have been the only person I can really talk to. I will pay you rent.'

I thought I was going to cry too. 'I wouldn't dream of charging you rent. You being here will be more than enough. Okay, Harry, let's get the ball rolling. I will phone the home to make an appointment to see the person in charge and we can take it from there.'

The following Tuesday, I met Clarissa who was in charge. She was very nice and said she would need to contact her line manager, talk to Harry to make sure it was what he wanted to do and let social services know. Someone from social services would come to my house with Harry to make sure it was suitable and look to see if there was any equipment Harry might need.

A week later the inspection took place. I had cleaned like mad the day before. My house was deemed fit to have Harry there and no equipment was needed. If and when that time did come, I would make sure he had everything to hand.

I went over to the home the following week to help Harry pack up his things and Kath put his cases and special items in her car and drove us over the road. Harry said goodbye to everyone in the home and promised he would come over and visit. At least with Harry staying with me, I wouldn't have to keep eating meals off my lap. We could actually sit at the table.

I spent time with Harry helping him to settle in. I had bought a new duvet set for him and put flowers in his room and showed him where everything was. I helped him unpack his suitcases and Harry decided where to put his photos and mementos. He was in the first-floor bedroom which had a good view over the park. We walked around the area and I took Harry into his local pub and bought him a light ale to celebrate his move. He looked more relaxed now and his smile had become broader and his laugh louder. We would get along. I could see it. I gave him his own keys and told him he could come and go as he pleased. It wasn't a prison. He could have his friends round, and, if he felt energetic enough, he could help in the garden. It would be totally up to him.

He couldn't stop thanking me. The first night he moved in, he cooked a special meal for me, one he had made many times for him and his wife. We shared a couple of glasses of wine. At about 9 pm, Harry stood up.

'Sorry, Beth. It has been a long day and I am very tired. So up the wooden stairs to Bedfordshire I go. Good night to you.'

The following morning, Harry came down resplendent in a new suit he had recently bought.

'Well, hello to you, Mr Savile Row. Did you have a good night's sleep, Harry?'

'I did indeed, thank you. When I was at the home, there was someone on my floor who would walk around at night and often came into my room and sat on my bed. There was also the noise of the night carers as they checked up on everyone. I am glad I don't have to worry about that anymore.'

'Well, I will make sure I don't come into your room during the night and sit on your bed then.' We both smiled.

We ate scrambled eggs on toast for breakfast and drank fresh orange juice.

'Would you like to do anything today, Harry? Anything take your fancy?'

'I think I would like to get some new underwear. Some of the ones the home gave me have someone else's name in them and I don't feel too happy about that. Most of them have gone a horrible grey colour too and there are holes in places where there shouldn't be holes.'

We went to a nearby department store and Harry got three packs of colourful underpants. I got him a couple of shirts too as he liked to look smart. I had put my outings with Kath on hold for a couple of weeks as I wanted to spend time with Harry.

We were out in the garden one afternoon. I was weeding some flower beds and Harry was deadheading old flower blossoms.

'Beth, I don't want to stop you doing what you have been doing with Kath. You know, all your days out. Please, I will be okay. I feel very happy here. I think I know my way around your home now.'

'Tell you what, Harry; let me get Kath to come over later today or tomorrow and we can look at something we can all do together. How about that?'

'I would love that, Beth, but please don't feel pressured to do that.'

'I'm not, Harry.' I called Kath and she was more than happy to have Harry come out with us.

Kath came over the following evening for dinner and we talked about things we would all like to do together. I didn't really expect Harry to try hang gliding but then again, he might be an ex-world champion and had forgotten to tell me.

As we ate a lovely dessert, Harry spoke.

'You know the only places we went to when I was in that home were the park, the seaside once or twice and a trip to see a pantomime.'

'Sounds like a hoot, Harry, or not as the case may be,' Kath said.

'Have either of you ever done paintballing before?' he asked.

'No,' we both said at the same time.

'Well, how about it? I am fit enough. I will try not to roll about, mind you, but I have always wanted to give it a try.'

We looked at each other. Was this a good idea? I was worried about Harry. It could get quite energetic.

'Are you sure, Harry?'

'Positive.'

'Okay then. Kath, Harry, let's do it!'

Harry clapped his hands together and poked me in the arm.

18

What a Load of Paint and Bull

I booked a paintballing place we could go to just out of London. I phoned up and spoke to a man, who in all honesty sounded like a child whose voice hadn't yet broken, and told him about Harry. I made sure Harry was out of earshot. The 'youth' said they had had a party of old aged pensioners, his words, in the week before and the centre had been rigorous with the health and safety aspects of their visit. It had all gone very well.

Kath drove us there and we sat through the preamble about how everything worked and how to keep safe. We then changed into our paintballing outfits. Mine was a bit of a squeeze and I found my helmet and face-covering particularly unflattering. It almost looked as if I was going deep-sea diving.

'Harry, you look very dapper in yours,' I said. You couldn't tell how old he was as he was so well covered up.

Harry smiled and stood tall. Over the last few days, I had noticed he had started to appear like he was enjoying life much better and seemed more refreshed. He liked being out of that care home.

'Let the bunfight commence,' he said.

We went out to a large forest and were joined by a few other people. One of them was a man in his forties who decided that now was the time to do his warm-up exercises. He stretched from side to side, did several squats and made lots of grunting noises. I think he thought he was actually in the army and was going out on a real reconnaissance exercise. He shook himself down a few times and then suddenly slapped his chest and shrieked very loudly, 'Let's do this!!' Kath and I both jumped.

Harry had the look of someone who didn't care. He just shook his head slowly. 'He's a bit of a twerp, isn't he?' he said.

One of the staff told us that the centre was celebrating its tenth anniversary so, as a special treat, we were going to be given twice the amount of time out on the paintball battlefield. We would also get double the amount of paintball pellets each. Everything would be special, he kept saying.

'If he mentions the word special once more, I will splatter him here and now,' Kath whispered in my ear.

At the end of our session, a horn would sound and staff would add up how many paintball splatters each person had received and the one with the fewest would be declared the winner. There would also be a second and third place and trophies would be handed out. The night before, we had worked out a strategy and had written lots of plans and drawn lots of pictures on paper at home. We had conveniently left all of our hard work behind so had to make up something else quickly.

We were put with four other people to make up a team. Harry was elected as our leader. He told us to fan out so we could see each other and could then let each other know when the 'enemy' was nearby. We moved slowly and tried not to step on any twigs. Suddenly, we heard a noise. A rustle. Harry pointed to the left and we could just see the grunting man from earlier trying to hide behind a large bush. We each hid behind a tree and waited. Nothing happened. It was a stand-off. We had talked about doing a pincer movement like the Roman army used to do - come at the person from left, right and in front. I beckoned Harry and Kath to take each flank as I crawled along the ground heading straight for the grunter. It worked. We surprised him so much that he screamed and winced. We each took a shot and got him. He wasn't happy at all. He accused us of cheating and said he would report us to the staff. I thought he was going to call the police too, such was his anger. He was almost frothing at the mouth. We smacked each other's hands in victory and continued to seek out and destroy. This was fun.

'He's a bad loser, isn't he? Look at him. Big-time Charlie. He is really getting on my goat,' Harry said.

It was only afterwards that Harry told us he used to be in a special army unit that dealt heavily with camouflage in order to reach their targets. Our team spent a fruitful three hours eliminating the opposition and, in the end, Harry was declared the overall winner.

I got hit twice, Kath once and Harry wasn't hit at all. He was very skilled at avoiding anyone and hid himself so well that he seemed to disappear at times.

We decided not to paintball each other in celebration and afterwards we each received a trophy. Harry was so proud and so pleased to get his. He held it on his head and danced around.

After changing back into our clothes, we put our trophies in Kath's car and went for a walk. There was an animal sanctuary nearby and we wanted to visit it. We paid the entrance fee and wandered around cooing and aaahing. We were the only adults without children in the petting area and spent a good half hour stroking sheep, guinea pigs and goats. We had tea and cake in the café area and each talked proudly about the trophies we had won.

'I will put mine on my mantelpiece,' Kath said.

'You were so good, Harry,' Kath said. 'You will have to teach me how to become invisible so I can avoid people I don't want to talk to in the street.'

Harry said that wouldn't be a problem at all. He was very pleased to have been declared champion of champions at the paintballing. He was so full of beans that he fairly skipped around the animal sanctuary. We went into the gift shop and I bought a large fluffy toy goat. Kath got a vibrant red scarf with parrots on and Harry got a chess set with animal characters. I saw a toy duck that made a particularly good-looking Queen with a crown on its head.

Next to the animal sanctuary was a farm and we assumed that it was part of the set-up. Harry pushed heavily at the gate and we went through to look more closely. I was a bit concerned as the lock on the gate seemed to have come loose, possibly by Harry barging his way through. We ended up in a field of cows.

Kath was way ahead of us.

'This is wonderful,' she said turning around and around with her arms out. 'Look how close we can get to these marvellous creatures.'

Harry and I walked back to the gate. We both had the sense that something wasn't quite right. Kath carried on walking quickly towards them. As she got closer, they parted like the Red Sea. Kath suddenly stopped. Behind them was the biggest bull she had ever seen. It was staring right at her with a look on its face which said 'Get out of my field and away from my ladies right now! Who the hell are you?!'

'Kath, Kath, Kath,' I said as quietly as possible but she couldn't really hear me. 'Move as quickly as you can back to us and take off that red scarf. You have heard of a red rag to a bull, haven't you?' Harry and I beckoned her back.

Kath stood as still as a statue for about three seconds. Then, quick as a flash, she turned, her arms now above her head and yelled her head off. She still had her red scarf on which was flapping wildly in the wind. This was like a starting gun going off for the bull who scraped one of his feet on the muddy earth and then took off like an Olympic sprint champion.

'Take your scarf off, Kath. TAKE YOUR SCARF OFF!' I screamed. She couldn't hear me as she kept turning to look at the bull who was making some very loud noises.

Kath was not the fastest cheetah in town and the bull seemed to be gaining on her. Harry and I clutched at each other. I suddenly noticed that there were lots of cowpats right where Kath was running towards us.

'Kath, mind the....'

Kath stopped and lifted up her feet, one at a time.

'Oh, for goodness' sake!' she shouted. She carried on running towards us with the bull getting even closer.

'This could end in tragedy,' Harry yelped. 'I have to do something.'

138

'Harry!! No!!!!' I shouted as he leapt into the field. He took off to the left and waved his hands in the air.

'Bull, bull, I'm a much tastier option. Come over here,' Harry yelled frantically. The bull suddenly stopped and looked at Harry and then looked back at Kath. He was confused about who to go for. Kath made it back to the gate, and Harry, after winning a Who Blinks First competition with the bull, finally came back and practically threw himself over the fence. We closed the gate as quickly as possible. As we did, we saw the farmer coming towards us on his tractor. He didn't look at all pleased.

'Hey, you!!!' he shouted. 'Get off my land!' Luckily, his tractor was not an Aston Martin farm prototype and we were able to get away from him without a shotgun being fired above our heads. One of the staff from the animal sanctuary came running up to us.

'Good God,' Kath said breathlessly. 'I thought I was going to be skewered as part of a delicacy for that bull.'

'That farm doesn't belong to us,' said the worried staff member. 'Are you okay? That gate should have been locked. I will have a word with Jim, the farmer. I am so sorry. We must put a sign up too, telling people not to go in there.'

Harry shuffled a bit and then coughed. 'I think that might have been down to me when I shoved it open. I can only apologise. I will pay for any damage.'

'Don't worry. I think the farmer should sort that out himself. It's been dodgy for a while now so don't blame yourself, sir.'

We got in the car and waited for Kath. She tried to wipe the cowpat off her shoes with a tissue, which had separated into several bits from constant use. She wasn't successful. She threw the tattered remains in a bin She opened the car door and sat down.

'You honk! Euwwwww!' Harry said and held his nose with his fingers. Kath got out, took her shoes off and put them in the car boot.

'It was either stand in the field and clean my shoes or run like mad, trying as I went not to get tossed up in the air by that raging bull's horns,' Kath said.

In the car on the way back, we went over everything that had happened and hooted with laughter. I was laughing so much I was crying. I felt like I was with family.

'What an udderly unpleasant experience it was with those cows and that bull in that field!' Kath chortled. 'Do you get my joke?'

'Oh, that's bad, Kath. That is terrible,' I said but laughed again anyway.

19

Back to the Past

Harry spent a lot of time looking at the photos of my family. I would watch him while I was in the kitchen. He would stare intently and stroke several of them slowly with his fingers. I could almost feel him remembering my grandfather and the antics they got up to. He would smile and sometimes laugh.

'Beth, could I ask a favour?'

'Yes, of course, Harry. What is it?'

'I am not getting any younger and I would really love to go back to this time of my life again.'

'My time machine is at the repair shop, I'm afraid.'

'Well, that is a shame but I was thinking of going back to the road I lived on and where your family lived too. Would you come with me?'

'I would consider it an honour. It would also take me back to that time.'

A couple of days later, we set off. We got the train to Croydon and walked from the station to Gloucester Road. Harry stood for a moment to take everything in. It had changed since he was last there. Houses had been demolished and factories had been put up. His house, my old family home and the pub were all still there. I took photos of everything. Harry stood in front of the pub pretending to hold a pint up as I snapped away.

'This takes me back, Beth. This really does. Could we go into the pub later and have a drink?'

'You don't have to ask, Harry. Of course we can!'

Harry spent time standing in front of his old house and pointing out which room was which and where his bedroom was. I could see someone inside staring at us. Eventually, they came out.

'Hello. Is everything okay? Nothing's fallen down from the roof, has it?'

'No, no, no,' Harry said. 'I used to live here a long time ago. I just wanted to come back and see the old place.'

The woman looked at both of us. 'Would you like to come in and have a look?'

'That would be lovely. Thank you,' Harry said and we followed the woman in.

'My name is Joanne,' she said and shook our hands. We introduced ourselves and were offered tea and biscuits. We sat down and I could see Harry looking around. Joanne noticed him too.

'I imagine it has changed a lot since you were last here. We knocked through to make one big room here and at the back, we put in large windows which we open up in the summer straight out to the garden.'

'Could I see the garden, please?' Harry got up before Joanne could answer and we all went out.

Harry did a quick scout around and then went over to the wall at the back. He went straight to a brick halfway up and pointed at it.

'Look,' he said.

We both moved closer and looked at where Harry was pointing. There was a heart engraved on the wall with H + E in it.

'Is that you, Harry? Who does the other letter stand for?' I asked.

'That's me, yes.' Harry didn't say who the other person was. 'Could I look upstairs if possible? I would like to show Beth my old bedroom.'

We all went upstairs. Harry knew where to go as if he still lived there. His room was used as a room for when Joanne or her husband's family visited.

'My daughter is at university now. Cambridge, studying archaeology. She comes home every two to three weeks just to get her washing done, I think. She stays in here.'

I could see signs of the younger generation on the walls. Posters of groups I hadn't heard of and a film star whose name escaped me.

'I had my bed in exactly the same place. I remember climbing out of that window when I was in my teenage years to try my luck at getting served a pint in the pub. Never happened though. The landlord of the pub knew my father and knew how old I was.' Harry walked around the room. 'I had a wardrobe there and a table next to my bed with a lamp on it. This does bring back memories.'

I looked out of the window. It was quite a drop down to the ground.

143

Harry came up beside me. 'I used to tie my sheets together to help me get down and get back up.' He winked and looked at Joanne. 'We never had an indoor toilet. We had to go out to the privy, as it was called, in the garden. Many a time I was in there slapping the walls with a newspaper if I saw a spider.'

We went back down to the kitchen. It had changed beyond recognition from Harry's time there. He looked disappointed but then he walked through the kitchen to a door at the back and opened it.

'Ah. I am glad this is still here. This used to be my mother's pantry.' It was now the laundry room with a washing machine and tumble dryer on top of each other. It smelt of fabric conditioner.

'If we wanted a bath we had to wait in line. We had a large tin bath that we kept in the garden and it would take ages to fill it up with hot water. The kitchen was a no-go area when someone was in here having a bath. I always wanted to have mine first as the water was clean but had to wait for my parents, brother and sister first as I was the youngest.'

I wish I had had a Dictaphone on me. I would love to have recorded his words and then written them down for him to read at a later date.

After an hour, we said thank you and goodbye to Joanne and went up to the Drum and Monkey, or Shit and Shovel as Harry called it, for a drink.

Harry got himself a light ale and bought me a glass of red wine. We sat in an area at the back. There were only a few people in the pub, old regulars by the look of it, who sat on stools at the bar with a Guinness in their hands, chatting to the bar staff.

'This takes me back. I had my first legal pint in here with some mates when I was eighteen. We used to sit near the door so we could watch all the girls coming in and then decide who to try our luck with.' Harry laughed at the memory.

I got us another drink each and we ordered lunch. We spent a good three hours in that pub. Afterwards, we went to look at my old family home which Harry remembered well. He pointed out all the rooms to me. We had to stand outside as there was no one in for us to ask if we could have a look around.

The weather was starting to close in. Dark clouds had appeared and rain was just starting to spatter down. We had a walk around the local area and then got the train back. Harry spent most of the journey looking out of the window.

'Could I have some copies of the photos you took today?' he asked me.

'I was going to get them printed off for you and then frame your favourite ones. You could keep them in your bedroom or in the living room. Up to you.'

On the way home, we got some fish and chips which we would warm up a bit later. I loved pickled eggs so got some and Harry got two pickled onions. I was glad neither of us would be kissing anyone later.

'Thank you, Beth. I don't think you realise how much that journey meant to me.'

'It was my pleasure, Harry, and as I said, it was a walk down memory lane for me too.'

Harry told me more about what life was like then. Croydon had been bombed heavily in the Second World War so there was lots of rebuilding going on when Harry and his family moved there. At sixteen, Harry got a job helping to build new homes. He only carried bricks but watched what the other builders did and was even shown how to plaster a wall after helping to put the bricks up. Harry had a lot of strings to his bow and could turn his hand at helping out with many things. He had helped me in my house when a tap started to leak and fixed a window when it got stuck.

We had our fish and chips in the garden as the weather had improved. Harry liked lots of vinegar on his chips and the smell made my mouth water. I preferred mayonnaise and tomato ketchup but also put some vinegar on my chips. It smelt like an acidic petrol station and I was thankful neither of us smoked. We would have been blown sky-high.

We both went to bed early as the day had been long and energetic for us. I slept better than I had for ages.

The next day, I started to type up what Harry had told me. It was good to do as it included lots of memories about my family too. I sat in the garden with my typewriter. It was my mum's old typewriter and would ping at the end of a line. I loved the noise of the keys when you pressed down on them. I had Tippex with me in case I made any mistakes.

Harry sat out with me. He closed his eyes and listened to the noise.

'That does remind me of listening to Doris in the office when I worked for my family. She was so quick when she typed. She sounded like she was playing all the instruments in an orchestra, tapping away on the strings or drums.'

It didn't take too long to finish. I straightened all the papers together and gave them to Harry.

'I will get a cover for it, Harry, so it doesn't get damaged.'

Harry thanked me and held on to the work tightly as if a strong gust of wind would suddenly carry it off like a kite flapping in the sky.

'I will keep this somewhere close to me always,' he said.

We went for a walk and popped over to see Kath who was in a quandary. She wanted to paint her hall but couldn't decide on a colour.

'Kath, may I suggest you pick a light colour as your hall is a bit on the dark side. What do you think? Daffodil White is always a good one to go for,' Harry said. 'You could also get those little sample paint pots and put lots of colours up and then see which one takes your fancy.'

'I will look into it, Harry. Good suggestions.'

We stayed at Kath's for a cup of tea and the usual large slice of cake. She was meeting a friend later so we didn't stay too long.

That night, we watched a dreadful comedy film on television. Neither of us laughed and we kept looking at the magazines on the table.

'Well, that wasn't at all funny. Not sure why it was called a comedy. We should have checked the Radio Times. There was probably something much better on,' I said. I got up to get a glass of wine but changed my mind and got some fresh orange juice instead. I gave a glass to Harry who took a little sip and then drank the rest in one go.

'Would you like some more?' I asked.

'Sorry, Beth. The orange juice they served at the home was one you had to mix with water as it was very concentrated. It was so sweet and tasted yucky. Didn't taste like fresh orange juice at all. I would love another glass, thank you.'

We finished off the orange juice. Harry washed up and sang a jaunty song as he did. I could see him moving his feet from side to side as he cleaned plates in the sink.

20

Re-Enactment the Old-Fashioned Way

Harry bounded down the stairs the following morning. He seemed to be getting younger every day. I wondered if he had got a portrait of himself upstairs that was gradually getting older as he was getting younger.

'Good morning, Beth.' He made some toast and went out to the garden.

I joined him after making coffee.

'Beth, have you ever heard of re-enactment?'

'Depends what you mean, Harry. I have heard of people dressing up pretending to fight in civil wars. Do you mean that?'

'Yes, I do,' said Harry. 'I used to be a member of The Sealed Knot. They do re-enactments of the English Civil War for schools and the public. You know, battles and skirmishes and such like. I met a friend recently in the park who is a member and they are doing another re-enactment at Edgehill in Warwickshire in a couple of weeks. My membership has lapsed but my friend Jack said he would sign me back up so I could take part. I would love to go. I was wondering if Kath would drive me there. I would pay for the petrol and for you both to stay in a hotel overnight. I have a lot of money that I am just not spending.'

'Harry, I am sure Kath would be up for that and she wouldn't dream of taking your money. You also don't have to pay for the hotel. It would be a bit of a day if we went up and then came back but Kath and I can pay for our rooms. I will pay for your room too, Harry.'

After a long discussion about who should pay for what, with Harry saying he wouldn't go if he couldn't pay for me and Kath and me saying well Kath and I wouldn't go either then if we couldn't pay, it was agreed that we would all go and pay our own way. I phoned Kath and she said she would love to go. I looked up local hotels and booked us all in. We would go up the night before so there wasn't a rush on the actual day. Kath and I wouldn't be taking part. We weren't members and neither of us wanted to cause history to be rewritten by helping the wrong side to win.

Over the next week, Harry went through all the ins and outs of the English Civil War. He should have given talks on it to the general public, he was so good.

'Now, the Battle of Edgehill took place on 23 October 1642 and was a battle of the First English Civil war. There was no real knockout blow, as they say, and so the war went on.' Harry told us about the cannonballs, the cavalry and the losses on both sides. It sounded like a fierce affair. He told us to read up on it too as he would be testing us just before we went up.

'Could we do something like Mastermind then?' Kath said. 'I have the music for that somewhere. It is called Approaching

Menace as far as I can remember. If I was ever on Mastermind, that music alone would send me into a frenzy, let alone having to answer loads of questions.'

'I think just having the questions fired at us by Harry will be fine. We can have a chat about the possible answers together.'

We did the quiz while eating dinner at mine. Kath and I did pretty well. We only got a couple wrong. I felt far more knowledgeable and confident about going now.

Harry came and helped me in Kath's garden. He knew a lot about plants and flowers and helped us put bulbs in. Kath had a special piece of equipment which meant Harry didn't need to keep kneeling down. He could use it standing upright by making a hole in the ground and then grab hold of the bulb with the equipment and plant it. Kath's garden was looking pretty good. It was a bit late to put in more bulbs and flowers but the ones we did put in looked lovely. Several were already starting to blossom.

'We could put in some winter-flowering pansies, Kath,' I said.

'Let's do that next week then.'

Harry said he would help take off some of the branches from the dilapidated tree. He started and then wobbled and fell. Kath and I rushed over.

'I'm okay. Just a little trip, that's all,' he said.

'Are you sure we can't do anything more? Are you in pain? Do you need an ambulance?' I was very concerned.

'No, honestly, I feel fine. Tickety boo, in fact. Nothing hurts. The grass made it a soft landing.'

We got him up and sat him in a chair.

I was still worried, but after giving Harry a cup of tea with lots of sugar in, he seemed to perk up. Kath and I carried on for a short while but I wanted to get Harry home.

'I will drive you,' Kath said. It was only across the park but I didn't want Harry to have a funny turn again if we walked.

We got in and Harry said he wanted to have a little lie down so I helped him up to his room. I got out a bottle of wine and Kath and I drank most of it together.

'That was a bit worrying,' Kath said. 'I hope he is going to be alright.'

'I know. I hope he will be too. I will keep an eye on him tonight.' I remembered that a few days ago, I saw Harry in my garden with his head in his hands leaning on the table. I asked if he was okay and he said he was just a little tired.

We were due to travel up to Edgehill the following week. Harry recovered and was back to his usual self. He kept making a joke about his fall. 'I looked like I had drunk a whole bottle of rum. A right stupid pirate falling off the plank,' he said.

Kath picked us up mid-morning for our next great adventure. It took nearly three hours to get there. We had to divert at one point because of an accident on the motorway and there was a lot of traffic. It was raining too with thunder and lightning. The countryside on the way up was stunning. We were staying at a hotel near Edgehill which meant a short walk to the battlefield the following morning. We unpacked our bags and met downstairs in the lobby. We decided to go for a walk but the thunderstorm had followed us up from London so we stayed in the hotel. We went into the restaurant and had afternoon tea and cake. This was the norm with Kath and me. Tea and cake. I declined the offer of sharing a bottle of wine and instead had an exceptionally fizzy elderflower drink. To say I didn't burp much after drinking it was a gross understatement. I sounded like a warthog grunting loudly. I couldn't stop. Kath had to pretend to keep coughing loudly so other people didn't look at us. One woman did tut rather loudly and Kath turned to her and said rather disdainfully, 'Well, excuse me!'

Harry had to stifle his giggles by stuffing a napkin in his mouth but I could see his shoulders going up and down. I finally stopped and said no thank you to another one when the waitress came over. I opted for plain water instead.

The thunderstorm finally stopped so we went for our walk. We all had proper walking shoes on, a practical thought I had suggested the day before. The sky was starting to turn dark but we did see a few ancient houses nearby and read up about the battle in a small museum. Kath and I kept nodding in acknowledgement as we already knew quite a bit about it thanks to Harry.

We all decided that an early night was in order as tomorrow would be a hectic day. I checked on Harry to make sure he had everything he needed. I sat up and read a book for a while but tiredness crept up on me so I put it down on the bedside cabinet. I was just going to turn the light off when Kath appeared with a towel wrapped around her middle.

'Look. This doesn't meet in the middle. I hope the fire alarm doesn't go off while I am in the shower and this is all I have to wear.'

'Prepare for it then and take a large coat in the shower with you,' I said.

The next morning, we were all up bright and early. Kath and I were sitting in the breakfast lounge.

'Good morning, Harry. Did you sleep okay?' I asked him as he came in and sat down.

'Yes. I feel fresh as a daisy. I am ready for battle.' Harry was looking quite nervous but he said he was just worried for us as it would be quite loud.

'Don't worry, Harry. I have brought earplugs for me and Beth if it gets too raucous.'

As we walked to the battlefield, we could hear the distant sound of people gathering and talking in excited voices. There was quite a crowd there already. Kath and I went to watch from an area that wasn't crowded. Harry walked off to find his friend Jack. When he did, he brought him over to introduce him to us. Jack was dressed up as a Royalist and told Harry to go and get changed. He would be a Royalist too. Jack had a lot of feathers in his hat, very boldly coloured. He wore a doublet jacket with a white linen shirt which was laced at the neck and wrists. I recognised him as the man Harry had a heated discussion with in the park back home.

As we waited for Harry, Jack told us a bit more about the Royalists.

'Everyone would have you believe that the Royalists, also called the Cavaliers, always wore floppy hats, all this lace and finery but…ah, here he is.' Harry came out of a large tent sporting the same uniform. He came over and bowed extravagantly, taking his hat off and hurling it in the air. I took some photos of Harry and Jack.

'Right,' said Jack. 'We need to go now and get ready for battle. There is a plan afoot. We will see you both later.' They waved and moved off to join their army. The enemy, the Roundheads, were gathering too. They stared and shouted at the Royalists. It was all very realistic. Kath and I couldn't see Harry as they were all wearing practically the same uniforms. We put our hands over our eyes as the sun was glaring down on us. There were people on horseback. The horses were rearing up and looked ready for action. There seemed to be hundreds and hundreds of soldiers on the field.

'Kath, I can't see this lasting just the one afternoon. I read yesterday that some of their battles can go on for two or three days.'

'We will only be here today. I can't see Harry lasting three days and I know I won't. I am already wondering where the toilets are.'

Kath and I rushed off to find the toilets and came back to find that the battle had started. The noise was unbelievable. I have never heard so many cannons going off at once. Men were screaming and shouting with a lot of close-contact fighting with swords and muskets were being fired off.

'Kath, KATH!! Have you got the earplugs handy? I might need them if this continues. If this was a real battle and I was a soldier and someone asked me what injuries I had sustained, I would just answer with a pardon, what did you say? This would be followed by oh yes, just deafness. That's all. That's my injury.'

Kath was standing stock still. She was mesmerised. She hadn't heard a word I was saying, not because of the noise but because she was enthralled by a portly middle-aged man on a horse who was galloping around in front of her.

155

'You know what, Beth? I might look into joining this society. I could act as a slovenly wench who has it away with any horseman who ventures near her.'

'Of course, Kath. I would never have guessed.'

The battle had been going for an hour or so and then stopped. Victory for the Royalists/Cavaliers. There was much cheering in the winning ranks.

'I think I have gone deaf, Kath'

'What?' Kath said. 'Speak up. I can't hear you.'

We went to find Harry and Jack. We found Harry sitting on a wooden chair outside a tent. Jack was leaning over him, handing him a tankard of water.

'Is everything alright? I asked.

'Yes, yes. Nothing to worry about,' Jack said and turned to look at Harry.

'I'm fine. Just overdid it somewhat on the battlefield, that's all. I haven't done that for a few years. I really should have done some exercise to get fit before doing this. Bit of a rum do, isn't it? Sorry if I spoilt it for you both.' Harry wiped his forehead with the back of his hand.

'You haven't, Harry. Please don't worry about that,' I said. 'We both thoroughly enjoyed watching it'.

I took Jack to one side and asked him what had happened.

'I'm not sure. I just found him like this. I was concentrating too much on running my sword through a Roundhead.'

I took Jack's contact details. He lived quite close to us and I asked if he would like to come round some time to see Harry. He said he would be delighted to.

'That home was no good for him, Beth. He needed to be doing more there. He missed out on a lot when he was looking after Maisie.'

The following afternoon, we packed our bags and left the hotel. Kath didn't drive as fast as she had done going up to avoid disturbing Harry who was sleeping on the back seat.

'Kath, I'm worried about Harry. He has had a few episodes where he has not felt right. Remember him falling in your garden?'

'I know, Beth. Maybe you should get him to see his doctor.'

'Yes, I will.'

We got back in the dark. Kath dropped us off, and, after I made a cup of Horlicks for both of us, I helped Harry up the stairs.

'Harry, I think you need to see your doctor. Just to make sure everything is okay.'

'I will but it is nothing for you to worry about. I have just had a few funny turns, that's all. Remember, I haven't been out and about doing lots of active things for a while. It's bound to have an effect on me. I'm not as fit as I used to be.'

'Okay. Let's make the appointment and I can come with you.'

Luckily, his doctor's surgery was close by. Harry insisted I sit in the waiting area while he went in to see the doctor.

He came out after a while and said everything was fine. He just needed a few pills that was all. I didn't believe him. He had a prescription which we took to the chemist. I couldn't see what was written on it and Harry wouldn't show me. When he got his medication, it was in a paper bag and he put it straight in his coat pocket.

When we got home, he went upstairs and appeared a few moments later.

'I feel better already,' he said.

I decided we wouldn't do anything over the next few days. Harry looked like he needed to rest and I would make sure he did.

21

Peace and Quiet....

Harry and I spent the next week pottering around my house and the garden. I certainly didn't want to suggest doing anything that could make Harry ill again. I did some gardening and Harry watched me. He kept pointing out any areas that needed maintenance.

'That bit there, Beth. It could do with a bit of a turnover with your spade. Need to get the air to it.'

After my gardening workout, I sat with Harry in the garden and asked if I could draw him.

'Okay. Please don't make my nose look any longer than it already is though. Hold on while I flatten down my hair a bit.'

I got my sketchbook and a fresh orange juice for each of us. Harry was easy to draw. He sat still, keeping his gaze over my left shoulder. I made him have a break halfway through and, after another ten minutes, it was done. I signed it and gave it to Harry. He looked at it and smiled.

'Thank you for not making me look like a hobgoblin. That is delightful. Thank you so much.'

I had a spare frame so put the drawing in it and hung it up on his bedroom wall in a place where he could see it from his bed. Relaxing was doing us both good.

I had stopped feeling so anxious and was in a better place emotionally. Having Harry staying with me had given me the opportunity to give my love to another person.

Kath came over a couple of times in the week and we enjoyed eating a food delivery in the garden. I didn't feel the pressure to cook for guests.

One day Harry and I sat on the bench outside and watched the goings-on in the park. A couple of men walked past us and then stopped. I could hear them having an animated talk.

'Here we go,' Harry said. 'Prepare for battle stations. This could be a bit of a humdinger.'

He was right. The man nearest to us stopped and turned to his companion.

'How could you? She is my ex-wife. How could you do that?'

The other man didn't know what to say apart from sorry a few times.

'Was this going on while Marion and I were still together?'

'No, of course not, Grant. What do you take me for? She was upset because of the divorce and we just became close. I was, sorry, am your best friend and she simply wanted to know if there was any chance, any chance at all that you would change your mind and you would get back together again. We didn't plan it. It just happened and once it did, we felt incredibly guilty. It's over now. I promise. Could I ask how you found out?'

'A friend of my adoring wife told me. She had seen you together. Listen, I don't want to see you for a while, Clive. I can't. To be honest, I just want to hit you right now so I need to go.'

Grant turned and walked away leaving Clive standing there looking at his friend getting smaller and smaller until he finally disappeared down a side road.

'That was better than watching television,' I said. 'I did feel sorry for Grant though. Goodness, what a thing to find out. I hope he wasn't the last person to know as that would be awful. You wouldn't know who of your friends to trust after something like that.'

Harry said nothing. He just sat there staring straight in front of him without blinking. 'Shall we go back, Beth? I fancy a cup of tea.'

'Of course. I have a Victoria sponge cake in the fridge from yesterday's online supermarket delivery. Let's indulge ourselves.'

We both ate two slices of cake and drank two cups of tea. I felt very full afterwards and kept rubbing my stomach.

'I shouldn't have done that, Harry. I was being a bit of a pig.'

Harry laughed. He had yet another slice. 'Do you have a bottomless pit in your belly?' I asked.

'I do, yes,' he replied.

That evening, we chose not to watch the television. We did other things instead. Harry was talking all about The Sealed Knot as he leafed through a book about the battle he had bought while in Edgehill. He kept asking aloud if I knew this and that about them.

I decided to look over my recent sketches to see if I could add anything. They all looked fine. While looking at ones I had drawn of people in the park, I noticed something. There was the man I had seen all those months ago who had been sitting on a bench near my house looking decidedly sad before erupting into happiness. He must live nearby. Why had I not remembered him?

'Well, this is odd.' I told Harry the story.

I showed Harry my drawing and he dropped his book. He grabbed my sketchbook from me.

'That looks just like my son. When did you draw this?' He was looking very anxious.

'Two or three weeks ago, I think. I can't remember where you were at the time. Maybe you were meeting Jack or something.'

'If this is my son and you saw him a few months ago and then a few weeks back he must be over here. He is meant to be in Canada. Why hasn't he told me he is here?'

Harry looked very upset.

'Harry, it might just be someone who looks like him. A doppelganger maybe. It does happen. It is only a sketch. I once saw someone who was the image of an uncle of mine abroad and then someone I knew had a real go at me as they said they had seen me on a beach in Barbados and had waved at me and called out to me and I had completely ignored them. I have never been to Barbados. Fear of flying.'

Harry shrugged his shoulders and gave me back my sketchbook. He returned to his reading.

We sat in silence for the next hour. I looked at him and thought that either one of us says something or this silence will last all evening.

'Harry, if you want to talk about anything I am a good listener.'

Harry put down his book. 'Thank you, Beth, but as I said once before, I am not yet ready to talk.'

There must have been something big waiting on the horizon that would come bounding towards me when Harry finally opened up. I went to the off licence to get a couple of bottles of wine and rang Kath to see if she wanted to come over. It would help with the intermittent silence and might take Harry's mind off his thoughts. Even I couldn't manage two bottles myself. Kath came over and brought over a Chinese takeaway.

'I was getting one for myself anyway so just ordered more. I hope you haven't eaten yet.'

'No, we haven't,' I said. I didn't tell her how much cake we had already eaten.

Harry cheered up and tucked into egg fried rice, stir fried vegetables and sweet and sour sauce. Kath was good for him. He loved her sense of humour and she loved his. She didn't treat him like a child.

'You two. I don't want you to think you have to watch over me or call me every minute of the day if you are out. This week has been good but if you both want to go off and do something together, please do. I really don't need looking after.'

Kath and I tried to reassure Harry that it wasn't an issue for us and we wanted to be there for him, but he was adamant that we should go off and enjoy ourselves.

'Okay, Harry.' I was still concerned though.

Kath and I agreed to go to the small local art gallery we nearly went to once before. We could walk to it rather than head out on the long and winding road into the centre of town. It was an Italian art gallery full to the brim with modern art. Paintings and sculptures were everywhere. I was so worried about knocking something over. I have never been a fan of modern art but told Kath I would give it a go.

We spent some time looking at a painting that was just different shades of blue.

'I don't get it, Kath. A child of six could draw something better.'

'Beth, for me, it's about the emotion it conveys to the person looking at it. How it makes one feel. What one reads into it; what you see in it.'

'It makes me feel like I was in the wrong job for all those years if it only takes a splosh of paint on a canvas to make money.'

I spent a lot of time turning my head from side to side, frowning and just not getting it. I looked at the sculptures and couldn't make head nor tail of any of them. One was entitled A Woman on The Verge of a Catastrophe. It just looked like a lump of stone to me. There didn't seem to be any defining features; nothing I could relate to.

We sat in the courtyard outside and had a coffee. We agreed to disagree on our understanding and appreciation of modern art. We walked to a few shops afterwards and I got a new top in one. Kath tried on various pairs of trousers but couldn't decide which ones to buy so ended up buying three different lots. She was a bit like me in that respect. If I couldn't make up my mind whether to buy a short-sleeved or long-sleeved top, I would buy both. One for summer and one for winter I would always say.

After two or three hours, we went back to mine. Harry was reading his book again. He smiled when he saw us.

'Did you have a nice time?'

'We did, yes, thank you, Harry. I have been trying to teach Beth the benefits and joy of modern art to no avail.'

'I didn't get any of it, Harry. It all looked like someone had simply got hold of a paint pot and thrown it at a canvas.'

'Ha, ha,' Harry laughed. 'I have never been a fan myself. I like a painting that looks like a painting; one you can recognise as being something, someone or somewhere.'

He had a point as far as I was concerned.

Kath changed the subject as she knew she wasn't going to win the argument.

'Have either of you ever sung before? I don't mean in the shower or bath. I mean as part of a choir.'

'I haven't,' Harry said.

'I did at school,' I said.

'There is a local choir very close by. You know that community centre at the top of the road in the side street? They meet there. It isn't far at all and I wondered if you would like to come along. If you don't fancy a sing-song, you can just sit and listen.'

Harry and I looked at each other.

'I would like to come along,' Harry said. I agreed. It sounded like a fun thing to do.

'Their next get together is this Wednesday evening. I know someone who goes so I will find out what time we need to be there. Harry, if at any time you don't feel comfortable or feel a bit wobbly, we can leave.'

On the Wednesday, Harry put on his best suit. Kath called for us and we walked up to the centre.

The choir leader was chatting to a couple of people, one of whom was a friend of Kath's. She saw us and beckoned us over.

'Lucinda, these are the people I was telling you about. This is Kath and…. sorry, I don't know your names.'

Harry and I introduced ourselves. Lucinda had an array of scarves around her head and neck. She reminded me of a female version of Harry when I first met him or someone who was in the process of being mummified.

'Lovely to meet you. Glad to see you, Harry. We are a bit short on male members. Forgive that double entendre. How rude of me. We could make a film about it. Choose a title like in the Carry On films. Carry On Singing and all that.' We stared at her without saying a word.

She asked us what section we would feel most comfortable singing in. Kath and I said alto. I tended to squeak if the notes got too high. Harry was with the men who were all basses or baritones.

We did several warm-up exercises which included stretching our arms out, turning our heads from side to side, breathing in and out and then doing several scales to warm up our voices.

Lucinda had decided we would have a try at Swing Low, Sweet Chariot. Harry looked pleased. I had heard him hum the tune at home a few times.

She went through the first part with the women in their sections and then came to the men.

As soon as she started to sing their bit with them, Harry's voice boomed out. It sounded like there were ten men in his section rather than the three who were singing.

My mouth fell open and I saw several other members of the choir turn to each other, their eyes raised in surprise.

Kath turned to me and whispered, 'Blimey, Beth. He kept that quiet.'

We carried on and afterwards Lucinda had a word with Harry.

'What did she say? I asked him.

'They have a concert taking place later in the year and she wants me to do a solo. I said no. I only came along as it was something I wanted to do and I have done it now. If the concert was sooner, I would have considered it.'

'You have a magnificent voice, Harry. Please think about it,' Kath implored.

'I only came along for a try and I don't want to put anyone's noses out of joint,' he reiterated.

He refused to talk about it further. Lucinda tried her best again and had a word with Kath and me. I said I would talk to him over the next couple of days. We had cups of tea and biscuits with the other choir members after we had finished and then left. We hummed the tune on the way home.

I was keen to keep going to the choir sessions. Kath was too. I decided not to mention the choir opportunity again to Harry. He had made it very clear that he didn't want to take part in the concert.

We came home and had a glass of wine in the garden to celebrate our latest endeavour.

22

Online Cooking and Party, Party, Party

I tried to convince Harry a few times to sing the solo in the choir but it was still an adamant no from him. Instead, he mentioned that he would like to learn how to cook more exotic food. I went through some cookery books with him but he wanted to be shown how to make a meal rather than have to keep referring to a book. I wasn't the best cook in the world so got Kath on board.

'Why don't we go online and see what is available?' she said. 'We can follow a class and keep helping each other if we need to go over anything.'

'I like the sound of that,' I said and Harry nodded his approval.

'I am not too clever with online stuff so I may need to stop and talk to you both,' he said.

'Not a problem, Harry,' Kath said.

Harry fancied making a Thai green curry. We looked up online cookery classes and found one that was live in a couple of days' time. Hopefully, we wouldn't have to keep asking each other questions. We looked up what we would need and wrote everything down. We booked ourselves for the Thai cookery class. On the morning of our cooking class, Kath and I went to the biggest supermarket near us to get all the ingredients. It would give us a bit of time to get acquainted with the food beforehand.

I got us all cooking aprons and gave Harry a chef's hat I had bought him from a cookery shop. We came back and organised ourselves on a table each that I had set up. I turned on the TV, went on the internet and put in the link to set up the class. It would be much easier for all of us to see it all on a big screen rather than have to keep leaning over to watch it on a laptop.

The class started off well. We seemed prepared.

Harry chirped up, 'Belt and braces then. Ready and able.'

The cook went through everything we would need again and we kept saying, 'Yes, got that,' and then we started.

'Can you turn the sound up, please?' Harry asked.

'She is talking very fast, or is it me? I'm not sure I can keep up,' Kath said.

'What was that she said about adding things to the sauce?' I yelled.

We kept asking each other so many questions that we missed half of what she was saying.

'I'm sorry, ladies. I think I have messed it all up,' Harry bleated.

I looked at what Harry had done so far. It didn't look great; like someone had just put lots of different types of food in a food processor and swizzed them all together. I really couldn't tell what it was meant to be.

We did cook the vegetables reasonably well which was the only thing we had managed to do properly. My sweetcorn was a bit too crunchy though. The sticky rice was an immense problem. We spent so long trying to remember what to do that it was overcooked. It looked like wallpaper paste.

We looked at what we had prepared to eat and divided it up in bowls. It all looked a dreadful sickly colour.

'Well, that didn't work out as planned. We can't eat this. We will probably get food poisoning,' I said.

We all giggled and put the disastrous outcome in the rubbish bin.

'Well, why don't we go out for lunch instead? Harry, you up for that?' Kath asked.

'Sounds good,' he replied.

While Harry sorted himself out upstairs, I took Kath to one side.

'Can we go to a restaurant nearby? I don't want Harry exerting himself.'

'Of course. There are a few at the bottom of the road.'

We all agreed to go to the local fry-up café. I had double egg and chips with two slices of white bread and butter, Kath had the same and Harry went for a full English breakfast. We all squirted lots of tomato ketchup onto our plates.

'Could you pass me the brown rocking horse, Kath?' Harry asked.

'The what?' Kath replied.

'The brown sauce. Cockney rhyming slang,' Harry said. We all gobbled the food down.

'That was worth it,' Harry said while patting his stomach.

We decided to sit in the park afterwards. It was a nice warm sunny day. There were lots of people out walking.

'This is lovely, isn't it?' I said. I snuggled down onto the bench.

Harry suddenly waved at a couple of older people who were walking with people who looked like care workers as they had uniforms on.

'Hello. How are you two? When are you moving to your new home?'

'Soon but no date as yet,' one of the older ladies said. 'We are all just taking in what we will be leaving behind. Going for walks, that sort of thing.'

I had an idea. When we got home, I told Harry. Kath was there too.

'Harry, why don't you ask some of your friends from the home to come over here? They can bring their carers. We could have a little farewell party for them.'

'I am not sure they would be allowed to come but I can ask. Thank you, Beth,' Harry said.

'Will there be a theme for this party, Beth?'

'Tarts and vicars, Kath.'

Harry and Kath both looked at me in silence.

'I jest,' I said.

'I will ring the manager, Harry. Save you the hassle. They could look at it as an outing for the residents.'

I phoned the manager who said it sounded delightful. She would sort out how many carers would be needed. They would all come over in their bus. I told her I had upstairs and downstairs toilets so there was no need to worry about any issues on that score. I went through who Harry wanted to invite. There were fifteen people on his list. With carers, that could go up to twenty. I wasn't worried about the space as we could use the garden.

I arranged the party for the following Saturday at 2 pm. Kath said she would come along as well. I sat with Harry and we ordered a lot of party food to be delivered on the Saturday morning. We were both looking forward to it. I hadn't been in a large gathering at my home for ages but now felt more confident. Harry was very excited. He asked if his best suit and shirt could be sent to the dry cleaners.

The food arrived early on Saturday morning. We unpacked everything and put some out on tables ready for later. I made sure there were covers on all the food until our guests arrived. Some food went into the fridge along with drinks. I got fresh orange juice and non-alcoholic wine. I also got the obligatory couple of alcoholic bottles of wine for me and Kath.

Kath drove over earlier than the 2 pm start to help out.

'I have brought a gallon of mead and some fold down chairs with me,' she said. After a couple more hours making sure everything was ready for our guests, we all flopped in the armchairs and enjoyed a glass of wine.

Harry kept a lookout and at 2 pm, shouted out, 'They're here!' He opened the front door and waved at everyone. It took a bit of time for everyone to get off the bus with help from the carers. They had also brought some food over from the home. I welcomed them all in and Kath helped put their coats in a safe place upstairs. I had also invited Harry's friend Jack who turned up just as people were getting off the bus. He gave me a bottle of whisky at the door and went off to find Harry.

When everyone had settled in chairs and on the sofa, Kath and I gave some of them a glass of fresh orange juice and others the non-alcoholic wine. One man drank some wine, licked his lips and said loudly, 'This isn't real.' He put down his glass and got a bottle of gin out of his bag. 'Have you got any tonic, miss?' he asked.

I looked at the carers for help and advice but they were all too busy helping people. 'I am not sure if I should let you have that. Are you on any medication?'

'No, I am not, dear. I am perfectly alright and all I want is a nice G&T.'

I made a bold decision. I got him some tonic and poured some of his gin in a glass. 'Keep going,' he said, lifting his hand up in the air. He put his thumb up when the glass was nearly full. Once word had got around that he was drinking it, several other people wanted some. By this time, the carers had finished helping everyone. 'One small alcoholic drink will be fine for them,' a carer said. 'None of them are on any medication which would cause a bad side effect.'

I wondered why they weren't allowed more than one drink then if everything was going to be okay. They might be old and a few needed some care but they were still adults after all. I decided to throw caution to the wind. I stealthily offered them all some gin and tonic or alcoholic wine. I sent Kath out to get some more bottles. Harry and Jack spent time chatting while drinking the whisky.

After a short time, a couple of people asked if we could have some music on. I asked if they had anything in particular that they wanted to listen to. I didn't have any old-time music to hand, but, after they had all reached a decision, I put on a compilation of old London cockney songs on the TV internet. Knees up Mother Brown came on. Luckily, I had cleared a large space to help people move about more easily. I had never seen so many people get up in one go and start jigging about. Even someone using a walking frame kicked his legs in the air. Harry, Kath and I joined in and sang along. Two of the carers held on to a couple of people and turned their hips from side to side.

'I thought elderly folk got tired easily,' Kath gasped at me as she was taken around the floor by a smartly dressed man.

'I don't think they do,' I said as she appeared near me again. The dancing went on and on. When the Hokey Cokey came on, everyone put their left arm in, then out and threw them up in the air. Harry had grabbed hold of one of his female friends and was twirling her around and around. I thought back to the parties I used to go to. They were never like this. People would just stand about, holding a glass of wine, talking to someone else, with the odd drunk person dancing like they had just been spun round several times and then let go and pushed forward. A few of Harry's friends were starting to look slightly tipsy and were laughing their heads off.

We all went out in the garden as it was still a lovely day. Several people walked around the garden with their carers while others sat down. Kath's fold down chairs were a godsend. People were still dancing in my living room and singing very loudly. I was worried about noise complaints from the neighbours.

When everything quietened down, I made lots of tea and brought out the biscuits and cakes. The music was still on in the background but didn't thunder out like earlier. Several people were out in the garden.

'I have thoroughly enjoyed myself. Thank you so much. Three cheers to Beth, Kath and Harry!' one of them said. 'Raise your glasses.'

Everyone put their glasses in the air and there was a loud rendition of hip, hip, hooray and they are jolly good fellows. I felt overcome. This had been a wonderful party. I couldn't find Harry so went into the living room to see if he was still dancing. I heard a couple of people talking in the hall. It was Harry and Jack.

'Harry, you must say something. It's not fair on her. You have to let her know.'

'You don't understand, Jack. Moving in with Beth has been one of the best things to happen to me in a very long time. I don't want to spoil it.'

I stopped but there was no more talk. I turned around and started to go back outside. Harry and Jack appeared shortly afterwards. I looked at them both. They weren't showing any signs of the nature of the conversation they had just had. I needed to know what it was about. Awful thoughts were racing through my mind.

I found Jack when he was alone. 'Jack, I hope you are having a good time.'

'It's wonderful, Beth. You have put on a very good show.'

'Jack, I caught some of the chat you were having with Harry in the hall. It wasn't deliberate. I was looking for some more wine. What were you talking about? It sounded serious.'

'Listen, Beth, it was nothing. Honest. In any case, Harry should tell you himself. I am, unfortunately, sworn to secrecy.'

Jack then pretended he had seen someone he wanted to talk to and quickly left me to walk to a small group of people.

I didn't know what to do. Was Harry a bank robber or a serial killer? Were the police due at any time to finally arrest him? Maybe he was going to leave me after making up with his children and move in with one of them. I wasn't sure I could cope with whatever it turned out to be. Should I ask him or wait for him to tell me? I decided to get advice from Kath.

At 8 pm, everyone left. As they were getting on the bus, several people yelled out, 'See you next time!' and waved at us.

We all felt exhausted by the activities that had taken place. I sat in an armchair drinking water. I had drunk too much wine. Harry and Kath started to clear up the glasses and plates.

'Leave that,' I said. 'I'll sort it out tomorrow morning. The kitchen police are not due this week. At least there is not much food left to sort out. Come and sit down instead. You have both been marvellous today. Thank you.' I raised my glass to them.

'Blimey, that was some party,' Harry said. He looked like he could hardly move.

'Not sure about making that a monthly event though. Maybe we could think about doing it again on a special occasion. I will see. I feel shattered.' I put my head on the back of the armchair.

We all fell asleep where we had sat down. An hour later, I woke up. Kath stirred and wiped her mouth as she had been dribbling. Harry's hair looked a sight to behold and my red wine glass had emptied its contents all over my beige top.

'Bugger!' I said as quietly as possible.

'Salt is good for that, I think, or one of those stain remover things,' Kath piped up as she got her focus back.

'To be honest, I might just dye it. Wake Rip van Winkle up, would you?'

'Okay, will do. I need to go home, Beth. It's been a busy day and I need my bed. I can collect my car and chairs tomorrow.'

'Kath, I will come with you. I could do with a walk, a long refreshing walk. Thank you so much for all your help today.' A walk would give me the chance to talk to her.

We walked around the edge of the park. I told her what I had heard between Harry and Jack.

'I would suggest you leave it until Harry is ready to tell you. If you say you had overheard him talking to Jack, he might not like it. He might think you were deliberately listening in, being a nosey nose.'

The trouble was I had been. I wish I hadn't.

When I got back, Harry had washed up all the glasses and plates. He was eating a couple of sandwiches with turned-up edges that he had found while tidying up. I found some cheese balls still in their packet behind the sofa and put them in a bowl for both of us to scoff down. We threw them up in the air, trying to get them in our mouths. It was not a successful enterprise. We talked about what had made us laugh earlier and Harry said how some of his friends had really surprised him with their dancing and energy.

'See what happens when you put on something that everyone enjoys doing? I can't remember the last time I saw Percy get up and jig around like that.' He laughed out loud.

I realised then how much happier I had been since Harry had moved in. It wasn't just the fact of having someone, anyone, there. It was having him in particular. He had added something to the place; his laughter, his willingness to be part of things, his graciousness and his thoughtfulness. Whatever was going on with him, I was sure he would tell me.

Early the next morning, I cleaned and hoovered everywhere. I put the wine bottles to one side. In the garden, I found glasses in the flower beds and a slice of cake sitting on a tree branch. I know I love cake, but I decided it wouldn't be the best idea in the world to shake off all the dirt and eat it in one go.

'The birds can eat that,' I said out loud. 'I hope they enjoy it.'

Kath conveniently came over after everything had been tidied up.

'That is a shame, Beth. I was coming over to help.'

'Like hell you were,' I scoffed. We both smiled. We were good friends, great friends even. I hoped I was helping her cope as much as she was helping me leap over this very high hurdle of despair. I did feel like the hurdle was getting lower all the time.

'Where is Harry?' Kath asked.

'He went out for a walk.'

'Have you said anything?'

'No, Kath. I took your advice and will wait for Harry to tell me his deep dark secret. If there is one. Let's finish this off. Be a shame to waste it.' I poured out some remnants of wine from several bottles for us. I decided not to talk about Harry and his secret again.

23

Community Gardening

Kath and I were part of an online group for our local area. Most of the time, people just wanted recommendations for opticians, hairdressers or plumbers or just wanted to complain about traffic noise and dirty streets. One message did stand out though. A man called Mike was looking for people to help out with community gardening in a couple of the smaller local parks every Saturday morning. There was a group who were already helping out but Mike needed more people.

'How many notices do people need to put up on this thing? Look at the time and there are already loads of posts about rubbish collections or the lack of them!'

I looked at the clock in the kitchen. It was 10.30 am.

'I know it's not something we said we would like to do but we could do this gardening thing and add it to our bucket lists when we finally get round to writing them. Who would find out?' I said. 'How about it, Kath? It sounds like it could be a real giggle.'

'I like the sound of it. Let's get in touch with Mike.'

I e-mailed Mike. He didn't want our CVs to see if we had any previous gardening experience and we didn't have to sit in front of an interview panel either being asked questions like, 'So how would you determine the best place to plant crocuses?' with people then furiously writing notes down on a pad when we answered.

Kath and I were put on the list to meet up the next Saturday in one of the parks at 10 am, along with a lot of other people, hopefully. It was a short walk away. We didn't want to have to lug lots of gardening equipment there but thankfully, Mike said he had plenty anyway to share with people.

I got a couple of trowels out though as we could put those in our coat pockets.

'I need to swot up on plants and the like,' I said. I looked at my books of flowers and trees the day before so I wouldn't look quite such an idiot and would hopefully recognise them. Kath had also done lots of revision on her mobile. It felt like we were heading out to take a practical examination.

'Look, Beth.' She showed me her phone. 'I have downloaded this app about flowers and plants. All you do is open the app, point it at something and it tells you what it is instantly. I know it could be considered cheating by some folk but if we get stuck wondering what this and that is in the park, I can just whip it out, so to speak, and have a check. We will look like experts.'

'Brill, Kath. I will put that on my phone too. The double cheaters. Here we come.'

We met up on Saturday morning and walked the few minutes to the park. On the way, we kept pointing at flowers and asking each other what we thought they were. The park was very peaceful. There was bird song again and squirrels were darting here and there or scurrying up and down trees. We met Mike, our leader. He looked like he needed a good wash. He had grime all over his face. He hadn't brushed his hair and it looked quite matted. *Not a good first impression*, I thought. There were eight other people there which was a good turnout. We stood around for another five minutes so Mike could get some spades and rakes from his garden. A couple of people went over to his front door and brought back two wheelbarrows and what looked like large builders' bags. Everything was placed on a bench and the bags scrunched down and put behind it.

'Hello, everyone, and welcome. Good to see so many of you for this session. My name is Mike. I know some of you already which is great.' He put his hands together as if to pray and quietly said thank you. A few people acknowledged this by smiling and nodding in acknowledgement.

'I will just say a bit about myself and what I hope we can all achieve together here. I was a gardener at Kew Gardens for a number of years but retired last year. Reached that age of no return.' He chuckled to himself. 'I still wanted to help out whenever and wherever I could, and, on my travels around our lovely borough, I realised that some of our parks were looking a bit sorry for themselves. I spoke to the council who are quite happy with us planting and clearing leaves. We will not be allowed to chop anything down as that would be for them to deal with. I am not an advocate of clearing whole areas anyway unless there are very good reasons to do so. Now, are there any questions?'

We were all silent with a few people shaking their heads. 'Right, what I think we should do now is split up into groups for today. There are eleven of us here including me, so a four, four and three. I have a list of what needs doing which I will share with you all. Let's just take it easy and get to know each other. Right, get into your groups and I will give you your jobs for today.'

We all introduced ourselves to each other and said hello, nice to meet you. Some people immediately gravitated to each other as they were friends already. Kath and I joined a couple, Colin and Poppy, who were also novices. They didn't say much and hadn't said hello to anyone else. They had just stood still and nodded with their hands in their pockets. Poppy spent all her time looking like she was chewing gum. As we were all newbies, we were given the unenviable task of sweeping up the leaves. I wanted to get involved in planting. I was hoping that if we made a good job of leaf-clearing, we would be upgraded to the elite group in charge of bringing life and colour to the flower beds. People were collecting bulbs to plant ready to come up in the autumn. It was too late for the summer display.

'My app tells me the names of flowers, not sodding bulbs. I have no idea what they all are.' Kath wasn't happy. 'Shouldn't have bothered. Maybe I should have looked up all the different types of leaves instead.'

Kath and I collected some rakes and we started on one side of the park. Kath almost poked Colin and Poppy with her finger as they made no effort to move.

'Come on, look lively,' she said to them.

She gave them a couple of rakes and they just stared at them. I thought they were going to ask Kath what they were.

'Why are they here, Beth? They don't seem to give a flying fig about gardening or indeed trying to make an effort to talk to anyone else,' Kath said out of the side of her mouth to me.

I shrugged my shoulders. 'I don't know, Kath. Maybe they had a different idea about what it would be like or maybe they are just painfully shy.'

We all swept back in unison. It wasn't hard labour but the rhythmic movement made me feel like it was. I imagined Mike coming over and saying, 'Listen, there's some very large rocks over there that need breaking up and then moving. The pickaxes are over there. Come on. Chop, chop.' We built up several large piles of leaves but as we went off to collect the bags to put them in, a huge gust of wind suddenly descended on us. I turned around and saw that most of the leaves had been scattered all over the grass again.

'Hashtag bloody hell!' Kath huffed. We brought the bags back and between the four of us, we raked again and filled most of the bags. Colin and Poppy picked up one leaf at a time, very slowly it seemed. It took about an hour to complete our task and once finished, I drank some water.

A lovely lady called Monica had come over to help us. She could see we were having difficulties with both the wind and Colin and Poppy. She had short grey hair with pinks bits in. I thought she might be an ex-hippy. She told us she meditated and did yoga every morning. She was in her early 70s, but looked younger. I liked her.

Mike looked over. 'Well done. Now you can do this side. It has been somewhat neglected of late.' He pointed to his side of the park which was again covered in leaves.

'Anything else? Does he want us to pick up all the bird poo and doggy do-do as well? Maybe he would like me to just go commando and pick them all up with my bare hands. I mean, I have all the time in the world. Other people go off to India or Bali or some other place to discover themselves and what am I doing? This. Anyway, why weren't these leaves swept up late last year?'

'Now, now, Kath. I think I heard Mike say that this was the first meet-up after the winter as a lot of people couldn't make the days before to help. Let's just smile and get on with it. We don't have to come back next week if we don't want to. Colin, Poppy, we have been summoned.' Colin and Poppy glanced at me and moved over at a snail's pace.

'Sorry, Beth. I just feel that most people know each other here and we have been given all the crap jobs because we are virgin community gardeners. I know it will get better. Hopefully.'

The garden was in a very opulent square surrounded by large Victorian houses. All the other people helping out in the park lived in the square surrounding it. One of them looked up and walked over to have a chat.

Hello. My name's Nerissa,' she said. 'I see you got the short straw today.' She was dressed for gardening but everything she had on looked like it had been bought from an expensive designer shop and this was its first outing. Her gardening gloves were pristine. *Never been worn before too*, I thought. I began to wonder if Kath and I needed to expand our wardrobe to include wellington boots, as seen on the catwalks in Paris, and jackets to be shown during the next autumn season in London.

Nerissa told us she worked for a large banking corporation in Canary Wharf. She was head of something or other and dealt with investments. I started to drift off and left Kath talking to her. At one point, I heard Nerissa say, 'That sounds like such a lovely thing that you are doing. Well done you.' She patted Kath on the shoulder and walked back to plant yet more bulbs.

'Patronising so and so,' Kath said when Nerissa was out of earshot. 'I was telling her about my job. I doubt I will be fulfilling any of her dreams. I wouldn't want to either as she could certainly afford to pay for her own dreams. Anyway, she would probably ask to go on a world tour of historically interesting sites'. Kath was sweating so I gave her some water.

We cleared the entire park of leaves, or that's what it looked like. I saw a few hiding under bushes but pretended not to notice. Mike wrote something down in a book; I imagined it was scores of achievement for today. I was expecting a gold star to add to my collection. Mike then asked us to turn over some soil for planting the following week. Kath and I were quite adept at doing this as we had been sorting out her garden for the last few weeks. I saw some rather fat worms as we arranged the soil from old to new. I wanted to pick one up and hurl it at Kath but thought better of it. She had turned a nasty shade of boiled beetroot. At this stage, Colin and Poppy looked like they had lost the will to live. They were both staring up at a tree looking at some crows cawing loudly. They hadn't said a word to either me or Kath while we were all meant to be working together.

'Have they never seen a crow before? Where do they live, underground or something? Never seen the light of day?' I asked Kath. They were very pale so I did begin to wonder.

'They do look very green as in they have never done anything like this before,' Kath said. We stood with our hands on the handles of the spades and looked at them. They hadn't even got themselves some spades. I think they had decided to finish and not tell anyone.

At 1 pm, everyone started to pack up. I thought a silent horn had sounded to tell people to finish, one that only people with a certain hearing sensitivity could pick up on. Mike got us and other people to help him take the spades, rakes and wheelbarrows through to his garden. He had a very large garden shed which also contained an electric lawnmower and defunct water fountain. We dragged the large bags of leaves to an area near one of the gates so the council could pick them up during the week. Colin and Poppy, meanwhile, had skulked off without saying goodbye.

'How rude. I doubt those two will turn up next week. They didn't seem that enthusiastic at all. Said nothing to us all morning. I felt like I had to keep pointing at things or miming what we needed to do next,' Kath said. She was rubbing clods of earth off her coat and from her hair.

'Not sure I will come next week,' I replied. 'My back is starting to really stiffen up.'

'I think I might, Beth. Even if it is just for the exercise. I feel like I have run a marathon this morning.'

After we had all checked there were no gardening implements left in the park, Kath and I realised we were alone. A quietness had descended until Mike came back into the square.

186

'See you next week, ladies,' he yelled and waved goodbye to us. 'I have your e-mail addresses so check for next week's extravaganza.'

We smiled, stuck our thumbs in the air and waved back.

Kath said under her breath, 'And have a bath before next week, sort your hair out and wash your clothes. It's not a good look.'

'See you next week, Mike,' I shouted back.

We decided to sit on one of the benches before heading home. Harry was seeing Jack again for a drink in the local pub. The park was now starting to fill up with people. Children were screaming and running over the grassy areas while their parents chased them. A couple of young lovers were wrapped around each other on a rug. A man was smoking a cigar like it was a precious gift. He was certainly making it last. Dogs were sniffing under bushes, peeing up against benches or bounding over the flower beds. I could see flowers being trampled and bulbs being uprooted. I was feeling quite protective about what we had all done earlier.

I wanted to stand up and yell, 'Excuse me, EXCUSE ME!! Could you please not trample over everything? We have just spent an excessive amount of time planting them all or hadn't anyone noticed? Hey, you lot with the dogs. Put them on leads.' I didn't though and took the easy option and turned to Kath instead to vent.

'I wonder how those people with children would feel if I suddenly turned up at their homes and ran amok in their gardens,' I said to Kath, who laughed.

'You have a point, Beth, but this is a public space so we can't really put a flag in the ground, salute and claim it as our

187

own.' We stayed there for another hour and then our tummies started to rumble.

'Do you want to come back to mine and have some late lunch?'

'I would love to, Kath.' We walked back quite quickly. We were both hungry and desperate for food and a toilet.

Kath put out some French breadsticks, cream crackers, cheese, pickles, hummus and mayonnaise and then, after rooting about at the back of the fridge, found some salad.

'I hope this salad is okay. It says it should have been eaten three days ago.' She shook it out a bit. 'It's fine'

It did look a bit limp but I really didn't care. We decided to go back the following week only if we hadn't planned to do anything that was far more exciting. I doubted that Mike would be ticking people off on an attendance sheet and then phoning parents up to see why we hadn't bothered to turn up. It was also a good way of meeting more neighbours. They seemed like a nice bunch, apart from Colin and Poppy who had remained silent and distant throughout.

When I got home, Harry was back and sitting at the table. He looked like he was writing something but put it away when he saw me.

'Hello there. Did you have a good time with Jack?'

'I did, yes. We had a pub lunch and a few drinks. Had a good chat too. How was the gardening?'

I told him what had happened and how everyone seemed. Harry said he might come along the next time we went, not to help out but to sit on a bench and keep telling us where we had missed a bit.

Seeing Harry writing put me in mind to write to David's parents. I wanted to keep that link going. My visit to see them hadn't ended well from my point of view. I was still unbalanced by discovering David had a child and had been married before. I told his parents what I had been doing and that I hoped we could meet up again under better circumstances. I walked with Harry to the post box to send it on its way. I hoped I had done enough as we had experienced a very up and down relationship so far.

'Everything will work out for the best, Beth. You know it will.' Harry put his arm around me and squeezed my shoulder. It was very comforting. Harry felt like a long-lost uncle or big brother to me. We had developed a very special relationship. I just wished he felt more able to tell me what was bothering him.

We went home and had spaghetti bolognese for dinner. Harry cooked the spaghetti and I made the rest with vegetarian mince, a tomato sauce and some vegetables. Harry didn't notice the difference with the meat-free option. At least this meal tasted a lot better than our disastrous attempt at making Thai green curry and we both had seconds. Afterwards, we sat in the garden with blankets over our legs and listened to a play on the radio. We stayed outside until the dark sky wrapped itself around us both.

'Right, up to bed I go. Good night, Beth. Sleep tight. Don't let the bed bugs bite,' said Harry.

'Sleep well too, Harry. See you in the morning.'

I sat in the garden for a while longer. The only light was coming from the living room. It made strange shadows on the ground. I thought I could see a square-shaped bird at one point. All of a sudden, I started to cry. It was uncontrollable.

189

Someone had turned a tap on and the tears gushed out. I hadn't even been thinking about David or anything else for that matter. I sat there for a long time. Eventually, I stopped and took a deep breath in. I folded up the blankets, left them on the chairs and went in. I had a quick drink and went to bed. I kept the television on all night. It was a distraction. I didn't want to start thinking about David. Just when I thought things were starting to become better, I found myself deflating like an old wrinkly balloon, losing any positive air I had gathered.

I woke the next morning annoyed with myself. I knew I would have good and bad days but wanted more good days to bring a smile to my face.

Kath came over to see how I was. I had phoned her earlier to tell her about my crying episode.

'Beth, we will have days when everything just disintegrates and life loses its sparkle. I have them quite often. I didn't want to offload to you all the time though.'

I had thought that Kath was coping, but like me, she had times when she struggled.

'Kath, you know damn well you can talk to me.' I sounded harsher than I meant to. I took her hand and apologised.

'I know I can, Beth. I know.'

24

Finding a Release

There was a gym practically on my doorstep but I had never thought about going in. I had always walked rather hurriedly by it. I didn't want to go to the doctor and ask for tablets to help me. I felt they would just mask my problems. Counselling hadn't worked. I felt pretty fit and healthy so went in and signed up.

The person I had gone through the form with was dressed as if she had just done a session in the gym; all Lycra and tight elasticated leggings. She smiled at me and made me feel comfortable.

'In order to use the gym, you will need to see one of our staff who can show you around and go through how all the different equipment works. You can have a session with a personal trainer this week too if you want. Shall I sign you up for that?'

I said yes to everything and the next day went and got some gym clothes and proper trainers. My appointment was in two days' time so I tried a few exercises out in the garden. Harry watched as I tried to touch my toes and then managed three sit-ups before collapsing. I struggled to get up and had to turn over onto my side to get on my knees and eventually hauled myself up. I felt like a turtle that couldn't right itself; legs going like the clappers.

'This is ridiculous,' I said between breathing in large gulps of air.

'You can only get better.' Harry was always right on the button. I could see he was giggling though.

On the day of my gym meeting, I had a shower before going. Not the best thing to do as I knew I would need another one when I got back home. I just wanted to look my best. I put my hair in an elastic band and put my gym bottoms on and a nice vest top. I have to say it was a bit of a struggle as I had put on weight and really believed I was still a size smaller.

I met with a member of the gym staff who showed me lots of equipment and how to operate them. She took me to the treadmill and started it at a slow pace. *This is fun*, I thought. *I can do this*. Then she pressed the button again and I started to jog slowly and then following another button press, I was running. I hadn't expected this. I ran for about three minutes and then pressed the emergency off button.

'Are you okay?' the woman asked me with a concerned look on her face.

'I just haven't done that much exercise for a while. I have been quite ill.' I didn't lie really. My mind hadn't been well with all my grief. It still wasn't and I knew it had affected me physically.

She took me over to a rowing machine. It had a screen attached so I could see an animated version of myself rowing along a river. I loved it. I tried it for about five minutes and that was enough for me. A shark got me. We went and tried a couple of other machines and then it was time to meet my personal trainer.

Paul was a big strapping man who looked at least a foot taller than me. He was a giant. His muscles were bulging out ready to pop. We went through the preliminaries. I lied again and told him I used to do a lot of exercise but had been forced to stop due to a long-term injury.

'Okay. Come over here and you can try some squats. I will show you what you need to do.' He led me to an area where there was no one else around, thankfully. He leant down on one knee with his other leg almost straight behind him. *This looks simple*, I thought.

'Have you ever used a kettlebell, Beth?'

I couldn't lie. 'I haven't, no,' I said.

He went off and came back with two round balls with handles on top. They looked nothing like a kettle but seemed easy to hold.

'Now, I want you to take hold of one in each hand and then, keeping your back straight, bend your knees and stand up slowly.'

I picked them up or tried to. They were incredibly heavy.

'Good God,' I said. 'How much do these weigh?'

'These ones are four kilograms each,' he said so nonchalantly I imagined he walked around holding them in the street.

I tried very hard indeed to hold on to them and do as Paul said but kept thinking I was going to topple over and fall flat on my face. The trainer made me continue until I had done at least four. Next, Paul made me do ten squats. I went around the area we were in and I thought my legs were going to give

193

way. If people saw this as a fun way to get fit, I didn't get it. All I wanted to do was go home and eat cake. Lots of it.

Paul could see I was struggling so made me stop. I could have kissed him. While he carried on talking, I looked to one side and saw something that made my heart flutter.

'Paul, could we go over there and try that? I think it might suit me better than lifting up these heavyweights.' I was looking at a large punchbag swinging gamely from the ceiling.

'Of course. Have you ever used a punchbag before?'

'No, but I'm willing to give it a go.' What I really wanted to say was '*no, but once I have been trained up I will find you and punch your lights out for making me do all those squats.*' I knew I wouldn't be able to walk tomorrow.

Paul made me do some warm-up exercises for my arms, legs and stomach and then found me some boxing gloves. I put them on and stared at the punchbag. It looked even bigger than Paul. I imagined his face on the front of it, smiling while I descended into exercise madness.

I took an almighty swipe at the bag. It moved back and then suddenly came flying forwards. I was still in the same spot and only stopped myself from being catapulted across the floor by grabbing hold of it. The bag and I moved from side to side and back to front. It felt like I was dancing with a man who had no idea what steps to take.

'You have got some punch there, Beth,' Paul said. 'Whoa.' He held on to the punchbag while I steadied myself.

This is what I should have done all along. I wasn't an aggressive person at all but I needed to take my stress and anxiety out on something and this was perfect. I felt like another huge weight was being gently blown away from my shoulders.

'I like this,' I said. I really did like it. I did several more punches at the bag and yelled out a couple of times, more to myself than for the entire gym to hear. I finished up warming down and came home. I had another shower and felt very refreshed afterwards. It wouldn't make me forget David but I hoped it would help me deal more positively with my emotions around him.

Harry was in the garden with a cup of tea. 'How was it?'

'Great, Harry. I loved it. I have discovered a new passion for hitting a punchbag. It felt really good.'

I got myself a fresh orange juice. This would be the start of the new me. I would cut down on the amount of wine I drank with Kath and stop eating so much cake.

The next day I couldn't move. I struggled to get out of bed. I had to get Harry to help me. My arms and legs felt like they had been hit with hammers. I spent the day in my pyjamas as I couldn't get out of them and certainly wouldn't have been able to put on a clean pair of knickers. I couldn't have asked Harry to help me in that department.

'I hate personal trainers,' I kept muttering. When I recovered and next went back to the gym, I decided I would ignore Paul. If he tried to speak to me, I would tell him to bugger off.

Harry brought me up a cup of tea and a couple of biscuits.

'I know you said you were trying to cut down on eating cake but two biscuits won't hurt you.'

'Thank you, Harry. You are a gentleman.' I went back for more biscuits. I kept telling myself that I needed them as I had just done a lot of exercise.

That evening I could move a bit more so I got up, got dressed and tentatively walked down the stairs.

Kath had just arrived. Harry had phoned her earlier to tell her about my predicament.

'Well, well, well. How are you, Rocky Balboa?'

'Better than I felt this morning,' I replied. I slumped into a chair and laid my head back.

'I have come round to cook for you both,' Kath said. 'What do you fancy?'

Kath then decided cooking was out of the question and went out to get fish and chips.

I didn't care about the new me. I gobbled down my food like it was my last meal.

To help out I put tomato ketchup, mayonnaise and vinegar on the table. That was all I could do though. I had to keep sitting down to recover from my exertion the day before.

'That.... was.... delicious,' I said. 'Thank you, Kath.'

I still felt a bit hungry so decided to start my new regime the following day and we all finished off the Victoria sponge cake.

Three days later I felt much better and went back to the gym. I continued pounding the punchbag. Luckily, there were three in the gym otherwise I might have been told to stop and hand the bag over to someone waiting for it. Whenever I hit it, I said something positive to myself under my breath. I went on the rowing machine and, after a couple more weeks, finally beat the shark. I actually put my clenched fist up to the screen and shouted 'Hah!! Got you!!' A couple of gym-goers looked at me and grinned.

I was losing weight and sleeping much better. I no longer had the TV on in the background all night either. I was starting to feel revitalised.

Kath and I decided to go for a very long walk towards the end of the week and treat ourselves to lunch on a boat moored on the River Thames. We wanted to go round the backstreets. The traffic on the main roads was too loud and neither of us wanted to keep breathing in the pollution.

'The sooner all cars go electric the better,' I said.

Eventually, we couldn't avoid the main roads any longer and ended up at the top of Shaftesbury Avenue. We took a detour to Covent Garden. There were a lot of tourists there all taking photos of their friends or family standing in front of places smiling broadly. We went into a couple of shoe shops but didn't buy anything. There was a market area at the back selling cheaper items so we had a look. I kept putting on silly hats and dancing around in front of a mirror. Kath, though, seemed a bit distracted.

'I'm retiring, Beth,' Kath suddenly said. 'I have to give a month's notice but then I will be free to do whatever I like, whenever I like. A recently deceased rich widowed aunt has left me a healthy legacy in her will. I won't need to work again.'

'I am sorry to hear that about your aunt, Kath, but also, congratulations on being able to pack in your job. Have you any idea what you will do with the money?'

'I have quite a lot of family living in New Zealand so I may go over there for a long holiday. Apart from that though, I don't have any set plans. I might look at investing some of it but will have to see.'

I didn't say anything at first. If Kath went away for a month or two, I would lose my support. I knew I was being completely selfish as she was still not over Christopher by any stretch. Eventually, I squeezed her arm.

'Your trip idea sounds amazing.'

'Why don't you come with me?' she said. 'My Kiwi family would love to meet you. I have told them so much about you.'

'Thank you but I couldn't leave Harry for that long, Kath. Maybe I will come along if you ever go again.'

I felt an obligation to Harry, a very nice obligation and I couldn't just waltz out the door with a very large suitcase and say, 'See you when I see you, Harry.' If I felt anxious or alone, I would go to the gym and take it out on a punchbag.

Kath agreed about Harry. We would plan something special in the future.

We enjoyed a splendid lunch on the boat. I didn't have a dessert and only drank one glass of wine. Lots of other vessels were making their way up and down the Thames. A tourist boat went by and it looked like everyone on it was waving at us. We waved back. The weather was starting to turn and the river was becoming a bit choppy. The boat we were on was starting to sway.

'Might be time to start thinking about making a move, Kath. You know what I am like on anything that moves up and down or side to side. I really don't want to bring the delicious lunch up.'

We got a black cab as neither of us fancied walking back home. We had done our exercise for the day. We both stretched our legs out in the back and wiggled our toes.

'My feet are aching like mad,' I said.

'I think everything is aching. Even places I don't like to mention.' Kath had taken her shoes off and was rubbing her feet.

'You ladies having a good day? Been anywhere nice?' A metallic disembodied voice floated towards us from the front of the cab. We could only see the back of the driver. He had one of those fat necks that I wanted to squeeze really hard.

'Well, we walked all the way down here, went to Covent Garden and then had lunch on a boat on the Thames,' Kath said.

'Sounds like you have had a lovely day then.'

'You probably get asked this all the time but have you ever picked up anyone famous?' Kath asked.

Now he was in his element. 'Blimey, yes, I have, darling. Only the other day I picked up whatsherface from that soap opera. Can't remember her name. Anyway, she was lovely and she gave me a big tip. Last week I picked up a newsreader from the BBC. Can't remember his name either but I have seen him on the news in the morning. Oh, and then there was......'

He went on to list several more famous people and told us that he lived out of London and how bad the traffic was coming in to work. He asked us what we did and we both said we had retired.

'Lucky you. I wish I could pack it all in but needs must and all that.'

He dropped us off outside Kath's. I wanted to walk back home across the park.

As we were paying, he suddenly looked at Kath.

'Kath? Kath Malone?'

'In a former life, yes. That was my maiden name.'

'It's me, Sam Somerset. We went to secondary school together. You knew me as Sammie.' He turned to me and pointed his thumb at Kath. 'She was my first love, you know. Well, I never.'

'Sammie? I am sorry I didn't recognise you. How are you?' Kath looked pleased.

'I'm good, thanks. Listen, here's my number. Give me a bell sometime. It would be good to meet up again after so long.'

Kath took his number which was written on a taxi receipt card. 'I will, Sammie. I will. Lovely to see you again.'

'Likewise, Kath. Have a good rest of the day.'

We both waved as he drove off.

'Well, I never. I didn't recognise him at all. He has put on a lot of weight and has lost all his hair since I last saw him which would have been about thirty-odd years ago.' Kath chortled. I popped into her place for a quick coffee and then left.

Later that day, Kath phoned me to say she had found all her old school photos and there were several of her and Sammie, holding on to each other and laughing. She would come round tomorrow to show me.

25

New Beginnings for Kath and Harry?

The next day over afternoon tea in my garden, Kath showed Harry and me the photos of her when she had been at school.

'I would never have known that was you,' Harry said. He was looking at a school photo of Kath.

She looked very prim and proper in her school uniform with her hair in an Alice band.

'We had to have those done. I was eleven at the time. I made a special effort to smile as you can see. No grey hair and certainly no wrinkles then.'

She was staring like a madwoman at the camera. She showed us the photos of her and Sammie together. They looked so young and seemed very happy.

'I bet you were good fun then too, Kath,' I said.

'I had my moments. Sammie and I were fourteen when we first went out with each other. We had such fun times together. We once did that thing from Lady and The Tramp. Remember? When the dogs were both eating the same strand of spaghetti and suddenly, they ended up with their mouths together. Our first kiss was nothing to write home about, I know that. We lasted about six months. I can't really remember

201

the reason why we split up. I think we just grew apart as you do. You always remember your first love though. I will give him a ring later. Be good to talk about the old days,' she sighed.

I could hardly remember anything about my first aborted attempt at a relationship. His name was Jamie Corrigan and he wasn't that interesting or exciting to be with. I had a few relationships after Jamie but David had been, and always would be, my first true love. Harry and Kath knew that already.

'My first love was a delightful lady called Mavis Fullerton. She worked for my family's firm and we went out for about two years. Her family didn't approve of me. They wanted someone better for Mavis, someone better educated than me who actually owned a company rather than worked for their dad in one. I mean, really, I did alright. They were such snobs. Never saw her again. Her family moved to Devon.' Harry finished and shook his head.

I got my old school photos out to show them.

'You haven't changed a bit, Beth. You still have that same smile.' Kath looked over at me and grinned.

'I can't show you mine,' Harry said. 'All those photos are at my daughter's, and, as she isn't in touch with me, I doubt I will ever see them again.'

I felt sorry for Harry. You could see how much he loved his daughter. When he did mention her, you could feel the affection in his voice.

'Harry, I know you say she hasn't kept in touch but have you tried to make contact again?'

'No, Beth. What would be the point of that? She doesn't want to talk to me.'

'Would you like me to phone her? I don't mind if it would help.' I waited while Harry thought about it.

'I wouldn't want to impose on you. She can have a bit of a mouth on her when she gets angry.'

'I think I can handle that, Harry. Don't worry.' I thought of my punchbag at the gym.

'Okay, Beth. Not now though. It will put a dampener on a good day. I will go and find her number for you. I hope she still has the same one. Thank you. At least if you call, I will know whether there is any hope at all.' He went up to his bedroom.

Kath went home as she wanted to phone Sammie. She said she would let me know how it went later.

Harry came back down and gave me his daughter's number. It was on a tatty piece of paper. 'Please don't lose it, Beth.'

'Tell you what, I will write it down in my address book so you can have this back. Do you know where she lives at all?'

'No, not really. I know it is in London somewhere but London is a big place.'

'No worries. I can always ask her. What is her name, by the way?'

'Sarah Millington. That's her married name. She might not be with the same man now though.'

The next day, Harry went out so I phoned his daughter. I was very nervous but had worked out what to say. I rang the number and waited. A woman answered.

'Hello?'

'Hello,' I said back. 'You don't know me but…'

'If this is a scam call, I am not interested. Go away.'

'It isn't. I know this is a bolt out of the blue but your father Harry is staying with me at the moment and he would really like to see you. To be honest, I don't think he is well.'

'Is he there now?'

'No, he is out.'

'Well, when he gets back, tell him I don't want anything to do with him. He knows what he did and it broke my mother's heart. God only knows why she stayed with him afterwards. He has never apologised. Please don't phone here again.' The line went dead.

Now I had another conundrum. How was I going to tell Harry?

'All I want is a simple life,' I said out loud. I made a cup of tea and waited for Harry to come back. Three hours later, I heard the front door opening.

'How was your trip out, Harry? Where did you go?'

'Here and there. Nowhere in particular. Had a little walk around. Sat down when I needed to.' He took his coat off and came into the living room.

'I rang your daughter.'

'And?'

'I'm really sorry but she said she doesn't want to see you.' He looked dejected. 'She said you knew what you had done and how it had broken her mother's heart.' I stopped short of asking him what she meant.

'That again,' he said. He got up and pulled out a bottle of beer from a bag he had. 'I did nothing that Maisie hadn't done. That was why I did what I did.'

I was confused.

'Harry, do you want to talk about it?'

'Yes, I do, as this is getting ridiculous. You aren't going to like it and if you want me to leave, I will accept that.'

Maybe he and Maisie were a couple of hustlers. A British version of Bonnie and Clyde. Maybe they had robbed banks together or forced people to hand over their money. Maisie got caught, spent time in prison and Harry had evaded the law. *No, that was silly,* I thought.

'Maisie and I had been married for about a year. She was pregnant with Sarah and I was working hard to get enough money together so we could care for the baby when she was born. We lived in a small two-up two-down house on a terraced street and my dad was helping me with the rent for it. I was working my socks off, even at weekends. Maisie needed a pram for Sarah when she was born and baby clothes. It was one of the happiest days of my life when Sarah arrived. I loved her so much. Still do.'

Harry drank from his beer and stared at the floor.

'I can imagine it was a happy occasion, Harry. For both of you.'

'Not for Maisie. She got very depressed. If it was now, they would probably call it, um, what is it?'

'Post-natal depression?'

'Yes, yes, that's it. She wouldn't care for Sarah. She struggled to feed her. I was having to get up in the night to help when Sarah cried. All Maisie did was sit in a chair and ignore her. I asked my mum to help out and thankfully she did. Maisie didn't seem to care at all. Then, one day, I came home from work and the house was a complete mess, with dirty clothes and nappies everywhere and the sink was full of cutlery and plates. Everything needed a good wash. I finally lost it.

Maisie told me she had asked my mum to leave that morning and to not come back.'

Harry had never been so open about his marriage.

'I shouted at Maisie and asked her what the hell she thought she was doing. I was working all the hours God sent and she was just sitting there. She told me to leave as well and threw me out. She chucked my clothes out of the bedroom window. Then she said something awful. She yelled out of the window so all the neighbours could hear that I might as well go as Sarah wasn't mine.'

I was shocked.

'That must have really hurt you, Harry.'

'I couldn't believe it. Why would she say such a thing? I spoke to her mother and told her what had happened. She went round and got Maisie to come back to hers with Sarah in tow. I missed out on seeing my daughter for what seemed like a lifetime. It was only a few months, but even so. My mum tried to help sort things out but she just got the door slammed in her face when she went round.'

I got up and went to the kitchen to pour myself a glass of wine. I brought the bottle back in with me. This might be a long session.

'During the time that I didn't see them, I went off the rails a bit. I started to drink more, got thrown out of some local pubs and stopped turning up for work. Henry and Elizabeth, your grandparents, were brilliant. They really helped me. They got me back on the straight and narrow.'

Harry paused and looked at me.

'It was during this time that I started to fall in love with Elizabeth. The path of temptation had been put in front of me and I chose to walk down it. She was everything I had wanted Maisie to be with Sarah. She was always there for her daughter, your mum. I loved watching Elizabeth play the piano and sing to her own daughter and hold her in her arms, always stroking her little face. One day, when Henry was out, we kissed. Elizabeth was coming down the stairs and tripped. She fell into my arms and it just happened. Please believe me, Beth, it wasn't planned but I think part of me did it because of what Maisie had said. I was angry and lost. Anyhow, eventually Maisie and I got back together but Elizabeth had told Henry, who then came rushing round to mine and hit me in front of Maisie. He told me to stay away and never to go near him or his wife again. Maisie asked me what was going on and I told her. I said it was only because of what she had told me about Sarah not being mine. Maisie started to cry and said that she only said what she had said because she wasn't herself. Of course Sarah was mine. I had been such a fool. Maisie was so upset and because of me, she had lost her best friend Elizabeth. The upset and arguments lasted for years and she never forgave me.' Harry wiped his eyes with his handkerchief. 'I am glad I told you that but if you want me to leave, I will go. Jack could put me up.'

'Thank you for sharing that with me. It must have been difficult for you. Of course I don't want you to go, Harry. We seem to have another connection then. I think your daughter needs to know though. It explains a lot and I do think Maisie has a lot to answer for.'

Harry asked if I could help him write a letter to Sarah.

'You don't know where she lives though,' I pointed out.

'I don't but I am sure I know someone who does. I once met Jack in the park and we ended up having an argument as

207

he let it slip that he had Sarah's address. She gave it to him under strict instructions not to give it to me. It was only in the event of an absolute emergency.'

I wondered if that was when I had seen them in the park. They had looked like they were having strong words with each other.

'Well, I think we can consider this to be an emergency,' I said. 'Come on, let's get cracking.'

Harry phoned Jack, and, after a bit of a heated exchange of words, Jack gave him Sarah's address. Harry sat down and started to write a letter to his daughter. I helped him with a few ideas. He added my home telephone number and address. He put a stamp on the envelope and then we went out. He kissed it before putting it in the post box.

'I hope this works,' said Harry when we got back. 'I really do.'

'You have done all you can, Harry. It will be up to Sarah to decide what to do next once she reads your letter. You have done the right thing by writing to her.' I knew Harry would spend the next few days pacing up and down, getting anxious.

Kath phoned later. She and Sammie were going to meet up for a drink that night. She would fill me in tomorrow over a glass of something.

I was happy for both Kath and Harry, but realised my two closest friends might well be slowly floating away from my orbit.

26

It's a No-No and a Yes-Yes

Kath phoned the next day and asked if Harry and I would like to go round to her place for lunch later. She had lots to tell us about her evening with Sammie. I had some French bread and fruit to take over.

Harry and I walked through the park. How things had changed since we first met on that bench. He was now an important part of my life and I hoped I was in his. I held his arm as we went. I was an only child and he was like the perfect close family member.

Kath had put out lots of nibbles on her garden table. She buttered the French bread and put the fruit in a bowl. There was a large jug filled with something which was a dark shade of purplish red.

'I hope that's not poison, Kath,' Harry laughed.

'I hope so too. Hopefully, it will taste just like Sangria and also, hopefully, not poison you both.' Kath got some fancy glasses and stuck cocktail umbrellas in them. She poured us a drink. It tasted fine.

'This is great, Kath. You have hidden talents,' I said.

After we had discussed how nice the weather had been recently and what the council were going to do with their empty office block at the end of the road, we got down to the nitty-gritty.

'So, Kath. How did it go with Sammie yesterday?' I asked. I was playing with the umbrella in my mouth but kept piercing my tongue with it so took it out.

'Sit back and get comfy,' Kath replied. We filled our glasses again and piled our plates with food.

'We met outside Covent Garden tube station. Sammie took me to a small wine bar nearby. I think we might have seen it on our travels when we were there, Beth. It was a very cosy little place with dimmed lights and low music. Each table had a candle on it. The wine menu was huge. Six pages to look at. Sammie ordered a bottle of their finest wine and then we talked. It started off okay. Sammie asked me what I did and how long I had lived near the park. That lasted all of five minutes. For the next two hours, all he did was talk about himself. I found my eyes wandering around to look at other people. I kept nodding and saying things like yes and how delightful, which was totally inappropriate when he started telling me about his wives. He didn't seem to notice though. He went on and on so much that I thought I was going to go into a narcoleptic trance.'

Kath took another swig of her Sangria and carried on.

'According to him, there were four of them. He told me about Carol, his first wife, who he had been married to for one year. He apparently discovered her in their bed with a woman. He was meant to have been working a night shift in his taxi but it had broken down, so instead of getting a replacement one, he went home and found them. Can you believe it? His next wife, Ana, was Portuguese and once they were married, she moved her entire family in. They were all living in Brixton at the time and she had decided that where Sammie lived would be much nicer for them. There were eight of her family in the house with two sleeping on the sofas and two on the floor. Sammie said they had no privacy at all. Once, when he was trying to have a relaxing bath, Ana's mother walked in. They talked really loudly in their own language all the time and Ana had refused to deal with it. He couldn't speak Portuguese so was unable to join in any conversations they had. That marriage lasted six months. When he had told them all to go, including Ana, he thought they were going to put him in the cellar and leave him there to die. He never heard from Ana again.

His next wife, Maria, was extremely argumentative, which he only found out about when they got back from honeymoon. All she did was go on and on about cleanliness. She spent all her time shouting at him at how dirty his house was and what he should do about it. She had a habit of running her fingers across the tops of cupboards, picture frames and along the mantelpiece. She regularly checked the bedding and looked under the bed for dust. Sammie said the funny thing was that she never did anything about it herself. She didn't work but instead seemed to spend all her time writing lists down or sitting on the sofa eating doughnuts, shouting at him that this needed fixing or that needed cleaning. It went on and on. After a year and a half, she went, leaving Sammie a note saying she couldn't live in such a disgusting hellhole. I pity the next man she meets. The next tale needs a glass of wine. Anyone else want

211

one?' Harry and I both said no. Two big glasses of sangria were enough for both of us.

Kath got up and brought out two bottles of wine seemingly just for her. She filled her glass and took a big gulp.

'Finally, there was Stephanie. She lasted five years. All that time, though, she was still seeing her ex-husband. You know, in the biblical sense. She got pregnant and when the child became ill and needed some platelets, it was then discovered that Sammie wasn't the dad. All very sad. I could see that Sammie hadn't aged well at all, but then, if I had had four wives like that, I would have got a head full of grey hair much earlier and loads more wrinkles too.'

'That is some story, Kath,' Harry said. I was hoping he wasn't thinking back to his dalliance with Elizabeth.

'I know,' Kath said. 'I really don't think I want to become wife number five any time in the future. I will see Sammie again, but any romance will be completely out of the question. I had thought about it once a long time ago but no, not now. It just wouldn't work. He held my hand at one point last night and I had to pretend I needed to go to the loo so he would let go. He kept going on about how perfect we had been together, how he had never forgotten me. We didn't go out for that long and we were in our teens. I had to tell him that our past togetherness was just that, in the past, and wouldn't happen again but all he did was shake his head. We gave each other a hug outside the bar and said goodbye. I was quite drunk by the time we said goodbye. I had to get a black cab home.'

Part of me was relieved that I wouldn't be losing Kath. I know it was very self-serving of me and I truly wished her well.

I just wanted to be able to call and meet up with her still, whenever and wherever.

We decided to finish off the Sangria after all and ate most of the food. My new plan to stop eating so much crappy food wasn't really working. I was still going to the gym though. I saw Paul the last time I went and decided not to be so childish and smiled at him.

'Has Sarah got back to you, Harry?' Kath asked.

'I only posted it yesterday, so she may not have got it yet.'

'Well, here's hoping.'

A week later, Sarah got in touch. She had been away on holiday with her husband and two children. She had written a letter. Harry read it out to me with tears in his eyes.

'Dear Dad,

Thank you so much for your letter. It feels funny writing, Dad. I have read your letter several times. I had no idea that Mum had said that to you or that she had thrown you out. I know she told me once she had been going through a tough time but I never imagined that she could have been so horrible to you. I am still quite angry with you but I have thought about what would be the best thing to do and I would like to meet up with you. It has been too long and we really need to talk about everything. Call me or write back. Let me know when would be best. I can come over to you.

With love

Sarah'

Harry put the letter down and erupted. He sobbed like a child. I sat next to him and held him.

'Harry, she wants to meet you. That's a good thing.'

'She called me Dad, Beth. She called me Dad.' He snuffled into his handkerchief.

Harry wrote back to Sarah. He felt it would be too awkward on the phone. She wrote back to him and said she would come over the following Saturday afternoon at 2 pm.

Saturday morning arrived and Harry was frantic.

'Do you want me here, Harry? I can go out.'

'Would you mind doing that, Beth? I really need to do this by myself.'

'Not a problem at all.'

I prepared a few things for Harry and Sarah to eat, put out some drinks and left at 1.45 pm. I went over to Kath's and we sat in the garden wondering how Harry and Sarah were getting on and what we could do to pass the time.

'Do you want to go out and eat, Beth?'

'Where, Kath?'

'Oh, I thought the local launderette, Beth. We could eat sandwiches in there and watch the machine drums go round and round! A restaurant or café, silly.'

We went to a local café and indulged in what seemed like half the menu.

Harry called me at 4 pm. He said I could come back. Sarah was still there and wanted to meet me.

'Well, he sounds okay, Kath.'

'Let me know all about it, Beth.'

I went back and Harry and Sarah were sitting next to each other on the sofa. She was holding his hand and both of them were smiling. Sarah was dressed very smartly in a trouser suit. She had long earrings on and beautifully cut shoulder-length dark hair. I could see Harry in her. She had the same chin.

214

'Sarah, this is Beth.'

We shook hands. A warm handshake.

'Beth, I wanted to see you to thank you for looking after my dad. He says you have become great friends.'

'You are welcome, Sarah, and we have, yes. It is lovely to have Harry living here.'

'We have had a good chat and it has become clear to me that I should have been here for him. I have spoken to him about coming to live with me.'

Here it comes, I thought.

'But he said he was more than happy to stay here if you are still alright with that. I can always visit and Dad can come and stay with us for weekends.'

'Harry, you know you can carry on living with me for as long as you like' I said. I was very relieved.

She didn't go into what they had talked about but it had obviously worked out okay. They both looked contented.

She left soon afterwards and I could hear them talking quietly in the hall.

Harry came back into the living room. He exhaled loudly.

'Beth, that went like a dream. She is going to look at bringing my grandchildren over. I will finally see them.'

'I am so pleased for you, Harry. I am glad you have worked everything out.'

'She kept saying sorry, that she had no idea what had really gone on. Maisie had never told her the full story and had laid all the blame firmly on me. She was still upset with me but said she could sort of understand why I did it. I told her that her mum had told me never to darken her doorstep again and that

I thought it was all over. I can't tell you how happy I feel. Now that…well, never mind. I am just so happy.'

He got up and did a little dance. I phoned Kath to say everything was fine and she came rushing over. She gave Harry a big bear hug. 'I am so pleased for you, Harry. So very pleased.'

There was still the issue with his son but Harry said he wanted to build up a loving relationship with Sarah first. His son could wait.

That night, we celebrated with an Indian takeaway. Harry kept telling us how happy he was. Kath went home and brought back some more of her Sangria. We raised our glasses to Harry. We ate, drank and talked well into the early hours.

The next morning, I felt terribly groggy from drinking the Sangria. Harry came bounding down the stairs.

'How are you this morning, Harry?'

'Fit as a butcher's dog. How about yourself?'

'Don't. I am never drinking Sangria again. I feel dreadful.' I threw my head into the nearest cushion and moaned loudly.

Sarah was as good as her word and the following Sunday afternoon, she came over with her two young children, Charlotte and George. I wanted to leave Harry and the children to get to know each other, so Kath came over so we could go out somewhere. When Kath arrived, they were playing in the garden. Kath said hello to them. They just stared at her. Charlotte put her finger in her mouth and George grunted.

'If that is your way of saying hello from your planet of origin, I gladly accept it,' she said to them. They continued to stare at Kath. Charlotte then ran off screaming.

George stood in front of Kath with his finger in his mouth.

'How old are you?' he asked her.

'I.......am...... one......hundred......years old,' Kath replied slowly and dramatically.

'Where do you live?' he then asked.

'I live in the woods at the top of a tree in a tent covered with leaves so I can hide from all the goblins and trolls as they like to eat human beings,' Kath replied.

George said nothing and then ran off to Sarah.

'Mum, Mum, Mummy, that lady says she lives in the woods and there are monsters there too. I think she is really old too.'

'Oh, I think she is joking with you, George.' Sarah looked up and smiled.

'That child is the size of a hog,' she whispered to me. 'He could do with running around all afternoon and all next week. What is she feeding him on? Ice cream and chips for every meal? I mean, I know I like the odd dessert or two, but goodness me, that really is too much. He could sniff out truffles.'

'I am not sure hogs do that, but even so, stop it. He might have a metabolism problem.'

'Doesn't look like it. He is stuffing himself silly but I promise not to say another word about him. Right, shall we go out then and leave them to it?'

I told Sarah where extra food and drinks were and we said goodbye. I was very nervous and hoped they would all get along.

We went to the local pub for a late lunch. It had a beer garden so we sat outside and each ordered a healthy meal with lots of salad. There were quite a few people there including a group of men and women who appeared to be getting drunker by the second. Kath and I had fruit drinks as we were both still feeling the effects of the Sangria from yesterday. Even the smell of alcohol was making me retch slightly.

'I thought pubs weren't meant to serve people who were drunk,' I said. They were not that close to us but we could hear their conversation which was starting to get louder and turn nasty.

One man in the group waved his pint of beer in the air. It spilt over the sides. 'What did you say, Dan? What was that about my wife?'

'Nothing, mate. Honest. All I said was she looked good in her tennis outfit.' Dan had his hands up in front of him. He looked scared and moved back a bit. I started to feel uncomfortable.

'Fancy her, do you? Is that it?'

'Terry, come on, calm down. Of course he doesn't. He was just paying her a compliment,' another man in the group said.

'I won't calm down. I want an answer now. Come on, you. Disrespecting my wife. That's what you are doing.' Terry started to move towards Dan. 'Oi!! Tell me!!'

Suddenly, all hell broke loose. Terry staggered, threw his pint at Dan and lunged forward. His first punch ended up mid-air and then everyone, including the women, started fighting and throwing their beer glasses around. People at tables nearest to them scattered. Kath and I hoped it would all settle down. We carried on eating as if nothing had happened and talked about the weather.

I started to squirm in my seat. 'Kath, maybe we should move. Like, right now,' I suggested.

'We will be fine, Beth. Don't worry. Look, they aren't that near to us. It will be fine. Let's just eat this lovely first course and then get a pudding.'

Suddenly, they were right on top of us. One man came flying over our table with his arms out in front of him like Superman flying through the air. We both yelped. We jumped up as our drinks and food went all over us. We were both covered from head to toe. The fight raged on. We paid for what food we had eaten, and, as we left, a couple of police cars pulled up. We walked back with people pointing at us and giggling.

'It's lucky we don't live miles away. We would have had to sit on a bus or a train to get home otherwise. Imagine what that would have been like. We would have been chucked off. A cab certainly wouldn't have brought us back,' Kath said.

'I look and smell terrible,' I moaned.

'Well, I hardly look like I am about to go to one of the Queen's garden parties, do I?' We both stopped and laughed.

We got home, still covered in most of the remains of our lunch. Charlotte and George thought it was hysterical. They kept pointing at us and running back to Sarah shouting, 'Mummy, Mummy, can we do that?' George went to get some food off the table but Sarah grabbed hold of him and said, 'No, George. You mustn't.'

Harry was laughing his head off. 'What happened to you two?'

'There was a fight in the pub garden and we seemed to have come off worse,' I replied.

'Beth, you weren't involved, were you? I hope you didn't throw the first punch after all your gym escapades. I couldn't imagine you doing that though.'

'No, Harry. We just happened to be in the wrong place at the wrong time, unfortunately.'

Kath went home to clean herself up and came back later. We ate what food was left and decided we did need a glass of wine considering what we had been through. Sarah told us a bit more about herself. She was the manager of a small team of IT support staff and lived about five miles away. She had been married for twelve years. This was the first time that Harry had met his grandchildren and they were getting on like a house on fire.

'I am so sorry I didn't bother to find out what had actually happened all those years ago,' she said.

'Well, you know now and it seems to have turned out okay for you both,' I said.

'Yes, it has.'

Harry had arranged to go over to Sarah's the following Tuesday. Her husband, Trevor, would be working from home and she wanted Harry to meet him. Sarah picked him up at 10 am. I stood at the door and waved them off. I was very happy for Harry. His life was starting to make sense again. I just needed mine too as well.

27

Getting Reacquainted Again

I hadn't seen a lot of my family or friends in quite a while. I used to have a really good friend called Sissy. We had been very close at one point, but after David had passed away, we lost touch. It was my fault entirely. I refused to answer any calls or reply to any of her texts. I decided now to send her a text. That was easier than initially talking again after so long. She replied within the hour and we arranged to meet up the next day.

I decided not to meet her in the local pub just in case there was a rematch planned between Terry and Dan. We met in a restaurant on the high street for lunch. It wasn't busy so I felt I could talk without having to whisper and could then open up to her. I apologised a number of times to her for not keeping in touch and she was very nice about it. She said that sometimes people just needed to shut themselves away to deal with the grief themselves. I agreed as that is exactly what I had done.

'Losing David not only affected me deeply, but it also made me think about all the other people I had lost. It was like a domino effect. The tiles just kept falling over.'

'That happened when I lost my mum,' Sissy said. 'I kept thinking about all my family members who had died. I just hoped they had all met up wherever that was and were happy. I am so glad you got back in touch with me. It has been far too long.' She took hold of my hand.

'I know, Sissy. I just couldn't cope and I didn't want to dump all my difficult emotions and unhappiness on someone else's doormat.'

'Well, we are back in touch now. How are things for you at the moment?'

I told her about my house and Kath and some of the trips we had been on. I talked about Harry and how he had just got back in touch with his daughter and grandchildren. I said I needed to get back to meeting up with people gradually and told her how Kath had just almost landed in my lap. It would have been too hard for me to get back in touch with Sissy right away.

'I get that. How is it having Harry there?'

'He is an absolute joy to have around. He gets on with his own things, as do I, and he has also been out on trips with me and Kath. He has really helped me without knowing it.'

Sissy and I talked for hours. By the time we left, the staff there were just starting to serve the evening meals. We said goodbye at the tube station.

'Don't leave it too long next time,' Sissy said.

'I won't. I promise.'

I walked back over the park and smiled to myself. I got home and found Harry dancing in the living room. He had got his old tape deck out and was listening to a cassette.

'Goodness, Harry. I haven't seen one of those in years.'

'I was sorting things out and found it in one of my boxes. Forgot I had it. I've got loads more cassettes too.'

I told Harry about meeting up with Sissy. He was pleased I had as he wanted me to move on. He said he felt he was starting to get his life back together again. When he was in the care home, he felt like he was starting to fade away, like a shadow when a cloud covers the sun.

I danced with Harry around the living room and we sang out loud. This was something I hadn't done in years. The last time was with David when we had first met in the pub. We were both a little drunk at the time and there was a DJ there. We kept asking him to play our favourite tunes.

When one of my songs came on, David had grabbed hold of me.

'Come on. Get your dancing shoes on and let's have a whirl.' David had laughed and put his arm around my waist and then held me close when the music changed to a slow record.

I missed those intimate touches with another person. No one had even come close to taking David's place and, at the moment, I didn't want anyone else to. I had had offers, believe me. Nigel at work had tried to tempt me with a meal out and then back to his place, but I declined. He also had an unhealthy interest in letting grasshoppers fly free around his house. I wanted to remain an independent spirit until the time was right for me.

Harry told me how he and Maisie used to go to the local dance hall every Saturday night before things went wrong between them. They had got dressed up and always met up with Henry and Elizabeth. They would spend all night there. When they weren't dancing, they would sit, talk and laugh. He said he missed that friendship so much. He had heard from

223

friends that Elizabeth had passed away following a car accident a few years ago. Harry stuttered when he spoke. I could tell he was still deeply affected by past events. That was why he was so pleased to have rekindled his relationship with his daughter. He told me all about Jack and how they had become friends.

'I was in a shop which sold things like miniature war figures, battlefields and everything to go with them such as cannons and horses. I went to pick up the same soldier piece as Jack and we just got talking. We arranged to meet up and I went round to his place the next week and we re-enacted the Battle of Waterloo. I am glad he is my friend. We have the same interests.'

I thought about all the other people who had cared about me and how I had let them fall by the wayside and completely dismissed their concerns and wanting to support me. I wasn't sure what the best way of resolving this was but Harry suggested something.

'Listen, you helped me with my daughter. I wrote a letter, remember? Why don't you do the same with some of your old friends? You sent a phone message to Sissy and met up with her. That went well didn't it?"

'It did yes. Why didn't I think of writing to them? I would rather do that than keep texting people. Thank you, Harry.' I got my address book out and looked up several people. I wrote a number of letters that weekend to those people I wanted to meet up with again. I didn't expect all of my friends to write back or call me. Time had moved on for a lot of them.

The following week a few had replied. They expressed their sorrow again at my loss and two said it would be great to meet up again. I arranged to meet Helen in town. We had worked together in the city. We went to a restaurant in Piccadilly and both ordered a goat's cheese salad with chips.

'How have things been, Beth?' Helen asked.

'Not great but I think I am starting to come through the other side and can see the light at the end of the tunnel,' I replied.

Helen was my age and had retired from her job at a bank. She was now running her own company helping people buy stocks and shares. She was basically in the same sort of job she had been in before and I couldn't think of anything worse. I would have run to the hills if someone had asked me to do that. We talked over lunch. We had both started going to the gym and Helen said she had found it liberating. I told her how I loved to hit the punchbag as it helped me with all my stresses. She said she took her angst out on lifting weights at her local gym. I did notice her arms looked toned. We went for a walk in Hyde Park afterwards. Joggers rushed by looking like they were being forced to run.

When we sat down on a bench, Helen spoke.

'Do you remember my daughter Tilly?'

'I do, Helen. How is she? She must be at university now, or is she working?'

'She went to Cambridge University, got her degree in Politics and then decided to marry one of her fellow students and settle down. I am a grandmother now. I had such high hopes for her though. I thought she would make it all the way to the top, you know, be our next lady Prime Minster.'

I was jealous of Helen. I was jealous of Sarah. Both of them had children. I had a blank canvas. No photos around my house showing a happy family with children, all smiling, all happy. I had nobody to carry on my name.

We got coffees to drink as we walked and talked a bit more before saying goodbye to each other. I got a bus home. I would keep in touch with Helen but not necessarily on a regular basis. She was nice enough, but things had moved on for both of us and we didn't seem to have that much in common anymore.

When I got back, Kath and Harry were watching a thriller involving several suspects who may or may not have killed the CEO of a large company they worked for. I watched it with them and near the end, we all got who we thought the murderer was completely wrong. It was the elderly lady who came round twice a day serving tea and coffee. She came across as a very sweet person. Apparently, her son had lost his job there after being accused of embezzlement or fraud, something like that. The CEO had made a big show of getting rid of him but it was later proved he hadn't done it. He had been arrested at work and taken away in handcuffs with everyone watching. He ended up in a psychiatric hospital unable to cope. She just wanted to get revenge. She had injected poison into her boss's biscuits. She thought that best as the biscuits were on show to everyone so anyone could have done it. Unfortunately, she had written the whole plan down in a 'How to kill the CEO' notebook at work which another tea lady had found and read.

'It's always the least likely person you suspect. We should have realised that,' Kath said. 'Anyone fancy a takeaway?'

I got out a large number of takeaway leaflets from a drawer and we decided on a curry each. I hadn't sorted out the drawer yet, and as Kath looked at the other leaflets for future food ideas, a printed piece of paper fell out. She opened it up.

'Well, well, well. I didn't know you were interested in this, Beth.'

'What's that, Kath?'

'Murder Mystery Weekends.'

'Oh yes. That was something David and I thought about doing but then his work got in the way as usual and then, well, you know.'

'Why don't we go on one of these then? We could do it in memory of David.'

Part of me wanted to cry but the other half thought, yes, that sounds like a grand idea.

'How exciting,' Harry said. 'Could I come along too? I will probably end up as the butler though. You know, the one who always does it in the end. I hardly think they are going to cast me as the dashing bachelor come to claim his maid of honour.'

'Okay. Let's go for it,' I said.

Kath looked at the website and booked us for an event in a month's time. Luckily, there had been some cancellations. It was Harry's birthday the day before we were going to it so Kath and I paid for his weekend there as a present. We would be going on Friday and coming home on Sunday.

Just under two weeks before the event, we all got an e-mail about who we would be playing. I had set up an e-mail address for Harry so he could get his. Harry looked at who he was going to be and smiled. *I hope he hasn't got the butler*, I thought. He refused to divulge anything. 'Wait and see,' was all he would say.

'It even says we might have dark secrets hidden away and what they are. You know, skeletons in our closets,' I said. 'This is going to be fun.'

Kath came over that evening and tried desperately hard to get us to say who our characters were. She even tried to bribe Harry. We stood firm.

'Did you see the costume suggestions, Kath? Not sure how we are going to manage that as we can't all go to the same place to get them,' I said.

'May I make a suggestion, Beth? We can all go to the same costume place to hire them. I really don't want to go trolling around London looking for places when there is one place within walking distance from here. All that needs to happen is that one of us goes in at a time. The people there will put our costumes in plastic covers and a bag so we won't be able to see anything.'

'Good plan, Kath.'

A couple of days before we were due to set off, we went and got our outfits. We had taken an oath on the bible to swear we would not try to take a look at each of our costumes. We had hired one for each day we were at the event. I hid mine when we got home, still in its cover and bag, on the top of my wardrobe. I had no idea where Harry put his.

Late that day, I saw Harry muttering to himself and walking around the garden. When I joined him, he stopped.

'What are you doing, Harry?' I giggled.

'Nothing. Just talking to myself. People do talk to themselves, you know.'

'You are practising for our weekend away, aren't you? You can't kid a kidder.'

We both laughed.

'You got me there, Beth. You didn't happen to hear anything, did you?'

'No, Harry. I want it to be a surprise just as much as you do.'

The day before our murder mystery adventure, we celebrated Harry's birthday with lots of food and lots of presents. Sarah and her children came over and we enjoyed a lavish tea party indoors. The weather had turned autumnal and was a bit too cold to hold it outside. Unfortunately, her husband was working so couldn't make it, she said. Kath thankfully didn't say anything about George this time. She had piled her plate high with food.

'Are you going to eat all that?' I asked her.

'No, I thought I might wear it as a hat or maybe turn it all into a pair of gloves.'

Charlotte and George played in the garden and ran around with their arms out pretending to be aeroplanes making loud engine noises. Then they pretended they were horses racing each other jumping over flower beds and logs. I had bought a big birthday cake and had got Harry's name put on it. We all sang Happy Birthday and Harry blew the candles out. By 11 pm, we were all exhausted. The children had been put to bed upstairs and Sarah and I carefully brought them down, as they were still asleep, and put them in the car.

28

Whodunit?

We set off mid-morning the following day. We put our costumes, still wrapped up in the bags, in the boot so none of us could try and take a sneaky look at them. Kath drove us down to Sussex and Harry and I felt like we were going back to our part of the country. We stopped off at a roadside café for an afternoon meal. The confirmation e-mail had told us that we would only be getting nibbles in the evening, but these would include some scrumptious desserts.

'Hooray!' Kath shouted when I reminded her. 'If this weekend is only worth the puddings and cakes, I will be a very happy bunny.'

We went up a long driveway surrounded on each side by tall rose bushes, hedges and trees until suddenly a beautiful Tudor manor house appeared with timber framing and stone and brick in between. Kath parked in a space. There were already six other cars there. The grounds looked extensive and I could hear a peacock somewhere.

'Well, this is all very la-di-da,' Kath said. 'Lovely.'

'What a beautiful place,' Harry said. 'Just look at the carving above the front door.'

'How splendid,' Kath added.

'I can see a lake over there,' I said and pointed. 'You know, if I ever won the lottery, this would be the sort of place I would buy and you two could come and live with me.'

'Love to do that, Beth,' Kath said. 'You know the odds against winning are stacked against you but good luck anyway.'

We got our names ticked off at reception, met the person running the weekend and were shown up to our rooms. As we went up to our rooms, we heard someone doing vocal exercises - 'Me, me, me, me, me, ooooOOOO, AAaaahhhh, la la, laaaaaa.' Whoever it was, was going up and down a musical scale. Up and down, up and down.

'We won't have to sing too, will we?' Harry asked.

'I doubt it,' I replied. 'Probably just someone who has a character who needs to speak a lot and is making sure their voice is up to scratch. Funny though, as we don't start until tomorrow.'

'Are either of you secret squirrels going to tell me who you will be?' Kath asked.

'No!' was the reply.

We unpacked our bags and then went for a walk. The grounds had yew trees covering large areas. There was a terrace at the back of the house which had tables and chairs set out on it. It was a bit nippy so I didn't think I wanted to sit out there first thing for breakfast.

Just before 7 pm, we got changed into our best clothes and went downstairs for the evening reception.

'Let me at the cakes,' Kath said. She headed straight for the table they were on. Harry and I were standing to one side watching her. Kath ate so many little desserts I thought she was

231

going to be sick. The evening wasn't part of the murder mystery so we didn't need to be in character. It just gave us a good opportunity to meet the other guests and try to see who might let slip some vital information. No one did though.

Everyone was formally introduced to everyone else and I immediately forgot most of their names.

'Hello there.' A man had quietly sidled up beside us. 'My name is Nathaniel. I just need to check who your character will be tomorrow.' He had a little notebook with him.

'Er…' we said.

He laughed. 'Don't worry. Just winding you up. I know you can't really say. This weekend should be good.'

He put his notebook away and signalled to a woman standing next to us.

'This is my wife, Alexis. This is our twenty-seventh year of marriage. Have you been to one of these before? We come all the time. Been to loads around the country. I was once the murderer but no one guessed as I was so good at not giving anything away. Kept everything neatly tucked in.' He patted his chest.

Bighead, I thought. 'Sounds amazing. This is the first one I have been to,' I replied. I introduced him to Harry and pointed to Kath who now seemed to have cream on her nose and jam running down her chin.

'Well, enjoy,' he said and went off with his wife.

'Kath, Kath, stop eating. You aren't leaving anything for other people.'

'These are sooo delicious. Try one.' She shoved a small slice of something in my mouth.

'Yes very nice,' I said.

I could see a man in the corner who looked like he had dressed up in character too early. He had a red velvet smoking jacket on with a large silk scarf wrapped around his neck. His hair didn't move at all. I was intrigued and went over.

'Hello. My name is Beth.'

'My dear, a joy to meet you. My name is Dorian.' He shook my hand but almost seemed like he didn't want to. He smiled at Harry who had joined me.

'Have you been to one of these events before?' I was using the same tack as Nathaniel.

'My dear, I am a connoisseur. These... events.... are... my.... life'. He flung a cigarette holder into the air with a flourish. His cigarette was unlit. I thought he looked and sounded like Noel Coward. I wondered if he was the person we heard earlier doing all the Oooooos and Aaahhs.

'I'm in theatre, you know,' he added. *I would never have guessed. He certainly thinks he is the big cheese here*, I thought.

'How wonderful,' I replied. Harry had stood beside me not saying a word until now.

'You know we aren't meant to be in character until tomorrow, don't you?' he said to Noel Coward's younger brother.

The man put his hand to his chest, looked in disdain at Harry and walked off in a huff.

'Well, I can see you have made a friend for life there, Harry.'

'Seemed a bit of a twit if you ask me. Very affected. I wonder if he is being paid to act the fool here or maybe he is the murderer and is using his stupidity as a distraction.'

233

We went and chatted with other people. A few, like us, were new to the murder mystery malarkey. Those who had attended them before made a point of talking loudly about how wonderful their previous experiences had been and what high hopes they had for this one. No pressure then. One couple had gone on and on about who they had played before and how they had worked out who the murderer had been. *Clever clogs*, I thought. I think some saw it as a competition and were being very serious about it all. I wasn't aware that there would be a prize to fight for though. We all went upstairs at about midnight. We met up in Harry's room to try and work out a plan of action. The last one when we went paintballing had worked out a treat. This was more difficult so we left it.

'We could just meet up every now and then to share how things were going and who we suspected. The best-laid plans of mice and men and all that,' Harry suggested. We agreed to do that.

The following morning, we enjoyed a breakfast that would have filled any normal person up for the entire day. Most people, including us though, went up for second helpings.

'I think I might just have fruit for today's lunch and dinner and then all next week. I feel completely stuffed,' I said. I could hardly move due to my piggery. My stomach was looking bloated.

The person in charge of the murder mystery weekend came into the room. 'Hello, everyone. I do hope you have had a good breakfast.' We all nodded. 'Good. Glad to hear it. This evening, we will meet at 7 pm and the mystery will begin so make sure you are all dressed up in character. You have all received details of who you will be and what will happen when we all meet later. Until then, please feel free to explore the grounds here at the manor house or venture forth into the surrounding countryside. See you all tonight then.'

Harry was looking a bit tired so he went back upstairs for a little sleep. When he came back down an hour later, we went out for a walk in the grounds. We went to the lake and sat on a bench. Nearby, a peacock was fanning out its plumage and pacing about. Its feathers were making a loud rustling noise. We all stared with our mouths open wide listening to it.

'That is some sound. What a grand specimen,' Kath said. 'Beautiful.'

'Can a peacock break your arm?' Harry asked. 'I am not sure that one is happy to see us. It seems to be warning us off.'

'I have no idea. I know a swan can,' I said. 'I think it is doing that to attract a mate though'.

I kept hearing another rustling noise like sweets being unwrapped. I could see Kath was stealthily going into her pocket and then quickly putting something in her mouth. Harry noticed it too.

'What ARE you doing?' Harry turned to Kath and grabbed her hand. 'Where did you get those then?'

'They were on the reception desk when we came in. I just kept going back for more last night. The receptionist didn't seem to mind. I told her I was getting them for everyone else.' Kath had loads of lemon sherbets in her bulging pocket.

'Well, share them out then.' I took a couple as did Harry. Then we took some more.

'You are welcome,' Kath said as her pile slowly diminished.

'You can always go back and get some more, Kath. There is a new receptionist on today so she won't know about your dastardly deed yesterday.'

'And I will, Beth.'

We sat there for an hour crunching on sweets and then decided to get in Kath's car and drive around the area. We came across a small town nearby and stopped for a drink at a pub. I made Kath have a non-alcoholic drink as she was the designated driver. Harry and I chinked our glasses together as we were having gin and tonics.

We got back a couple of hours before the murder mystery started. This gave us time to relax, have a shower or bath and then get dressed. We were to meet each other downstairs and be in character. No messing about.

I got washed and changed and then went downstairs. It was just after 7 pm and Harry and Kath were already there with the other guests. I was the last to appear.

Harry was dressed up to the nines. He had a beautiful black double-breasted suit on, a waistcoat decorated with flowers and a red bow tie. His hair was immaculate and he had a monocle covering one of his eyes.

'Good evening, my dear,' he said as I came down the stairs. 'My name is Lord Stanley Higginbotham-Smythe. My family and I have owned this place for over a hundred years. Welcome.' He kissed my hand and his monocle fell out.

'Good evening, Your Lordship. My name is Georgina Jenkins. Your daughter Iris invited me to this sumptuous occasion. I am delighted to meet you.' I didn't know whether to curtsy, so just bent my knee a bit. I was wearing a tight full-length black velvet dress that had a large fabric white rose on one shoulder. I hoped I wouldn't have to keep sitting down as I doubted very much I would be able to get up again without help.

Kath stepped forward. She looked like a Charleston girl. She was wearing a straight loose dress which was just below her knees. It was sleeveless and covered in gold beads. She had a long pearl necklace wrapped several times around her neck, a headband, which was also in gold and a lovely dangly silver bracelet. She looked stunning.

'Hello there. My name is Jane Howard. I am engaged to the son and heir here. Delighted to meet you.' She gently shook my hand.

'Enchanted,' I replied.

Kath winked at us both and shoved her head in the direction of the drinks table. *Please no*, I thought. *She has a plan in mind.*

'I'm going rogue at some point tonight,' she whispered. 'If we are still going to work as a team, I think it might be a bit of a whizz if I listen to what the other characters are talking about. You know, sneak up and point my ear like an antenna at them.'

Suddenly, Dorian appeared beside her and picked up some more drinks to put on a tray. He was the butler, Aloysius, and looked very glum indeed.

'Oh yes, my dear,' Kath suddenly spoke in a loud voice. 'I do think that we should abandon the hunting season totally. Not a good show for the animals, is it? I am sure Lord Higginbotham-Smythe agrees with me. Yes, Stanley, do you agree?'

Harry looked at her and mumbled 'Er, yes.'

Kath whispered again while getting some drinks for us. 'Well, well. Dorian looks so annoyed at being the butler and having to be at everyone's beck and call. I bet he wanted to be the murderer or the person who solves it.'

'We need to stay in character, Kath.' Harry was sounding a bit annoyed.

'Yes. Sorry. Forgot where I was for a moment. Here we are. Georgina, a lovely glass of bubbly for you. Stanley, one for you too.' Kath thankfully then stayed in character for most of the evening.

We went around and chatted with the other characters. One man was the head of the local hunt so Kath as Jane got into a heated debate with him about how ripping up foxes for fun was not something she found amusing. I saw a group of people move closer to her, desperately trying to listen in on their conversation.

Fifteen minutes later, all hell broke loose. We heard a blood-curdling scream and a woman came running into the room which fell silent. She was dressed as a maid but I discovered later she was an actor, recruited for the part. She had some 'blood' down the front of her.

'He's been killed!! He's dead!! Heaven's above. Someone's done him in!! Never have I seen such a thing.' She was crying and scrunching up her uniform with her hands. 'Mrs Haverstock has called the police, your Lordship.' Mrs Haverstock was also an actor playing the part of the housekeeper. I looked around for Kath and Harry. They suddenly appeared behind me.

'Do we know who it is? Does anyone know?' Kath asked the room.

I had a quick look round and realised Dorian, as Aloysius, wasn't with us.

'It might be the butler who has been killed,' I said. 'I can't see him.'

Harry whispered in my ear, 'So the butler didn't do it then.'

Kath nudged my shoulder. 'I reckon it was Colonel Mustard in the library with the lead piping.' She nudged Harry in the back. 'Go on then, Lord Fauntleroy, do your stuff. Tell them what to do.'

Harry stepped forward as Lord Stanley Higginbotham-Smythe. 'I propose we wait here until the police arrive. Ladies and gentlemen, please make yourselves comfortable and do have more food and drinks. We shouldn't have to wait long.'

The police, all actors, arrived soon afterwards. They were led by Inspector James Conway of Scotland Yard. He told us he was in the local area on another matter but had made a quick exit to get here. He introduced himself to us all and then got down to the nitty-gritty. He was in his forties with an intense look on his face and a large bushy moustache.

'As you are now aware, a man has been killed here. We will be removing the body as soon as the doctor arrives to confirm the death. The sitting room where this occurred will be sealed off while we collect evidence. An incident room will be set up in the library and I, along with my sergeant, will interview you all over the next day or two. I would appreciate your full co-operation in this matter. Thank you. Rogers, Smith, come with me.'

He walked off with two police constables to the sitting room. There was more than one sitting room at the manor house so we all watched to see which one they went into. A doctor arrived a short time later and the body was brought out on a stretcher. It was the butler. His body was covered with a blanket but one arm had slipped out and I recognised his jacket. *I bet he did that deliberately*, I thought, *just so we knew it was him*. The police spent some time going backwards and forwards with evidence bags from the sitting room to the library.

Several women started to swoon and were helped to sit down. I looked around to see if anyone was acting suspiciously. A couple of the men were deep in conversation, some people were drinking wine and others were staring at their feet.

Inspector Conway started to call each person into Lord Stanley's office. Kath, Harry and I were the last to be interviewed. I went in when my name was called.

'Now, Miss Jenkins, could you tell us your whereabouts when the murder took place? The doctor has stated that it took place between 7.30 pm and 8 pm.'

'I was in that room with everyone else. I never left. Hold on. Yes, I did. I went to the ladies at one point but that isn't anywhere near the sitting room. It is in the opposite direction over there.' I pointed over my shoulder and waggled my finger about.

'You say you went to the ladies. Did you notice anyone acting oddly on your way there? Anyone who was in the vicinity of the sitting room?'

'I can't say that I did, Inspector.'

'Did you know the butler?' asked the sergeant.

The sergeant was taking notes.

'No, not before coming here. I didn't really notice him, to be honest. I just saw him walking around with a drinks tray a few times or standing near the door looking bored.'

'Do you have any thoughts as to who may have committed this terrible crime? Did any of the others say anything that you may have thought was a bit strange under the circumstances?' The actor playing Inspector Conway was really getting into his role.

'No.'

'Did you notice anyone missing when the maid came in to say what had happened?' he asked.

'No.' I did though. I remembered I was looking for Kath and Harry as I couldn't see them. I didn't say anything.

'Well, thank you, Miss Jenkins. That will be all for now. However, we may need to speak to you again.'

'Well, you know where I will be. Thank you, Inspector.'

Kath went in next, followed by Harry. When they came out, neither of them said anything to me.

We all went upstairs to go to bed. I heard a soft knock on the door. Kath and Harry were both in pyjamas.

'Let us in, Beth,' Kath whispered and came in anyway.

She sat on the end of my bed. 'Well? What did they ask you?'

'The usual. Probably the same as they asked you and Harry. Where was I, did I see anyone acting suspiciously? You know.'

'Yes, they asked me those questions too. I said as host and Lord of the Manor, I was with all my guests making sure everything was running smoothly and that they were all having a jolly good time.'

'Kath, what about you?' I asked.

'Oh yes, the same,' she replied. 'I told them I was in the room all the time.' She leaned forward. 'I did say that one of the guests was acting a bit off and left the room at one point though.' She leaned back.

I had my suspicions. The following morning, we ate a hearty breakfast still in character. The police had set up a few boards and tables in the library incident room and had put photos and what they considered to be vital evidence on display. Kath, Harry and I went in to have a look. There was a photo of the butler, Aloysius, lying on the floor with blood on his back. I started to make some notes.

'What are you doing?' Kath asked.

'Just writing stuff down. Might come in handy.'

The physical evidence consisted of a handkerchief, a torn piece of fabric, a metal clasp to hold a necklace or bracelet together, a bead and an empty champagne glass.

'They could get fingerprints off that glass,' Harry said.

'That would make it too easy. It would all be over with by lunchtime then,' Kath said.

We walked around the grounds again and found a little summerhouse. We sat in it. Kath was fiddling with her wrist.

'This bracelet keeps coming undone,' she said.

I kept quiet. I realised one piece of evidence on display was a clasp. Was it Kath's? She put the bracelet in her coat pocket. We walked back to the manor house. On the way, we met a couple of people. We all remained in character. Lunch was a fine affair and again we helped ourselves to second helpings.

I decided to sit with other people this time. I told Kath and Harry about my plan as I wanted to subtly question people about the previous night's events.

'So, Frank, what do you think about the goings-on?' Frank was his character's name but was also his own name. He was in his seventies and was a seasoned pro having already attended three other murder mysteries in the last few months. I imagined he spent most of his pension on gadding around the country hoping one day to be named as the murderer.

'I think I know who did it,' he whispered.

'Care to share your thoughts?' I whispered back.

'You remember that servant who appeared with the food dishes and was a bit late setting everything up? Well...'

He didn't finish as suddenly, the housekeeper came rushing in. She was holding a bloodied towel with the knife wrapped in it. Someone called for the Inspector. He carefully took it, still in the towel, and went off to the incident room.

'They could get some prints off that if I am not mistaken,' I could hear Harry say as Lord Stanley to a man sitting next to him.

I turned to the person sitting on the other side of me. She was a meek little character who didn't say much. I asked her who she thought had murdered the butler and told her about my ideas. She looked at me and squeaked so quietly back at me I couldn't understand what she had said. I didn't think she was capable of murder so I crossed her off my list of suspects. Kath and Harry were talking to other guests. I could hear Kath interrogating someone.

'So, where were you last night? I don't remember seeing you in the room before or after the murder.'

That afternoon, there were games going on, ones linked to the weekend. Harry decided not to play and went upstairs for an afternoon nap. Kath and I decided to give it a miss too. We got changed into our normal clothes and drove to the nearest town. We went into several shops, bought some souvenirs, took

243

lots of photos and then drove back. We went to look at all the evidence again. I, for one, had made my mind up. I was fairly sure I knew who the murderer was. We relaxed and ordered afternoon tea and cream cakes at reception and ate it out on the terrace.

That evening, there was a dinner and dance. We were all dressed up again in character. Kath tried to do a few twirls when dancing but failed miserably, almost falling flat on her back.

The music was suddenly turned down and then off. Inspector Conway came in, looking very angry.

'I have just been into the incident room and someone, someone here, has taken a vital piece of evidence. I have told my constables to search the entire house. You will all be searched too. It will be found, I can assure you.'

We were all given a pat-down by male or female officers. Then, we waited for what seemed like an age. Inspector Conway appeared again with a tiny object between his thumb and finger. It looked like the clasp I had seen earlier in the incident room. He held it up and deliberately and dramatically walked slowly towards each person, looking them straight in the eye.

'Well, well, well, and what do I have here then?' he said. He stopped and put it in the palm of his hand and showed it to everyone again. 'This was found upstairs in one of your rooms, ladies and gentlemen. One... of.... your.... rooms.'

God, he loves this role, I thought. I was beginning to believe he was a real Inspector. I bet he already had his Oscar acceptance speech written out, laminated and kept in his safe with a copy saved on his laptop just in case the original went astray.

'We are waiting for some results from the lab to come back and then we will be ready to make an arrest. No one, I repeat, no one is to leave this house tonight. I will be placing a police constable at each exit to make sure you all stay here.'

'That looks like one of your clasps, Beatrix. You always said you hated Aloysius as he took the butler's job away from your son. You told me that Aloysius had falsely accused your son of stealing a vase from here, didn't you?' An elderly lady whose character name was Isabella Walters was speaking.

'Isabella, how dare you. Yes, I hated Aloysius but I am not a killer. How can you accuse me?' Beatrix was beside herself with worry that she would be carted off by the police at any second. She kept playing with the pearls around her neck.

'And you, Herbert Longstaff, my most loving husband, told me before we came here how you wanted to take revenge on the Lord here because you lost all your money buying shares that he had told you to buy. How better than to hurt him by killing his longest-serving and most loyal butler?' The woman who spoke in character was Petunia Longstaff.

'I said that in anger. I would never have gone through with it. You know I wouldn't.' Herbert was indignant with rage.

All the secrets were coming out now.

Before we went up to bed, we were all given a secret ballot paper each. We were asked to write down who we thought the killer was along with our reasons why and then put it in a box at reception by 9 am the following morning. Inspector Conway said that he would gather us all together after breakfast and go through all the evidence, what dark secrets the police had discovered, explain what our characters' motives were and read out what we had written. The murderer would then be arrested.

'Oh, this is so exciting,' Kath said.

Before going to sleep, I wrote down who I thought the murderer was on my ballot paper. I put down Kath's character. She had appeared late after the murder had been discovered and then kept complaining that her bracelet wasn't fastened the way it should be. Had her bracelet clasp fallen off while she was killing the butler? Was that the vital piece of evidence that had been taken from the evidence room? I couldn't think what her motive would be to commit such a foul deed so left that bit blank.

On Sunday morning, we went down for breakfast. Everyone was still in character and we were all discussing who we thought the murderer was. I couldn't really say anything to anyone as Kath was right next to me.

Inspector Conway came in after an hour and told us to gather ourselves in the incident room. Chairs had been put out for us to sit on.

'And where is Hercule Poirot, I ask myself?' Kath said as she sat down.

'Right, settle down, please, and make yourselves comfortable.' Inspector Conway clapped his hands together several times. 'I am now in a position to go through all the evidence with you. I know yesterday you were able to hear a couple of possible motives concerning Beatrix Ambercombie and Herbert Longstaff. After much careful consideration, I do not believe either of these people murdered the butler, Aloysius.'

246

A few people tutted. They obviously had them down as the guilty parties.

Inspector Conway continued. 'Then we looked at other staff. The housekeeper, Mrs Haverstock, seemed a likely suspect as Aloysius had spread lies about her character to Lord Stanley which stopped her from getting a good reference. She was then not able to take up a new more favourable position elsewhere. The maid who found the body also wanted to leave as she had been falsely accused by Aloysius of stealing some food which he said she had wanted to give to her family. She was very angry with him but Aloysius had apologised. Whether the maid had forgiven him is another matter. However, they both had very strong alibis for the time of the murder.'

Inspector Conway went through the other guests. The mousey lady I had sat next to at lunch yesterday was completely dismissed as a suspect. Frank, the seasoned performer at murder mystery weekends, had apparently been Aloysius' father-in-law. Aloysius had treated his daughter dreadfully and had pushed her so hard one day she ended up unable to walk for months afterwards. He dismissed everyone else and then came to Kath and Harry.

'Lord Stanley Higginbotham-Smythe, you had a strong motive to get rid of Aloysius. You had shared many secrets with your trusted butler. You told him, for example, how you had forced the farmer next to your land off his farm by sending in a heavy mob to scare him away. You then bought his land at a knockdown price. You also shared tales of the many other salacious activities you were involved in. I have been told by your guests that you were not with them when the murder was announced and were not seen for up to half an hour before.

However, I am discounting you as a major suspect, Lord Stanley. Your maid has since vouched for you and told me you were checking the freshness of the food in the kitchen.' Then he turned to Kath.

'Now we come to you.' Everyone looked at Kath. There was only her and two other guests the Inspector needed to talk about. Kath wriggled about a bit and scratched her nose.

'You, Jane Howard, are NOT Jane Howard.'

'Yes, she is,' said Harry as Lord Stanley. 'I have known her for years.'

Inspector Conway pointed at Kath. 'This, ladies and gentlemen (dramatic pause ensued), is not Jane Howard. She is her twin sister Cynthia Howard.' There were loud gasps and several people said, 'Well, I never.'

Inspector Conway continued. He was in his element. 'Unbeknownst to you all, Aloysius had written down all his findings in his diary which we found on our search. He had overheard this lady making a telephone call, to an accomplice, seemingly.' He got out Aloysius' notes and started reading aloud from it to us.

'Today has been one of surprises. Coming down from His Lordship's bedroom, I overheard his son's fiancée, Miss Jane Howard, on the telephone. Well, I thought it was Miss Jane Howard but what I heard turned my head. I waited at the top of the stairs as I could see she was looking around to make sure the coast was clear. She was telling the person she was talking to that it was all going to plan. No one had suspected she was her sister's twin and soon the house would be theirs once she married the son and eventually did away with him and Lord Stanley. I decided to tell Lord Stanley but he was out for the day and it was all hands on deck preparing for the party. I will find time to tell him tomorrow. I will leave him a letter on his desk to arrange a meeting.' Inspector Conway closed the diary and continued. 'We did some of our own research and found out that Miss Jane Howard has in fact been in a mental institution for the past ten years having been placed there by her family. In our search, we also found the clasp that had been taken from the evidence table hidden in a bag in, as we now her know as, Cynthia Howard's room along with the letter that Aloysius had written. She had to get rid of Aloysius as she would have lost everything.'

'It's a stitch-up!!! You are all rotters!' Kath, as Cynthia Howard, was now enraged and spitting feathers. 'Damn you all to hell!!' Kath was playing her part to perfection.

'I am sorry but the evidence is overwhelming, Miss Cynthia Howard. Take her away, constable.' I could hear Kath being read her rights. Inspector Conway then read out all our ballot papers. I was the only one who had thought it was Kath and won the Best Sleuth in Town trophy. It was a dagger stuck in a circular piece of wood with a question mark curling around it.

The event was due to finish at 1 pm but we stayed on for lunch.

'I can't tell you how many times I wanted to let you both know it was me,' Kath was saying. 'I nearly let it slip so many times.'

We were now in our own clothes again and out on the terrace.

'I knew it was you. You were conveniently absent when the murder occurred and you kept going on about your bracelet being loose when we were in the garden. Remember?' I said.

249

'Oh yes,' Kath replied.

'I had no blinking idea who it was,' Harry said.

We ate a scrumptious lunch, put our bags in the car and bade farewell to a wonderful weekend of murder, mayhem and fun.

29

The Discovery

A couple of days after we got back, Harry came down the stairs and said good morning to us. He was very smartly dressed. I noticed he was walking more slowly.

'Are you really going to wear that to help me do some gardening? I would change if I were you. It's a dirty job out there you know,' I said.

'You are a wit. I am going out, Beth. I got a card through your door last night from my old care home across the way as they have found a couple of my shirts in the laundry room. I want to spend some time catching up with some friends there too so I won't be back for a while.' He waved goodbye and disappeared. I watched him out of a window and noticed he stopped a few times and twice sat down on a bench. Kath was with me again as we wanted to look at more flowers ready for next Saturday's gardening exercise.

'Damn. I forgot to tell him that I wanted to wash his duvet set.'

'Well, go and get them now. I'll help you. You can put them in the tumble dryer and hopefully, they will all be back in place before he comes back. He will never know. I know you said he particularly liked that set. If it isn't dry enough, I can help you put another one on.'

I didn't want Harry to think I was intruding so I said to Kath that I would leave it until he came back.

'You must have to go into his room to hoover though. I would like a quick look at the drawing you did of him. Please?'

'Okay, Kath. Just a quick look.'

We went up to Harry's room and I opened the door. Harry's room was very tidy. You could tell he had been in the army. Everything was spick and span. Kath went over to look at my drawing and said how marvellous it was. 'You have really caught his character, you know.' As she turned, she spotted something.

'Kath, let's get the duvet set and go. Harry told me he was a very private man with his possessions. I don't want him to know we have been in here poking about.'

Kath was holding a small box.

'Beth, is there anything wrong with Harry?' She showed me the box. It contained morphine patches.

'I… I have no idea,' I stuttered. 'I know he has had a few odd turns but he has never said anything to me about having these. Maybe he suffers from really bad back pain or something.'

'I think it is a bit more serious than that,' Kath said. 'I don't think people have these for back pain.' She put the box back exactly where she had found it.

'What are you going to do? You have to ask him, Beth. This looks serious.'

'I will think about it when he comes back,' I said. Deep down, I knew I didn't want to have to face this.

We sorted out the duvet and then sat in the garden but the conversation was muted. I kept tapping my finger on the table as Kath munched on biscuits. Neither of us really knew what to say. We were waiting for Harry to come back. I heard the front door going later in the afternoon.

'Kath, would you mind going so I can talk to Harry by myself? He might find it easier. Sorry.'

'Don't apologise. It's not a problem at all. I will make myself scarce.' Kath got up and said goodbye to Harry as he came out to the garden.

'Fancy a cup of tea, Harry?' I asked.

'That would be lovely. Thank you.' I heard him cough several times while I was in the kitchen.

'You alright?' I asked.

'Yes, yes, just got a tickle in my throat.'

Harry told me all about his visit. Everyone was fine but none of them were really looking forward to the move to their new home. A few bits of furniture had already been taken to the new place. He had a plastic bag and took out his shirts.

'Blimey, they could have given these another wash. Look at them.' He held one up. There were dark marks all along the sleeves and several red marks on the front of one of them. I could see that the staff had written his name on the collar. He looked at his other shirt.

'This looks like someone else has worn it and dropped jelly all down it.'

'Why don't I get you some new ones? I can take those to the clothes recycling bin nearby. If they aren't good enough for other people to wear, they can sell them as rags and still make a bit of money.'

'Are you sure? You paid for my murder mystery weekend. I don't want to take advantage of you. You have done enough already.'

'That was for your birthday, Harry. Please let me buy you some new shirts just because I want to.'

After a bit of persuasion, Harry agreed. We sat and chatted some more and then I decided to grab the bull by the horns.

'Harry, I hope you don't mind. Kath wanted to see the drawing I did of you, the one hanging in your bedroom. You were over at the care home so I couldn't ask you if it would be okay for us to go in so I could show her. The thing is, while we were in there, Kath found a box of morphine patches. I promise you we weren't looking at your things. She just spotted them. Harry, is everything okay? You can tell me, you know. I want to help.'

Harry's face turned red with rage. 'How dare you! How DARE you! Those are my things, not yours. MY things.' I had never heard Harry shout before. He got up and flew out of the house, slamming the front door on his way. I didn't even have time to apologise.

He came back half an hour later with a bottle of wine under his arm. 'I am so sorry, Beth. What must you think of me?' He squeezed my arm and kissed my cheek.

'Please don't, Harry. I am the one in the wrong here. It wasn't deliberate. Kath only wanted to see the drawing. That was all.' I poured out two glasses of wine and gave one to Harry.

Harry sat back and downed his drink in one go. 'I didn't want to say anything. I was worried that you would see me as a patient and not as a friend and send me off to hospital.'

I was starting to get worried. 'Harry, why do you have those patches?'

There was a long pause and then Harry looked at me. His eyes were starting to well up.

'I have far fewer days ahead of me now. I have cancer, Beth. I don't have much longer to live. A matter of months, if that.'

To begin with, I couldn't reply. I just stared at him. Eventually, I got up and hugged him tightly.

'Harry, I am so sorry.' My mouth was dry. I couldn't say any more. My stomach felt like it had been ripped out.

'I hope you don't mind but I have spoken to my doctor and consultant and told them I wanted to stay here. I was going to tell you, I promise, but it never seemed to be the right time. You know that I have been going out every week. I told you it was to meet up with a friend or go for a walk. It wasn't all of the time. Several times I had ordered a taxi which I picked up round the corner so you wouldn't see it and I was either going up to the hospital for treatment or to see my consultant. Why do you think I didn't want you to come in when I saw my GP?'

I remembered that time with his GP. He had insisted I sat in the waiting area for him.

'Listen, of course you can stay here, Harry. I wouldn't have it any other way.'

'I saw my consultant last week to get some results and the chemo isn't working. The cancer has spread. Those patches Kath found help me with the pain. I prefer them as I really don't like injections.'

I tried so hard not to show Harry, but I felt distraught. I felt hollow. My stomach was turning inside out.

'Have you told Sarah?'

'No, and I don't want her to know.'

'Harry, you must. You have to. She needs to know. She is your daughter.'

'I don't have to and I won't. Please don't say anything to her, Beth. I beg you. I don't want it to become the only thing in our relationship now. I love her too much to land this bombshell on her. We have only just started to get to know each other again. Telling her this would be too much.'

'You know that Sarah, Kath and I would have come to the hospital with you. We all love you, Harry. You are like family to me.'

We sat together on the sofa all that afternoon. Harry reminded me about all the times he had fallen over or looked exhausted and how he had explained them away to me as being him just feeling tired or a bit hot. He said I could let Kath know. He would talk to Sarah at a later date. He didn't say when though. I phoned Kath and she came over.

I needed to find strength from somewhere. I had to. I couldn't lose someone else so precious to me after David. Kath sat with Harry and clutched him close to her. I went upstairs to my bedroom under the pretence of having to get something. I threw myself on my bed and sobbed. I came down a bit later having washed my face and put more make-up on.

Harry looked up.

'Look, you two. Please just act normally. If I need any support, I promise I will let you know. I don't want you tip-toeing around me not wanting to say anything. You know now. It is out in the open. I still want to do all the things we have been doing. Alright?' Harry took our hands and held on tight.

I could see that Kath had been crying too. Her eyes were very red and she was sniffing.

'Okay,' we both said. I got up and made us all a cup of tea.

Life was changing again. I felt like I was on a roller coaster careering along the rails through up days and spinning round corners heading towards down days. Now I found myself stuck in the tunnel. I began to wonder if someone had got it in for me. It felt like a curse had been put on me to suffer always. I knew I was being selfish again though. What I needed to do was keep the boat stable, stop it listing for Harry's sake and give him as much support and love as possible.

A few months wasn't long enough for us to do everything we wanted to do but it would include Christmas and I would make sure it was the best one ever for Harry. Maybe Sarah would want him to go over there. Another bridge to cross.

'Is there anything you would especially like to do, Harry, you know, before…? What can I do to help you?'

'There is something I have always wanted to do. Pooh sticks.'

'Pooh sticks as in Winnie the Pooh?' I asked.

'Yes. I want to go to the bridge in Ashdown Forest where Winnie the Pooh and his friends played Pooh sticks. You know. You both drop a stick in the river on one side of the bridge, rush to the other side and the one whose stick appears first is the winner. When I was a child, it was my favourite book and I always wanted to go and meet Winnie the Pooh, Piglet, Rabbit, Roo and Eeyore and play that game with them. My mother and father promised they would take me there but we never went. Later, I asked Maisie if she wanted to go but she just laughed at me. Sarah and the children could come too. I could read the

257

book to Charlotte and George on the way down. It is what I want to do. Apart from Christmas and all the jocularity around that, the Pooh sticks will be it.'

'There is time to do other things, Harry.'

He didn't reply.

I felt I had to let Sarah know, even if it meant asking her not to say anything to Harry. I knew it would be going against Harry's wishes but she would be so angry and upset otherwise. They had only recently found each other again and I didn't want to be held responsible if Sarah wasn't told.

Over the next few days, I tried hard not to cry. I realised that grief was just love which had nowhere to go. I would turn it on its head and give Harry as much love as possible. I kept clasping my hands together and spoke in an exaggerated tone to him. Always happy.

'Beth, please don't feel awkward. I know this is affecting you. Just act naturally. I would really like you to do that. If you need to talk about it, we can. I know I will need to.'

'I am sorry, Harry. I am finding this very hard but I will make an effort, I promise. If I cry, you know it is because I love you.'

Kath and I looked up the route to the Pooh Sticks Bridge. Going back to Sussex again would be good for Harry and for me.

'There is a place to park called Pooh Car Park, funnily enough. It isn't that far from the bridge so we could drive down and then walk to the bridge.'

'Kath, I think it might be a good idea to get a wheelchair for Harry. He is becoming somewhat unsteady on his feet and

I want him to enjoy the experience rather than run out of steam.'

I asked Harry if he was okay with that and he said it was fine as he might have needed some help if there was a lot of walking to do. He had now started to relax more and felt much more able to let me know when he wasn't coping.

'Good idea,' Kath said. 'A friend of mine has one. He used it when he broke his leg badly and his wife had to ferry him about everywhere. He loved it. He kept pointing out where he wanted to go with a walking stick. His wife was not best pleased. I will give him a ring and ask if I can borrow it.'

After letting Sarah know about our plan, we all decided to go the following Saturday. We thought it would be good if Harry went down in Sarah's car with Charlotte and George. I got him a copy of Winnie the Pooh so he could read it out loud on the journey down. It would also give Harry and Sarah time to talk. Sarah would come over to my place and then follow me and Kath.

Kath brought over the wheelchair for Harry. He sat in it and I had a little practise taking him up and down the road.

30

The Forest and Sticks

Sarah drove over to mine and we all set off in convoy at 8 am on Saturday morning. Kath and Sarah wanted to avoid the traffic. Harry walked to Sarah's car. He insisted. Kath and I would make sure we left Sarah and Harry to spend more time together when we were in Ashdown Forest. I was hoping he would say something to her about his condition. I didn't want to be the messenger of such bad news. Sarah, Kath and I brought along some sandwiches and drinks.

The traffic through London was pretty dreadful. It took us an hour just to cross over the River Thames. There were several snarl-ups to contend with and lots of diversion signs in place which didn't help. I thought Kath was going to explode at one point when a car zipped in front of her.

'Riddle me this, wise soul that you are, Beth; where is everyone going at this hour of the morning? Is there a huge million-strong fan-based gig on route that we haven't been invited to?' Kath spluttered. 'Actually, I hope they aren't all making the trip down to throw sticks off that bridge. It will be a bit like a rugby scrum otherwise.'

'I have no idea where they are all off to today. I bet they are thinking the same as you though,' I replied.

Two minutes later.

'Second riddle. How does bubble tea work, Beth? What is it exactly? Surely, if you want bubbles in your tea, you could just put it in a sealed container and then vigorously shake it up and down or use a straw and blow air into it.'

I couldn't answer that either.

When we finally got out of London, a lot of the traffic left us to go to Gatwick Airport. The rest of the journey was quite blissful. Swathes of rolling Sussex countryside flew by, often in a blur. Cows and sheep occasionally looked up but seemed to find it much more interesting to put their heads down and carry on munching grass. A pheasant almost collided with Kath's car while darting across a road. Kath was tempted to run it over and cook it later but decided that it wasn't the moral thing to do and the plucking of its feathers would take an eternity.

We reached the Pooh Car Park after a couple more hours. We had to contend with numerous toilet stops and Sarah's children wanting to stop to get sweets. There were several cars already parked there but we couldn't see or hear anyone else. Sarah got her phone out and looked up how far the bridge was from the car park. It would take us about half an hour, give or take, on foot. Harry asked for the wheelchair. He said it would take us a very slow two hours if he walked there otherwise. Sarah and I would take it in turns to push him. I went first as Sarah had to make sure Charlotte and George didn't run off and disappear into the forest. She was worried they might become feral, eat squirrels and wear animal fur as clothing if she didn't find them. I put a blanket from the car over Harry's legs as the weather was getting a little colder.

The walk was an absolute delight apart from Sarah's children interrupting the beautiful sound of birdsong, the cracking of twigs underfoot and the sound of leaves blowing in the gentle breeze. They ran here, there and everywhere, yelling their heads off and calling out, 'Hello, hello, hello!'

'Charlotte, George, please calm down. Have a little bit of respect for other people. Not everyone wants to hear your horrid little voices,' Sarah said in a serious tone of voice.

I looked around and then looked around again. 'Does Sarah mean respect for us? There's no one else here,' I said. 'That's very nice of her.'

'I think she was just expressing herself, you know, talking aloud, to all the trees and creatures who live here. They don't want to hear screaming and shouting any more than we do. Why don't we climb up that tall tree? We would get a fantastic view. Maybe we could take Charlotte and George up there and leave them there for the day.'

'Kath. That's naughty. Actually, I am not really up for the Duke of Edinburgh's Award for depositing children in trees this year, thank you.'

On the way, Harry kept asking me to stop so he could look at numerous sticks. He had quite a collection in his lap. The trees were losing their leaves as it was now autumn so I had to keep bending down to brush them off Harry's wheels.

A family of seven were just moving away from the wooden bridge as we arrived so we quickly walked to place ourselves on either side of it. I imagined A. A. Milne and his son, Christopher Robin, doing exactly what we were about to do.

Sarah and I helped Harry get out of his wheelchair. He stood for a moment to take everything in.

'I have waited for this moment nearly all my life,' he said. He took a deep breath in and started to sort out his sticks. He told us which ones were best and gave us all two each.

'You and Sarah go first, Harry,' I said.

They stood on one side of the bridge and looked down as the water flowed below.

'Right, Sarah, on the count of three we both drop our sticks in the water. Then we go over to the other side and see which one comes through first. Here we go then. One, two, three!'

They dropped their sticks and both practically ran to see who had won. He had suddenly got more energy. Harry's stick appeared first. He was delighted and we all cheered.

'Let's have a competition,' he said. 'Anyone got some paper and a pen?'

I did so I wrote our names down and made a list of who would face who. Sarah sidled up to me and asked me not to put Charlotte against George. It might get a bit too competitive between them and she didn't want either of them stomping off or crying.

'Okay. Here is the running order. First up will be Kath versus Charlotte, then George against Harry and then Sarah and me.'

Kath and Charlotte stepped up first and dropped their sticks. I noticed that Kath let her one go a second after Charlotte. When we all looked over the opposite side, Charlotte's stick won. Harry was a bit too eager when it was his turn to face George. Harry won and George wasn't happy, but they did a rerun and George was victorious. Sarah and I stepped up, threw the sticks in and when we went to the other side, only Sarah's one came through. On checking, I could see my stick had got caught up on something and was languishing under the bridge. We then kept changing partners and when I totted it all up, Harry came top. *That was fitting*, I thought. He was like a big kid and clapped his hands. We all raised a plastic cup of fresh orange juice to him. We spent time on the bridge looking at the surroundings and the water flowing underneath. We could see more people coming towards us so we moved on.

Sarah was pushing Harry in his wheelchair now and he asked her to stop. He looked at me, Kath and Sarah. 'Thank you for making this dream come true for me. I know that is your job, Kath, so you can tick it off as done now. You have all made me so happy.'

We all snuffled into tissues and mumbled things like, 'That's alright Harry' and 'It was our pleasure'. Sarah got her phone out again to look at how we could follow two routes in the forest where many of the characters in Winnie the Pooh had lived, met up or larked about.

We decided to do both walks. Sarah was fine continuing to push Harry. We found some tall pine trees, otherwise known as The Enchanted Place, the Heffalump Trap and Roo's Sandy Pit. On the longer walk, we went to the bottom of the valley after walking through some open heathland and found the site of the North Pole. We came across a picnic area and ate our food and drank our juice. The view of the pine forests and valley was stunning. Charlotte and George discovered there was an echo when we looked down onto the valley below. They kept shouting out 'Hello. My name is Charlotte. Hello. My name is George'. A reply came back almost immediately. They both thought it was the best thing ever.

'They are going to lose their voices if they carry on,' Sarah said.

This is somewhere I could live quite happily, I thought. We all took lots of photos.

We decided to call it a day after eating some more as the children were starting to get grumpy with tiredness. I pushed Harry's wheelchair back to the car. Sarah had got the short straw earlier as some parts of the trail were very much either downhill or uphill. I loved the sound of sticks breaking under the wheels.

'We certainly couldn't creep up on anyone with this noise, could we, Beth?' Harry laughed out loud.

We found some toilets which were an essential requirement on any trip out. Kath and I only did long journeys and outings if toilets were freely available. We would often mark them on maps with a big red cross.

We went to a gift shop and stopped off at Pooh Corner. Sarah got Charlotte and George a Winnie the Pooh bear each and I got a Piglet for Harry. Kath pushed a bag into my hand.

'Here, an Eeyore for you.'

'Thank you, Kath. I got you a Heffalump. You didn't happen to see any Pooh fudge on your travels, did you?'

'That sounds really unsavoury, Beth.'

'I meant as in Winnie the Pooh, not what you're thinking of. You know, fudge with his image on.'

'Of course you did,' Kath said. We both giggled and ate some toffees instead.

The journey back was less fraught than the journey there and we only did two toilet stops. We stopped at a café to get more drinks. Harry drove back with Sarah, Charlotte and George again. We arrived home and Sarah and the children came in for a drink. Harry had loved every minute of the day. He went over it again and again. I was so pleased for him. It had taken his mind off his troubles for a while. We all collapsed on the sofa and armchairs and laughed ourselves silly for what seemed like ages.

I got up. 'Who wants a nice cup of tea, hot chocolate or a Horlicks?' I made the drinks according to the requests and we sat there sipping them. There was a lot of contentment in my house.

I had decided to take a bit of a break from the gym. I had been going every week and was starting to feel much fitter. I no longer wanted to hit Paul. Now I wanted to concentrate on sorting out Christmas. It was a bit of a while off but there was nothing like being prepared.

31

The Nearing of the Festive Season

The weather became much colder. On walks, my breath came out of my mouth like I was exhaling cigarette smoke. I had started to wrap up more. Harry had started to spend more time indoors. Christmas was beginning to creep up on us far too quickly. Harry was now unable to go out for walks unless he was in his wheelchair. I had a hospital bed delivered for him and made it up for him in the living room. He could no longer manage the stairs. He was starting to spend a lot more time lying down and he was losing weight. A nurse now came in once a day to help give him his medication. If he needed to go to the toilet, I would help when the nurse wasn't around. Harry had not told Sarah about his condition but she had begun to realise something was not right with him. She phoned me to find out what was going on but I told her it was best she came over so Harry could tell her. I told Harry and said I would go out to see Kath so they could talk. When I got back, I closed my front door and I could hear Sarah weeping loudly.

She looked up when I walked into the living room and smiled half-heartedly at me. 'I asked him why he hadn't told me and he said he didn't want to upset me again but look at me now. Just look at me.'

'I am so sorry, Sarah. Harry made me swear not to tell you. I kept telling him he had to let you know. It has been very tough keeping it all in.'

'I am here, you know,' Harry said. He had made a special effort and was sitting on the sofa, holding his handkerchief.

Sarah said that she had spoken to work and if I was okay with it, she could spend every day here, help out and work from my place. Her husband could look after Charlotte and George and bring them over to see us. It would have been too hard to move Harry to Sarah's and I didn't want him becoming stressed about it.

'How does that sound to you, Dad? I can be with you every day now.' She held Harry's hand as she spoke.

'As long as I am not a burden to anyone.'

'Right, well, that's sorted then. Sarah, that is fine by me for you to be here, and Harry, you are not a burden in the slightest. If you ever need to stay over, Sarah, there is Harry's bedroom upstairs as he is down here now.'

I took Sarah upstairs so I could ask her about her brother Simon.

'Will you let him know?' I asked. 'I don't know what the issue is with him and Harry but time is running out.'

'I will, Beth. The problem is, was, the same as my issue with Dad. Now I have sorted it, I will let Simon know that he had got it all wrong. I am still struggling to understand why Mum did what she did.'

Over the next week, Sarah started to settle in. She used Harry's bedroom as an office but was always on hand to help out. She had brought a bag of overnight clothes and toiletries and had stayed over for a few nights, particularly when he needed extra care. I felt a bit like an intruder in their relationship. Sarah was, after all, his daughter. I decided to talk to Sarah. Harry was asleep so I went upstairs to see her.

'Sarah, could I have a little chat? If it is inconvenient, I can come back as I know you are working.'

'No, it's fine. I need to take a break anyway.'

'Sarah, I need to clear the air, really. Harry is your dad and he is here but if you ever felt like I was taking over you must let me know.'

'Beth, you are not putting my nose out of joint at all. He has told me you are like a second daughter to him and I feel like you are a sister to me. I knew if he had stayed any longer in that care home, he would have gone up the wall. He loves being here and I am so incredibly grateful to you. You didn't know about me and my relationship with him wasn't the best, but we are starting to rebuild it now. That is down to you. You have helped us to get to know each other again. Harry would not have found living with me relaxing. The children can run riot a lot of the time, as you have seen. He has spoken to me about it to make sure I didn't feel put out with him being here and I can assure you I don't. He might not have said this to you but he has told me you saved him, saved him from a life of boredom and, as he put it, hell on earth. You have helped him to smile again. After he lost Mum, I thought his world would implode. I know they didn't always get on but she was his wife and they did love each other.'

I got up and gave her a big hug. I still wasn't used to being in such close contact with people but this felt right.

'I am glad I spoke to you, Sarah, and that you are okay about all this. What Harry said has really got to me in a happy way. He is such a lovely man.'

'I am here to help so please don't think you can't ask for it. Being here means I can spend more time with my dad and not have to worry too much about Charlotte and George. They are coming over this weekend anyway and I talk to them every day on a video call or my phone. I am taking some time off work from next week so I can spend more time here if that is alright with you.'

'I look forward to it,' I said. Sarah had missed out on so much with Harry. They were having to do a big catch-up in a short amount of time. I would make sure I gave them the space they needed.

Two weeks before Christmas, we all sat down to order food for an online delivery. I put the delivery date down for a couple of days before Christmas Day. This meant that if we had forgotten anything, it would still give us time to dash to the supermarket rather than get in a huge panic. Kath would be spending the festive period with us as well. Her family in New Zealand wouldn't be coming over as they couldn't get a flight and she had left it too late to get over there. Sarah confided in me that things had started to go awry with her husband and he would be spending Christmas with his mother and father. She asked if she could spend Christmas with us.

'Sarah, I never expected otherwise. Your dad is here. You are all most welcome. There is enough room for you and the kids to stay over.'

Harry had given me some money to get presents for everyone. He wanted to get Kath a vase as she always had lots of flowers around her place. He wouldn't tell me what he was getting me. Sarah was sorting that out, he said. He had something in mind for Sarah too but I didn't need to worry about that. He asked me to get some toys for Charlotte and George.

At the weekend, I got out the Christmas tree and all the decorations. Charlotte and George were being brought over by their dad and Sarah went out to get them when he arrived. I looked out the window and could see them having an animated discussion. Charlotte and George were standing to one side trying hard not to look. Sarah eventually brought them in.

'Mummy, why were you shouting at Daddy?' Charlotte asked.

'I wasn't shouting, sweetie. We were just having a loud talk. People sometimes talk like that but it doesn't mean they are shouting. They just like their voices to be heard.'

She looked at me and raised her eyes. 'Sometimes I would prefer to have my head shoved down a toilet after someone has done a particularly large and smelly poo than talk to him. This was one of the main reasons I couldn't have my dad over to stay. I wouldn't have been able to cope with trying to play happy families and it would have upset him so much to hear us arguing.'

'I understand that, Sarah. Listen, you and the kids will have a splendid time here. We will all make it a very festive occasion.'

Charlotte and George were standing quite close to us, giggling, so I looked at them and clapped my hands together. 'Right, you two. Who wants to help me put the Christmas decorations up?'

Charlotte and George both shoved their hands in the air, jumped up and down and screamed at me, 'Me, MEEEEE!! PLEEEEASSEE!!!!'

'Okay then, to be fair, both of you can help. Come on then.'

They continued to jump up and down and then ran around the living room.

I got drinks for everyone. Sarah wanted a stiff gin and tonic.

'You two little munchkins can have some fresh orange juice.' I gave them a glass each and they went over and sat on Harry's bed to talk to him.

I took the Christmas tree out of the box, put it together with help from Kath and Sarah and then realised I had forgotten how massive it was. It towered over all of us.

'I hope you have got a very tall ladder to get up there,' Kath whispered in my ear and chuckled loudly.

'I didn't put it up last year, did I? Forgot it was a total giant of a tree. Look at it. It's like a fully grown pine tree. People will walk by and think I am growing a forest in my living room. I will get reported to Environmental Health or the Environment Agency or some tree charity. I have a big ladder in the garden shed which we can use.'

I got all the decorations out of a box and worked out by height order who would do what and where. Charlotte and George would add decorations around the first three layers of the tree and the adults would take it in turns to reach up and throw glittery things and attach baubles. I had bought five bags of Christmas chocolates to tie around the ends of the fake branches. I say five bags but we all helped ourselves to the contents of one bag and I had to keep slapping Kath's hand gently to stop her from eating all the other bags.

'Need to check they meet quality standards, don't we, kids?' Kath said.

'Yeesssssss!!!' they replied. They hadn't really understood what she was saying but went along with it anyway.

The most difficult part was adding more decorations, and wrapping the lights around the top of the tree. When it came to that part, we drew straws to see who would go up. I lost but was quite happy to do it.

'Make sure you have got your parachute on Beth and some oxygen,' Sarah said laughing. 'And don't forget your climbing boots.'

'Oh, very droll, Sarah.'

As I went up, everyone else held on to the legs of the ladder tightly so it didn't wobble. When I had completed the task, I got Kath to close the curtains and then I turned the lights on. We all stood back and admired the tree.

'We have forgotten something,' Harry said from his bed and pointed to the top of the tree. 'The Christmas fairy. Have you got one, Beth?'

'Oh goodness, yes, I do. I had a Christmas fairy that I used to put on my mum's tree. It always marked that the tree was now ready for viewing by others.' I found it in the box, went up the ladder again, and, with much ceremony and trumpet noises, placed it at the top.

'That looks absolutely wonderful,' Sarah said.

Everyone else murmured their approval.

It reminded me of the Christmases I had spent with my mum and with David. I felt myself welling up as I knew both of them would have been very proud.

I turned the lights off and opened the curtains. The tree would look best in the evening when it could sparkle itself silly.

Sarah stayed until the evening. She needed to get back to talk to her husband as he was going away soon and had presents for Charlotte and George. The children needed to calm down from all the excitement.

Harry was lying on his bed looking at the tree as I had turned the lights back on.

'Wonderful,' he said.

That night, we watched Midnight Mass on the television. As the programme had the words running along the bottom of the screen, we all joined in. Loudly.

32

Christmas

Christmas Day was fraught with all sorts of anxieties. It was all about the timing of the food for me to make sure that everything was cooked to perfection. I didn't want to serve up plates with half the food raw and the other half burnt to a crisp. Not a pleasant mixture. It had to be the perfect Christmas Day. I got the sherry out and kept sipping it along with a couple of Baileys. I put the radio on and started some preparations.

Sarah had arrived the night before. I had a fold-down bed for one of the children to sleep on but in the end, they both wanted to roll around on the big bed and sleep with their mum. She was now off work and was more than willing to help out without having to contend with job-related issues and queries. Kath came over at 10.30 am on Christmas Day. She was in a bit of a fluster. She had made a number of video calls to family and friends to wish them all a Merry Christmas which seemed to go well until she realised she had completely forgotten about the massive time difference when calling family in New Zealand. They had already celebrated and the day for them was almost over.

We decided to open all the presents in the morning. I had always done this with my mum and wanted to keep the tradition going. Besides, Charlotte and George were too excited to wait until later in the day. They had been up since 6 am, squealing their heads off, and as a consequence, we were all woken up really early. I felt sorry for Harry as he was down there with them while they touched and shook every present under the tree. They had even started to peel back the wrapping paper on some but Harry had got them to stop. Sarah apologised to him but he said he was fine about it. He was just as excited as they were.

Charlotte and George got their presents first. They got the usual array of toys from us all plus a Christmas jumper each and some little gloves and scarves. Sarah told them to put the jumpers on for the day. They rushed upstairs and bounded down again wearing them. Charlotte had a Christmas tree on hers and George had a reindeer on his.

Harry gave Kath the vase which she loved and a framed photo of them both together. Kath got me a huge set of new gardening tools and some perfume. I gave Kath a gardening book, a bracelet and a silk scarf. Sarah gave me some expensive toiletries and a wine cooler bucket. I got her a weekend treat at a spa.

Harry gave Sarah his mother's favourite necklace, a beautiful pashmina and another framed photo of him with Sarah and the children. I had been tasked with getting that and the one for Kath. Sarah was overcome with emotion. She gave him a book that Charlotte and George had written with help from Sarah. It was a story about how they had met their granddad and all the things they had done together. She also got him a warm jumper and a new shirt. Harry had asked Sarah to get my present, a lovely new overcoat and a framed photo of me and Harry laughing together.

'It is the year of the photo present!!!' Harry said. 'I wanted you all to have something to remember me by. It's not much but they all mean a lot to me and you all mean so much to me.'

'Oh, Dad,' Sarah stuttered. 'Everything is wonderful. Thank you so much for my lovely presents. I shall treasure them forever.'

We also gave Christmas jumpers to each other which we had to wear.

'Are penguins really associated with Christmas?' Kath stared at my jumper which had a penguin with a Christmas hat on and a present under one wing.

'No idea, Kath,' I replied.

We started to organise lunch. Harry watched Charlotte and George as they played with their new toys. I had written up a plan of action including a list of who would do what. I had stuck it on the fridge door. Kath was in charge of crossing the Brussel sprouts and sorting out the carrots. Sarah was peeling the potatoes and parsnips ready to be roasted and I was in charge of cooking a turkey for everyone and a veggie roast for me and anyone else who wanted to try it. Sarah ended up helping me with the turkey as I wasn't too comfortable touching it. The turkey, veggie roast, potatoes and parsnips went in the oven. The peas, carrots and Brussel sprouts were to be cooked later in saucepans, the cranberry sauce and apple sauce were in jars and the bread sauce and Christmas pudding would be put in the microwave to heat up. Tasks were gradually being ticked off the list.

'At least we aren't making another Thai green curry, Beth,' otherwise no one would get fed,' Kath said. I told Sarah about our online cooking lesson disaster. Thankfully, this time, the meal was cooked perfectly.

We served it up at 1.30 pm. 'My word. This looks splendid,' Harry said. 'You have done yourselves proud. Thank you so much, ladies.'

'We have made a good feast here,' Sarah added while Charlotte and George went, 'Yum, yum'.

'High five, Beth.' Kath had her hand up waiting for me to slap it. I was holding a dish so just looked at her and smiled.

'Okay then, maybe not. Leave me hanging then' she said. She went and grabbed a dish piled high with parsnips and put it on the table.

I had put a nice Christmas cloth on the table and crackers beside each plate. When we sat down, we all pulled them with the person next to us or across from us. There were enough crackers to have three each so I got the rest of them out of the box. We all moaned at the dreadful cracker jokes and then put on our Christmas paper hats. Everyone helped themselves to the dishes of food. Harry made an effort to sit at the table and asked for brown sauce so he could put it on his turkey. He also had lashings of bread sauce, cranberry sauce and apple sauce. In fact, everything looked very saucy indeed.

'I like to try every sauce going,' he said. 'They all add to the overall taste of any meal. This could do with some mayonnaise and tomato ketchup too,' he said in between munching food down.

'Goodness me, Harry. I think you would prefer just having a pile of sauces on your plate,' Kath laughed out loud and Harry nodded.

'Oh yes, most certainly. Fiddle–dee-dee-dee-dee and all that,' he said.

I got them for him and he squeezed the bottles until a small mountain of each appeared on his plate.

We made sure the lunch lasted as long as humanly possible. If it was going to be Harry's last, we wanted him to enjoy every single minute of it. There were requests for seconds and Kath spent time slicing off more bits of turkey for people. Kath tutted slightly when George asked for thirds but hid it well from Sarah. When we finally cleared our plates, we decided to have a little break before eating the Christmas pudding. We watched the Queen's speech and all sang the national anthem. What a change from last year for me when I was alone and feeling very depressed.

Later on, when we finally had space in our stomachs, we ate the Christmas pudding with brandy sauce or double cream. Charlotte and George had the cream with theirs. Kath tried to give George a little bit of the cream but he grabbed hold of the pot and the spoon and scooped out dollops for himself. I had another lot of cream in the fridge so it wasn't a problem.

'I can't even bring myself to ask you about him verging on the ridiculously enormous and the reasons why but I cannot unsee what I have seen,' Kath whispered in my ear.

I chose to ignore her remarks and asked people if they had everything they needed. I felt like my stomach was going to burst.

People had always told me that the trouble with turkey was that it made you sleepy after being eaten and indeed it did. I was sorting out the plates and bowls to wash up later and when I looked up to say something, everyone, including the children, had their eyes shut. Harry had gone back to bed and was snoring a bit. Charlotte and George were curled up either side of him. They all looked so relaxed, all snuggled up together.

I started to bang a few metal saucepans about and then made the fatal mistake of accidentally dropping a large china dish on the floor. It smashed and made a terrible noise.

Everyone immediately woke up.

'What, what's going on?' Kath mumbled.

After a lot of eye-rubbing and stretching, we played charades and Who Am I? I wrote down Winnie the Pooh on a post-it note for Harry and stuck it on his forehead. He got it after asking three questions. Someone, and I believe it had to be Kath, had put down a Satanic Leaf-Tailed Gecko on my post-it note. I couldn't get it at all and had to look it up later. 'It's tiny. Look at it. It has a tail that looks like a leaf.' I showed an image on my phone to Kath.

'Really? That must be why it's called a Leaf-Tailed Gecko then. Duh,' Kath replied.

I decided that the next time we played this game I would find the most obscure animal or insect on earth for Kath.

The day had been quite exhausting for all of us so in the evening we all sat sprawled out on chairs and the sofa and watched television. I could see Harry was looking tired but I could tell he was making a special effort to keep up with everyone else. He looked very contented. I put bowls of nibbles out and two tins of chocolates. I would start my diet in the New

Year. I made numerous cups of tea and refilled glasses of wine. Harry showed Charlotte and George how to dunk a biscuit in a cup of tea and time it so you could whip it out before it fell apart.

'We should all go for a walk tomorrow,' Sarah said.

'Yes, that sounds like a wonderful idea. I need to work off some of this ballooning fat I have started to develop again around my waist,' I said as I gave my stomach a poke. 'I could do a bubble and squeak tomorrow with all the remnants of food from today.'

Sarah had put the children to bed at 8 pm as they were practically falling asleep standing up but we stayed up. There were still lots of chocolate sweets to eat.

'What a day it has been,' Harry sighed and patted his belly. 'Thank you, one and all. It has been the best Christmas ever. I don't think I will be able to eat anything else for a week.'

'You are most welcome, Harry,' we all said in unison. It had been a splendid day.

When we had gone on a walk once before, Harry had told me that Christmases with Maisie had never really been that happy. He had never really enjoyed any of them. When he was younger, his own family Christmases had been full of arguments and door-slamming.

The following morning, we all woke up late. After coffee, tea, toast and a choice of croissants or breakfast cereals, we gathered ourselves together and went out for a walk.

Sarah was pushing Harry in his wheelchair. He had a blanket over his legs. The air was crisp and cold and managed to wake us all up. I had to keep wiping my eyes to stop them watering and Kath and Sarah kept blowing their noses. There were several other families out and we all exchanged smiles. Children were proudly riding new bikes or scooters and I could see adults wearing Christmas jumpers under their coats. We went up to the main high street. I always found it a pleasure on Christmas Day as nearly all the shops were closed and there was nowhere near as many people out and about. It was far more relaxing than having to keep moving out of the way of people coming towards you on a normal working day. We looked in shop windows and found a small food store open so got a few more things to add to the bulging collection of items already at home. I was glad I had a store cupboard to put extras in. After a long walk, we came home and I cooked up all the bits left over from yesterday for lunch. We all smothered the food with an array of leftover sauces. Harry managed to eat some food and squeezed out more brown sauce on his plate.

Later, Sarah took Charlotte and George over to the park before it got dark. Kath and I looked out the window at them. It made a change from just me looking out.

'Look at them. They are having the time of their lives. How I wish I was young again, running around without a care in the world,' Kath said. She sounded very thoughtful.

I went and sat with Harry. 'I am so glad everything is okay with you and Sarah.' I squeezed his shoulder as he lay in bed.

'Yes, I can't tell you what it means to me. Thank you so much for helping me sort everything out, Beth.' Harry's voice was starting to sound quite weak and he was coughing more than normal.

33

The End of the Beginning

Harry started to deteriorate quickly after Christmas. It was like he had saved up all his strength to get through Christmas Day and was now letting go of a greasy pole. The nurse was now coming in three times a day to help out more with his medication and some of his care needs. Sarah and I helped with bed baths and toileting and he was now on a much higher dose of morphine. He was sleeping more and getting muddled in his thinking. I was happy for Harry to stay downstairs as I wanted him to still be part of everything that was going on. I couldn't bear the thought of him being in the bedroom upstairs alone.

When he slept, I would go somewhere else in the house and read or go on my laptop and Sarah would take the kids out for a long walk. I had stopped looking out of the window for David now. I finally knew he wouldn't be coming back. I still thought about him and still cried, but I needed to give my attention to Harry. Sarah had sat down with Charlotte and George to tell them about Harry and they were very good. They sat on his bed to chat with him and didn't create havoc by running around indoors and yelling. They went out in the garden or to the park to get rid of any excess energy.

Harry enjoyed our company and would try and join in conversations but often struggled and would lie on his bed with his eyes closed and just listen to us. Sarah and I would help him sit up in bed when food was served. We would cut his food up for him and help feed him as he now found it too difficult to use a knife and fork. We made sure he always had a choice of sauces on his plate.

Sarah's husband was still living in their shared home so I invited Sarah and the kids to stay with me full-time until she was able to sort out what to do next. Her husband, Trevor, had the children every other week. They were working towards a divorce which was another stress for Sarah to deal with. She hadn't told the children what was going on. She simply said that Mummy and Daddy weren't best friends at the moment, like when Charlotte and George were annoyed with someone they knew and then later everything would work out okay and they would make up. Charlotte and George often sat on Harry's bed and chatted with him or showed him their toys.

We had a muted New Year celebration with Harry. We listened as Big Ben chimed in the New Year and watched the fireworks. We raised our glasses to each other with pretend happy faces. None of us wanted to wish each other a Happy New Year as we knew it wouldn't be. We kissed each other and kissed Harry. Harry told us stories about his past life, stories we hadn't heard before. He told us about the time he had helped a neighbour put a TV aerial on their roof and was nearly struck by lightning. He had ended up clinging to the side of the roof shouting his head off for someone to help. He had saved someone from jumping in front of a train and he had played Father Christmas at a local community centre. Sarah had asked him if it was okay to tape him as he spoke as she wanted to write all his memories down. He was fine with that. His voice was quite weak so I wrote down what he said just in case his words weren't picked up by the microphone.

We felt quite helpless as there was nothing we could do other than make his last days comfortable and happy for him. His son had not got in contact and Sarah was furious. She had told him what Harry had told her about his fractured relationship with Maisie but Simon didn't want to know. She vowed never to speak to him again.

'He is such an arrogant stubborn man, Beth. He will never change. I don't need someone like him in my life, family or not.'

She had built up such a strong relationship with me that she again said she looked upon me as the sister she had always wanted and that was enough for her. I was family to her. I felt very flattered. She was a lovely person and I was glad we had got to know each other. She had built up a really good friendship with Kath too and I would often hear them chatting away over a drink. I was so glad she was staying with me.

Harry's passing came on a Monday evening. During the day, he managed to say some words to Sarah, Kath and me. We took it in turns to sit with him. He had something he wanted to say to each of us. His voice was very weak and we all had to lean in to hear him.

He spoke to Sarah first. They held hands as she sat on his bed.

285

'Sarah, my lovely daughter. I am so pleased we are together again. I can't tell you how much I missed you. You are a beautiful, caring daughter and mother. I will miss you so much but I will never forget you. Please live your life to the best. Don't waste a minute of it. You are far too precious to Charlotte and George. Be brave. I will always be near you and look after you. I love you, my angel, to the ends of the earth and back. Tell my grandchildren I love them very much. You have all brought such joy to my life. I love you my darling Sarah'

Sarah held his hand and cried.

'I love you too, Dad. I wasted so much time not seeing you. I hope you can forgive me. I will always remember you for the wonderful person you are.' She started to sob. She kissed his head and cheeks and grabbed hold of him and held him tight.

'I have nothing to forgive you for Sarah.'

Sarah came to get me.

'Beth, you have been there for me and I cannot tell you how much I love you for everything you have done. If I had stayed in that care home, I would have gone bonkers, but you saved me. You gave me a better life than I ever had before. Have the best life you can. Don't hide away after I am gone. Please. Be strong and brave. Life is too short. Make the most of it.'

'Harry, I am going to miss you so much. You have brought such happiness back into my life. I love you.' I held his hand, stroked his face and kissed him. I left him and cried.

Kath was next.

'Kath, you are such a good friend to Beth. You have made me laugh and helped me when times have been difficult, like now. Stay happy and caring. I love you....' Suddenly, his voice started to trail off.

Kath shouted at us to come back in. We all held on to Harry, not wanting him to float away and leave us. He looked at us, smiled and then he was gone.

'No, no, no, no. Please no. Dad! Please!' Sarah was weeping. She laid her head on the bed. I held onto her and Kath sat on the other side of the bed and held onto his arm.

We stayed with him for ages and then I nodded to Kath to leave Sarah alone with him. She sat with him and held his hands until the early hours of the morning. We had to go through all the formalities and Sarah then registered his death.

His loss was enormous. It was like being punched in the stomach, being left unable to breathe. There was a space at the table and on the sofa. There was one less plate to put food on. One less person on our trips out. One less person to share a joke with or seek advice from. It was these things, amongst everything, that played heavily on all of our hearts.

I decided to make a large donation to Cancer Research. I told them I wanted to leave a legacy in memory of Harry. I wanted to help other people in the future get the right treatment and survive.

Kath and I helped Sarah plan Harry's funeral. He loved sunflowers, pansies and freesias so I ordered a large wreath of them to put on the top of his coffin along with an Arsenal scarf. The funeral was attended by many people. There were his friends from the care home, members of staff, his friend Jack and other people I didn't recognise. Sarah had contacted the remaining younger members of his family and several had come. Harry had never spoken about his family at any great length to me and I had assumed they had all passed away.

People got up and read their own eulogies about Harry. People laughed, cried or stayed silent. Sarah read out Harry's favourite poem beautifully, The Lake Isle of Innisfree by WB Yeats and spoke about Harry in such heartfelt words. *I want that poem read at my funeral*, I thought.

Kath and I did a joint eulogy about Harry and told those present about some of our many trips out and about his love of sauces.

We all went back to Harry's favourite local pub afterwards. I had asked for an area where we could go and had ordered nibbles and sandwiches for everyone. I also put some money behind the bar for drinks. We drank a toast to Harry. Funerals are never great events to attend but everyone seemed more relaxed now.

A couple of days after Harry's funeral, we sat down for tea. Sarah said she would like to have a memorial service held to celebrate his life. She asked if it would be okay to have it at my home. I, of course, said yes. The care home had won a reprieve for another year so I contacted the manager to invite them all over. I asked if everyone could wear bright colourful clothes as I wanted them to share their happy memories about him. I wanted smiles and laughter. Sarah and I arranged it for a Saturday in two weeks' time. I invited Jack over too and he said he would be honoured to attend. Sarah collected Harry's ashes a couple of days after the funeral and had put them on the mantelpiece in the living room. I could hear her talking to him every day. *Nothing wrong with that*, I thought. I still talked to David.

I got lots of photos printed of Harry, including some the care home had given me. There was one of him wearing a straw hat with a large lollipop in his mouth. It had been snapped when the home had taken the residents to the seaside one hot summer day. He had his arms wrapped around friends standing on either side of him. He looked so happy and full of life.

I stroked the photo. 'Harry, I wish you were here now. I miss your voice. I miss you.' I kissed his face and put the picture on the table in a frame I had bought earlier that day. I not only missed his voice, but I also missed his humour, his wise words and his presence. Missing David was still something I felt acutely and I missed the intimacy we had shared. I knew I would miss Harry just as much but for different reasons. We had bonded and now that bond had been snapped in half.

The care home bus pulled up outside my home just before 2 pm on Saturday. I was pleased to see that everyone was wearing cheerful outfits. I could see blouses with flowers and birds on, brightly coloured suits and ties and an array of beautiful scarves and hats. As they came in, they gave us a kiss and a hug each and expressed their sympathy. Many were crying. Some gave Sarah bouquets of flowers.

To begin with, people were quite muted, not really knowing how to behave or what to say. Once they had settled into chairs and on the sofa, people started to share stories of Harry. I heard people laughing, talking about antics he had got up to. I got drinks for them and made sure they all tucked into the food I had put out. I put on background music which included Harry's favourite songs and tunes.

Sarah stood up and clinked her glass with the ring on her finger. Everyone stopped talking.

'Hello, everyone. Thank you so much for coming over to celebrate my dad's life. I want this to be a happy occasion so please share some memories with each other or out loud if you would like to. Do enjoy yourselves. Harry wouldn't want us to be miserable. If anyone needs a refill, please let us know.' She smiled and sat down again.

People started to look at the photos I had put out around the living room and several started to chuckle when they reminisced about a trip to Brighton.

The man who had worked out that the non-alcoholic drink was just that, non-alcoholic, the last time he was here, started to tell us a tale about Harry. His name was Bill and he had a lovely light blue checked suit on and a flowery tie.

'I remember when Harry and I sneaked out of the care home once to go to the pub up the road. We told the care staff we were just going outside for some fresh air. We drank so much that we had to walk around the park a number of times to try and sober up. It didn't work so when we got back we went straight up to our rooms to lie down. We drank lots of water before the evening meal. We both felt dreadful the next day.'

'I remember when that happened as you made me act as lookout when you went out and then got back. I could have got detention for a week if they had found out what was really going on,' someone else said and they all laughed.

'He was a character,' another person added.

Sheila was next. She had been a good friend of Harry's at the care home.

'I remember when the home put on a dinner and dance. Harry asked me for a dance and swept me off my feet. He was such a good dancer. He twirled me this way and that. He would sing along to the songs. He had such a wonderful voice. I often asked him to sing to me after that and he did. Beautiful. I will remember him fondly.'

I told them what had happened when we had joined the choir and how we had all stood, mouths agape, listening to him. I realised now why Harry had declined the offer of doing the solo later on in the year. He knew he might not be around.

A carer called Rosaline told us how Harry had helped with the boiled eggs for the Easter festivities and had painted caricatures of the staff and residents on the shells. People didn't want to eat the eggs as the drawings were so good and some residents still had his eggs in their rooms.

'He was a very kind soul,' Jack said. 'When I was having problems paying my rent, he gave me the money and refused to accept any money back from me when I had sorted my finances out. Once when I was ill, he came and saw me every day to check on me, get me food and clean my flat. Not many like him around now.'

They started to nod their heads and agree.

'Yes, he was one of God's own. Harry, I will miss you. Keep on being kind and funny wherever you are.' Stan, another care home resident, looked up and raised his glass and we all joined in.

After everyone had left, we sat in silence for a while. I looked at the photos of Harry around my living room.

'He would have loved this,' Sarah said.

'Yes, he would,' I added.

'He was the best of the best,' Kath said and we all raised another glass in honour of him. Kath stood up and saluted him.

I have always believed that people who have passed away still live on if we continue to remember them and talk to them and talk about them to people. They would still be part of our lives and be with us everywhere we went.

I had listened to what Harry had said to me and kept his words close to my heart. I would be strong and brave. I was no longer a kite, tethered to a tree in a storm, unable to gain height. I was now free to fly upwards and go anywhere I wanted to. I would grab life with two hands and enjoy it. Life was worth living now. Harry had taught me that and I would always cherish his memory. New beginnings.